Sikes hugged himself with both arms, shivering from more than the cold now. "We've got to head back to the hotel now. If I don't get dry clothes, I'm gonna freeze. Damn." He vented the edge of his frustration on a snowplowed ridge. "When we find Vegas, I'm gonna kick his ass. Doesn't he have the faintest idea how much trouble he's caused?"

"I don't think he had any choice."

Sikes turned, stilled by the odd tone in George's voice, and saw his partner stopped in the middle of the sidewalk, staring downward. "What?" He hurried back to him. "George, what are you talking about?"

George stooped and peeled a scrap of muddy paper off the pavement. It was almost transparent with meltwater, the jagged tread mark of one of the Purists' shoes obscuring the pasted-together words in one corner. What it said was easily readable, though, and made Sikes itch with anger even as he thought about the three Purists who had gotten away.

We have the slag Ross Vegas. Do like we tell you or everybody dies.

Alien Nation Titles

Published by POCKET BOOKS

#7 ALIEN NATION™

EXTREME PREJUDICE

A NOVEL BY L. A. GRAF

POCKET BOOKS

New York   London   Toronto   Sydney   Tokyo   Singapore

An *Original* Publication of POCKET BOOKS

POCKET BOOKS, a division of Simon & Schuster Inc.
1230 Avenue of the Americas, New York, NY 10020

ISBN: 0-671-79570-8

First Pocket Books printing March 1995

10 9 8 7 6 5 4 3 2 1

POCKET and colophon are registered trademarks of Simon & Schuster Inc.

Printed in the U.S.A.

To Ricia—We named it after the dog,
but we based it on you.
Roos editors, babe.

ACKNOWLEDGMENTS

Special thanks to Margie Marks of the Pittsburgh Zoological Society for her immeasurable patience with our bizarre questions as well as her insights into the workings of the Pittsburgh Zoo. It's nice to know that a zoo so beautiful and precious is cared for by someone so caring. Good luck with the lions, Margie, and thanks.

CHAPTER 1

"Matt, fasten your seat belt."

Sikes lifted the arm he'd thrown over his eyes half a flight ago only long enough to squint at Cathy and ask, "Why?" She'd opened the window's sliding shutter, and the sharp winter sunlight hurt his eyes.

"Because," Cathy said, reaching across their shared armrest to tug one end of his seat belt out from under his leg, "the airplane's landing, and the flight attendant asked you to." She dropped the metal buckle on his lap. "And I'm asking you to."

The plane's wheels thumped down on the runway, and Sikes grimaced against the engines' decelerating whine. "Cathy, we crossed an entire continent at thirty thousand feet without wearing seat belts. How much more dangerous can it be going five miles an hour on the ground?"

He felt her seat move with her sigh. "We've got to

do something about this problem you have with authority."

"We've got to do something about me not getting any sleep," Sikes compromised. "We can worry about authority later."

"Forty minutes? That's impossible." In the seat behind Sikes, George Francisco muttered unhappily to himself amidst a rattle of loose papers. Sikes resisted an impulse to unhinge his seat and let it fall flat onto the lap behind him. "How could I possibly have talked for forty minutes?"

"Try it again," Susan, seated out of sight beside George, suggested quietly.

Sikes snorted a little laugh, but it came out sounding more like a groan. "George, you've been talking ever since we got on this plane. What I'd like to know is how to get you to shut up for forty minutes."

Cathy elbowed him. "Matt, hush. These talks are going to be televised all over the country, and the symposium organizers were very specific that each speaker only has thirty minutes in front of the camera." She jerked the other half of his seat belt onto his lap. "Fasten your seat belt."

"You're talking at this Newcomer gabfest, too," Sikes grumbled, squirming upright in his seat but ignoring her suggestion as he glared at George over the back of his seat. "I haven't had to listen to you muttering about interspecies cooperation in law enforcement for the last six and a half hours."

George's alien pale eyes darkened a shade, and he pulled his lips into the thin line Sikes had come to recognize well over the last year. "Cathy had time to practice her talk before we left," George said stiffly.

"Instead of practicing, *I* was assigned to stakeout duty with you all last week—"

"I *know* that!" Sikes broke in. "That's why I've had maybe three hours of sleep in the last two days! You and your community service speech haven't helped any."

"You should have slept during the flight," Cathy pointed out reasonably. "George wasn't talking the whole time."

Sikes flopped back into his seat. "When he wasn't talking, the engines were going." He scrubbed at his eyes as the plane finally slowed to a stop at the gate. "I couldn't sleep through that even when I was a kid."

Cathy looked surprised. "I found the engine noise rather soothing."

"You grew up on a spaceship." Sikes tossed his seat belt parts aside and sighed. "You'll probably love the hotel heater, too."

As if inspired by Sikes's actions, the overhead seat belt light blinked off, and a trio of soft chimes sounded through the cabin. "Welcome to Pittsburgh International Airport. The local time is 1:57 P.M. The temperature is a brisk twenty-nine degrees, with snow and . . ."

"Come on, sleepyhead." Cathy half stood in the window seat, computer case in hand, and nudged Sikes toward the aisle. "I want to get out of here and stand up for a while."

Sikes didn't fight her, knowing from experience that it was useless. Catching his overnight bag between his feet, he dragged it into the open, then fumbled his way into the aisle while trying to pull his heavy peacoat from under the seat. *At the hotel,* he promised himself.

I'll get some sleep once we're at the hotel. If he survived that long. He felt like he was going to keel over and start snoring as soon as he stood still for more than a few minutes.

Which might be a problem sooner than he expected. By the time Sikes had worked clear of his seat, the aisle was clogged with bodies. He turned sideways, leaning back against an empty armrest with his bag and coat bumping his knees, and looked at the people sharing this plane with him for what felt like the first time. A shiver of weirdness went through him. He pretended distraction with the zipper on his travel bag to try to hide his reaction.

The plane was filled with Newcomers, jostling about just like human passengers, squirming to join Sikes in the aisle, struggling to open the overhead compartments or free their luggage from under adjoining seats. Their smooth, spotted heads looked unreal against a backdrop of airplane windows covered with falling snow, and the soft click and hush of their excited words sounded like some Japanese recording played backwards and very slow. A rail-thin Newcomer female, her spots as fine as leopard skin, skittered into the aisle ahead of a tall, broad Newcomer male who was probably her mate. The male squeezed past Sikes without seeming to notice him, but his wife offered a thin smile in apparent apology before being hustled away. Sikes smiled back at her, then looked away.

It had never occurred to him that getting used to the aliens in L.A. didn't mean he'd be used to them everywhere. It had seemed so self-evident—they were a thing unto themselves, and their location shouldn't have mattered to his reactions or feelings. Still, here he was, pressed chest to back with them in a too-warm, gamy-smelling airplane, the only human in sight, and he was overwhelmed with a feeling of threat and revulsion just like what he'd felt the first time he'd waded among a crowd of them as a cop, sent to help break up a riot in the Little Tencton district of L.A. The revelation embarrassed him. Six years ago he'd been a rookie detective, trying like hell to make ends meet from the losing end of a bad divorce. Then, he'd have laughed at anyone who suggested there was life on other planets. Now . . .

"You're blocking the aisle." Cathy slipped her free arm around his waist, tugging at a belt loop on his blue jeans with the other. Her pale eyes glowed above her puckish smile. "Don't you want to go to Pittsburgh?"

Sikes felt a rush of color and heat into his face and nodded awkwardly. "Yeah, sure." He brushed the back of his hand against her temple without thinking about it and was both touched and ashamed of his earlier thoughts when she leaned her cheek into the caress. "Let's go," he said softly, and took her hand in his before following the chain of displaced Newcomers down the aisle and out the hatch.

A blast of cold air caught them at the seam where the off-loading ramp met the door. Sikes squinted against the sudden chill, and Cathy's hand seized tight on his, hurting just a little. He pulled her up next to him as they moved into the tunnel beyond, fitting her under one arm in an effort to relieve her shivering. "I told you it would be cold here."

Cathy nodded. "But this is *terrible!*" He touched the

side of her neck, and she was as cold as the plane window glass. "Can humans actually go outside in temperatures like this?"

He disentangled himself from her just long enough to shake out the long peacoat and drape it across her shoulders. "Believe me, humans can go out in temperatures a whole hell of a lot worse."

She shuddered, her hands closing whitely at the throat of the coat. "That's amazing . . ."

Sikes grinned and pulled her aside as they cleared the gate into the terminal. "At least there's something we do better than you," he said, fastening the heavy buttons for her. "You know, I really ought to just give you this thing—you wear it more than I do." In fact, L.A. weather gave him little opportunity to make use of the heavy wool mantel. Cathy, on the other hand, bundled up inside it whenever the sky clouded over or the temperature dropped below sixty.

"That's okay," she said, rewarding him with a little touch of her forehead to his. "I'll just take it for the weekend whenever I can't keep warm close to you."

He smiled and turned up her collar. "You've got a deal." The softness in her eyes filled him with a warmth more than equal to any comfort the coat might have provided.

George and Susan joined them inside the terminal. They both looked at least as uncomfortable as Cathy, their grips overtight on their luggage handles, George's lips pressed with worry as he chafed one hand against Susan's arm in silent sympathy. Sikes shook his head, sighing. "We've gotta do something about getting coats for you people." He sandwiched both of Susan's hands between his and was startled at how thin and frigid her fingers felt against his palms. "Didn't you listen to a damn thing I said about the weather out here?"

"I brought a coat," Susan said between shivers.

"Where is it?"

"In our checked baggage." Before Sikes could do more than snort, she added, "I thought we'd have time to get it out before going to the hotel. I didn't think it would be so cold inside!"

It wasn't, but Sikes didn't think it worth pointing that out right now. "All right, let's see if there's a gift shop or something on the way to the baggage claim. We'll get you some souvenir jackets for the trip." Meanwhile, he pulled his own sweater off over his head and tried to ignore the chill prickling up his arms when he was left with only a short-sleeved sport shirt for warmth. "It ought to fit over your head," he commented, handing it to Susan.

She looked dubious but took it anyway. "I don't see why they had to have a business conference for Newcomers all the way out here, anyway," she said as George helped her tug the heavy sweater on.

"Because when eastern businessmen want somebody else to pay for a party, they hit up other eastern businesses," Sikes told her. "And the radio station or TV station or whatever it was that agreed to pick up the tab is here in Pittsburgh. I guess it's cheaper to ship all of you out here than it is to fly all their people and equipment to L.A." Besides, he had a dirty suspicion that even the most open-minded event organizers subconsciously wanted reassurance that the 'spotted menace' stood no chance of expanding into their own backyards. He kept that opinion to himself, though. "Come on—let's go find that gift shop."

"Shouldn't we wait for the symposium organizers?" George followed along behind while Sikes herded the women toward a cluster of lighted signs a few gates away—shops and eateries, apparently, wedged between gates at the end of a long moving walkway.

Sikes kept them off the conveyor, not wanting to encourage human rudeness by putting the Newcomers in too close a proximity. "I'm not taking them to Shanghai, George. We're just going to the gift shop." He flicked a glare at a staring woman on the walkway, and she hurriedly looked away. "Besides, they know how many of you they're supposed to have. They're not going to leave without you."

"It isn't a matter of being left behind," George said. "It's a matter of principle, of what sort of image we want to project as serious professionals—"

"Anal, George," Sikes cautioned him. "Here—" He threaded a path between two clusters of human travelers, his eye caught by a headless, armless mannequin sporting knitted black and gold. "This joint has sweaters." Even if they were kind of ugly sweaters. "We can always get you something better at the hotel."

"Oh, Matt," Susan chided him, swatting him lightly on the arm, "I think they're lovely." She slipped past Sikes to close in on one of the hanger-filled carousels, pulling George behind her with one hand. "I should probably get one for Emily, too."

Cathy joined Susan and George at the sweater rack, and Sikes paused inside the doorway to lean against the window. Watching the startled gift shop cashier and the trickle of curious people in the hallway outside both at the same time almost proved too complicated for his sleep-deprived brain. He hadn't really lost that feeling of being crowded when he left the airplane, only now it was the overwhelming presence of human people that made his back itch and his jaw clench. Maybe he was just antisocial, he decided. Or maybe he'd just been a cop too long to expect anything good out of anybody, regardless of which planet they were from. Not wanting to deal with either issue, he closed his eyes and tipped his head back against the window glass while he listened to the Newcomers' quiet chatter.

"Susan, look—puffins! I didn't know they had puffins in Pittsburgh."

"I think that's a penguin, George." A rustle and click of plastic hangers underscored Susan's thoughtful comment. "This must be a team sweater for another of those social warfare equivalent bonding groups, like the Pillagers."

"Pirates," Sikes told her, sighing. "The Pittsburgh Pirates. The Penguins are a hockey team." He decided it was probably best to avoid explaining the rules of chasing little black pellets all over indoor ice. "Can we just pick the sweaters and come on?" He wanted to sleep so bad he could taste it. "We're gonna miss our escort."

"I'll pillage," Susan said brightly.

Cathy laughed with her. "I'll puffin."

"Pirates," Sikes corrected, and George remarked, "I don't believe 'puffin' is a verb."

I shoulda shot myself in the foot, Sikes thought wearily, scrubbing at his eyes. *Then maybe they'd have let me stay home.*

"'Scuse me . . ."

Sikes startled upright when someone brushed past him, blinking his eyes into focus on the curly blond head passing in front of him. The man was taller than Sikes by maybe a handspan, but thinner, with a look of whipcord meat on his bones. Something about the frown that creased his narrow nose combined with the dark intensity of his stare and made Sikes's stomach crimp. He caught the blond man by the waist of his pants. "Where're you going?"

The blond skidded to a stop, reaching back to catch at Sikes's hand with a glare. "Do you mind?"

Sikes shrugged but didn't let go. "That depends." He flicked a glance across the shop at where George counted bills into the cashier's outstretched hand. "Why don't you just let them buy their stuff and get out of here so you don't have to look at them anymore?"

"What are you?" the man asked, jerking free. "A slag lover?"

"You want to spend the rest of the holidays in a body cast?"

The man shook his head in disgust and disbelief. "I should have known." He waved at someone out of sight behind Sikes, and it occurred to Sikes with a thrill of anxiety that the man was here with friends. "I hear it takes two guys to do it to them. Which one are you—the one who does it or the one who helps?"

Sikes slammed the guy hard with the heel of his

hand, then clenched his fist in the front of the bastard's shirt to keep him from stumbling backwards. It would have been easy to beat him then, to knock him senseless before he even figured out they were in a fight, and Sikes couldn't even have his badge lifted for it or anything because he wasn't a cop in this city. Sikes understood the principle behind public relations, though, and knew George would probably lecture him for a week if he hospitalized somebody fifteen minutes after landing in Pittsburgh. So, instead, Sikes stared the guy down with the guy's shirt wadded up under his chin, and tried to content himself with imagining what that jaw would look like held in place with surgical wire. "Yo, George . . . ?"

Sikes didn't break his attention to turn and look, but he heard Susan murmur something in alarm, and George prompted evenly, "Matthew? Do you need something?"

"Yeah." He flashed George enough of a look to let his partner see his concern, then had to look away when he glimpsed Cathy's eyes sparkling with fear. "Let's take the girls back to the gate. The shit's getting a little deep for my taste." He flashed his captive a bloodless grin. "No offense."

George slipped an arm behind each of the women to urge them forward. "Perhaps we should contact airport security."

"Trust me, George, security's probably waiting for us at the gate." Sikes rotated sideways as the Newcomers went by, dragging the blond bigot along with him. "Just get the girls on the walkway, and let's get out of here."

It wasn't that Sikes had expected the bigot to try and cut his legs out from under him, just that he'd handled too many gang bangers and druggies to get caught completely by surprise. When he felt the other man's leg scissor behind his, Sikes jerked a knee up between them without even turning his attention away from George. Both Sikes and the bigot toppled, Sikes on the bottom, but the bigot had curled into too tight a huddle to notice much when Sikes rolled out from under him. Scrambling to his feet, Sikes shouted, "Go on!" to George, even though the Newcomer *gannaum* showed no signs of stopping.

Two other men converged on the mouth of the walkway, one of them wearing the knotted white armband that was just becoming popular among Purists on the West Coast. Just what they needed— local color that was just as separatist as the color back home. Slamming to a stop just before the moving conveyor, Sikes planted one hip against the rail and jerked his elbow neck-high just as one of the Purists tried to rush past him. The guy clotheslined himself and dropped with a grunt, his heels thumping on the end of the walkway. Sikes hopped over him and pivoted, grinning maliciously when he caught sight of the last Purist just off the foot of the walkway, looking from one downed comrade to the other.

"Coming?" Sikes called.

The guy didn't answer, just stared at Sikes as the conveyor pulled them steadily farther apart. It was suddenly a disturbing image. Sikes turned away from it with a growl. Cathy, Susan, and George were already off the end of the walkway, having wisely hurried ahead to join up with the other Newcomers and a phalanx of airport security. But running ahead to join them seemed just as unnatural as leaving the human Purist behind, so Sikes just stood his ground and let the walkway carry him. Somehow he felt better letting something else decide his allegiances for him.

CHAPTER 2

A DRIVING GRAY snow closed around the chartered bus when it pulled away from the airport. George Francisco stared out the window at the winter landscape, catching indistinct glimpses of dark hills and bare-boned trees beyond the edges of the highway. Mostly what he saw was the reflection of his own grim face against the glass, smeared by streaks of splattered snow.

"George." Susan's hand curved around his wrist, a welcome bracelet of warmth in the chilly air of the bus. "Don't take this so hard. It's really no worse than what happened to us in Los Angeles."

George had to duck his chin to loosen the angry muscles of his throat before he could speak. "Susan, large-scale Purist protests in L.A. died out almost a year ago. Since then we've only had to put up with vandalism and occasional youth fights."

14

"Like every other minority in the city," said Cathy, turning from the seat in front of them to join the conversation. Her face looked pale but calm above the glitter of her new black-and-gold sweater and her dark blue peacoat.

"Yes." George turned his hand to catch Susan's and press it tightly. "I thought we'd seen the end of mass Purist demonstrations. I didn't realize we'd have to fight this battle over and over again in every city we entered . . ."

The bus labored up a long hill, with smaller cars passing it in a steady stream. Two hills away, George could see the swift silver gleam of the public mag-lev train they were supposed to board before the Purist demonstrators changed their plans. Too dangerous, airport security had decided at the last minute. Wouldn't the Newcomers feel safer on a crowded, smelly bus while the unpleasant humans stayed out of their way on the clean and quiet new mag-lev? George sighed regretfully. "I'm afraid it's going to be a long trawl before we're accepted as equal citizens everywhere."

"Long *haul,* George," said Sikes morosely. Unlike Cathy, he hadn't turned to look around from the bus seat where he sat. "Welcome to the Civil Rights Movement. Just don't drink out of any water fountains and you'll do okay."

"Really, Matthew, I don't see what the quality of the public water supply has to do with Purist demonstrations in Pittsburgh." George frowned at the back of his partner's head. "You're not suggesting they'd try to poison us, are you?"

"Forget it." Sikes slid down further in his seat, his

voice muffled in disgust. "It was just a historical reference."

"I think your friend's talking about the old segregation laws," a deep voice said from across the bus aisle. George glanced over at the stocky older *gannaum* who sat there, and felt his stomach clench when he saw the telltale ring of tattoo half hidden beneath the expensive shirt cuff. The former Overseer met his gaze pleasantly enough, however, and George tried to suppress his instinctive spurt of dislike.

"What do segregation laws have to do with the drinking water supply?" George asked, puzzled.

The other Newcomer grunted. "In many states, albinistic humans had laws that kept melanistic humans from drinking out of the same water fountains they did. Didn't you learn about that in your quarantine classes?"

"No." George hoped his voice didn't sound as uncomfortable as he felt. "I suppose my teachers were more concerned about the recent segregation laws than ancient ones like that."

"Oh, the water fountain laws aren't ancient." An older *linnaum,* elegantly spotted, looked up from the seat next to the Overseer. Her face was gaunt, with a faint wrinkle of radiation burns along one cheek. "They were still enforced in this country as late as the 1960s."

"Really?" Cathy sounded startled.

"Ask your human friend." The Overseer's deep voice turned quizzical on the word "friend" and George felt the skin around his eyes tighten with his effort not to scowl. "He probably remembers the crowds of humans that demonstrated against the repeal of those laws." The bus plunged into the orange mercury light of a tunnel, throwing odd shadows across the Overseer's blunt face. "Maybe he even attended some of the demonstrations."

"The hell I did!" Sikes jerked around to glare across the aisle, ignoring Cathy's restraining tug at his shoulder. "I'm not even old enough to remember when those riots happened!"

"Ah. Forgive me." The stocky *gannaum* smiled politely. "I find it so difficult to judge age from human faces."

"Because we all look so much alike?" Sikes demanded acidly.

Knowing his partner's tendency to transfer anger to the nearest available target, George decided to intervene. "Matthew, you must admit that you also have difficulty—" He broke off, blinking painfully, as the bus rolled out of the tunnel and into a blaze of winter brilliance.

"Oh, George, look! It's beautiful!" Susan leaned across his shoulder, pressing close enough to their window to mist it with her breath. The snow had stopped while they were inside the tunnel, and the scudding clouds had cleared just enough for the sun to break through. The winter light reflected off glittering water onto a triangle of mirrored buildings, then warmed itself against bright golden bridges over more water again. On either side, snowy hills folded the city in a close embrace. Unlike the barren mountains of Los Angeles, these slopes were quilted by houses and tree-lined streets, odd onion-shaped church domes, and the steep gray tracks of inclined trolleys.

Throughout the bus, George could hear the soft

chatter and clicks of Newcomer appreciation, and even a faint grunt of surprise from Sikes. In all the publicity and preparation for this visit, no one had bothered to tell the southern Californians about Pittsburgh's wealth of water. Three broad natural channels surrounded the city, full of rippling water from bank to bank—an astonishing contrast to the dry concrete gullies that L.A. called rivers. Two of the channels hemmed in the triangular wedge of downtown buildings, merging at its point to form a wider and darker third. The water caught the reflected colors of the bridges, the tall glass buildings and even the clouds and sky above, breaking them down into separate moving glints across its rippling surface.

The sunlit brilliance faded back into winter gray while the bus lumbered across one of the gold-painted bridges. Susan made a small, regretful sound as Pittsburgh lost its magical aura of light and became just another industrial downtown, crammed with cars caught in the late afternoon rush hour. Their bus slowed when it neared the curving ramps at the end of the bridge.

"There, look at that," said Cathy, pointing over Sikes's shoulder so George and Susan could see. On the far bank of the river they were crossing, a huge sign lit in blue neon proclaimed, Welcome, Newcomers! "The symposium organizers said Pittsburgh was a very friendly town."

"They also said there wouldn't be any snow this early in the year," Sikes retorted. To George's relief, he seemed to have forgotten his antagonism toward the former Overseer, although George saw that the big *gannaum* still watched the human. "If you ask me, I think they were being overly optimistic on both counts."

"Oh, Matt, don't be so grumpy." Susan leaned forward to pat his arm. "This is a free vacation for you and me. Don't let a few Purists spoil the whole trip."

"I'll try not to." Sikes scowled out the bus window as they rolled down an exit ramp onto a narrow city street. "But I can tell you right now, it's not going to be easy."

"Why not?" Cathy swayed against him while the bus braked to a lumbering stop.

Sikes snorted and rapped his hand against the windowpane. "See for yourselves."

Frowning, George leaned forward and wiped droplets of mist left by Susan's breath off the cold glass pane. The bus had stopped a block away from an expensive-looking brass and brick hotel tower that was obviously their destination. The reason why it had stopped was equally obvious.

The entire street in front of them was filled with silent, sign-carrying humans.

Through his misted window, George measured the length of snow-covered sidewalk separating them from what he hoped was the safety of the hotel. The Purists could throw a lot of ice and snow at them between here and there, he thought, and that was about the *best* scenario he could envision. The sensitive skin of his back shivered painfully at the mere thought of ice-cold water dripping down it.

"Oh, not again!" Susan sounded more exasperated than dismayed by the discovery of the waiting crowd. George glanced down at her, comparing the resolute set of her small, firm chin to the worry and fear on the other Newcomer faces around him. In many ways, he thought with brief amusement, he'd rather have his wife beside him now than anyone else. Somehow, Susan could make almost any disaster seem like nothing more than a mild annoyance. It was a gift he'd always admired in her, even back aboard the ship.

"Why can't the bus drive through them?" she asked now, practically. "Even Purists would have enough sense to get out of our way."

George shook his head, wiser in the ways of crowds than she. "There are too many of them to do that. The ones at the back of the crowd won't be willing to move further away, so the ones at the front won't be able to. We'll have to walk past them."

He heard Cathy take a deep breath. "Well, what are we waiting for?" she asked, steadying her voice after a quickly swallowed quiver. "They're not going to go away, are they?"

"No, but I think we're going to get an escort through them." Sikes dropped an arm around her shoulders almost absently, as if he had responded to her tension without realizing it. He stared out the window in the direction of a distant siren. It howled closer through the traffic, coming nearer and finally stopping with a skirl of red and blue warning lights beside them. "About time. I was beginning to think there weren't any police in the entire city of Pittsburgh."

Doors opened at the front of the bus, letting in a thin draft of cold air and the ragged sound of a few people chanting. A human female in a thick blue jacket climbed into the main aisle and pushed back snow-flecked hair to survey the Newcomers. "I'm

Captain Protzberg of the Pittsburgh Public Safety Department," she announced. "Please forgive the inconvenience, but we have a scheduled and licensed demonstration going on outside the Hilton Hotel. We also have three units of police on the scene, with more scheduled to arrive momentarily. As soon as they're all in place, I'll escort you out to your hotel."

Protzberg paused, glancing around the bus to gauge their reaction to the news. If she felt any discomfort at what must be her first face-to-face meeting with Newcomers, she didn't show it. George's respect for her increased. "Please don't panic," she said over the rising murmur of comment. "We do have an area roped off for you to walk through, and the demonstrators have been told that if they shove against it or throw anything at all, they will be arrested. So far, they've been cooperating."

Sikes snorted. "Of course they have. We haven't gotten off the bus yet."

"That's true." A grin lit Protzberg's snub-nosed face and was quickly wiped away, as if her sense of humor had fought with her sense of duty and lost. "We're not expecting much trouble, though. You might hear a few nasty comments from some people in the crowd, but if you refrain from making any reply you should be safe."

She glanced out the open bus door while another siren wailed to a stop nearby. "Okay, it looks like my reinforcements have arrived. You can follow me out to the hotel now. Just take your time and be careful not to slip on the sidewalk—it's still a little slushy."

The police officer started down the first step of the bus, then paused and threw a rueful look over her shoulder at them. "Oh, yeah, I almost forgot. Welcome to Pittsburgh."

"Some welcome," said Sikes dryly. "I can't wait to see the send-off party they give us." He stood and shouldered out into the aisle ahead of Cathy as the Newcomers in the front seats started filing out. "George, as soon as we get off the bus, I want you on the other side of the sidewalk. That way we can put Cathy and Susan between us."

George frowned, taking a moment to peer out the window while Susan gathered up her new sweater and followed Cathy into the aisle. He hurried after her, careful not to touch the Overseer getting up from the opposite row of seats. "Matthew, I don't think the sidewalk will be wide enough for all of us. I suggest that we stay on the right-hand side. It looks to me as if the worst part of the crowd is—" He broke off abruptly as his wife gasped and froze on the bottom step of the bus. "Susan, what's wrong?"

Her delighted gurgle of laughter reassured him even before he heard the noise of the crowd. The roar was so thunderous and deep that it took George a long time to realize why he couldn't make out any words. It was applause.

"It *is* a welcoming party, George!" Susan turned to catch at his hand and pull him off the bus after her, warm excitement in her eyes. "They're not Purists after all!"

"They're not *all* Purists," George corrected her, his police-trained eye catching the scatter of hostile faces amid the crowd. The enthusiastic clapping continued as they walked down the rope-cordoned sidewalk, punctuated by occasional protesting cries of "No more spongeheads!" and "E.T. go home!"

"Look, Matt." Cathy tugged at him, smiling and pointing toward the entrance portico of the hotel. "They're filming us for the TV news! Smile at them."

Sikes grunted, refusing to be distracted from his wary scanning of the crowd. "They can always edit me out later. George, where is that shouting coming from?"

George swung his head to focus his hearing more carefully and spotted the protesters along the icy sidewalk. The group of about twenty denim-coated young humans stood lined along the outer rope, carefully positioned beside the TV cameras so their shouting would sound more impressive to viewers. "Coming up on our left now," he said quietly. A ripple of scornful cursing sped through the group when they spotted Sikes and Cathy, the only mixed pair among them. George felt his feet stiffen with tension.

"Matthew," he said urgently. "Move Cathy over here to my right—"

It was too late. A little human girl cradled in her father's arms reached across the left-hand rope, shyly offering Cathy a spray of golden chrysanthemums. Cathy smiled and thanked her politely, then staggered and fell as a snowball hit her in the face. The little girl shrieked.

"Goddammit!" Sikes dove over the rope, hurling himself at the young human male who'd thrown the snowball, heedless of the police whistles shrilling around him. The crowd surged, most of them trying to back away from the fight that had exploded in their

midst while the TV crews struggled to come closer. The little girl's father bent, bravely trying to pull Cathy from under the shoving mass of humanity. Susan ran to help him.

George spat out a fierce Tenctonese curse and waded into the milling crowd, careful not to knock down any humans with his greater strength. As much as he sympathized with Sikes, he couldn't allow his partner's anger to trigger a riot—not here, where TV cameras could record the tragedy for the entire nation to see.

"Matthew!" George heard the cursing first, then spotted the familiar leather jacket inside a struggling clot of denim. One good strong tug broke the knot of protesters apart and let him drag Sikes out of its center, back toward the clearer space of the sidewalk. Blows rained down on him from all sides, but George merely hunched his shoulders and ignored them. Unfortunately, he couldn't enforce the same decision on Sikes. He had to grab his partner by the shoulders and throw him against the far rope to stop his furious attempt to dive back into the crowd.

"It's not going to do any good!" George held Sikes with a warning hand at his throat while police swarmed the protesters and started cuffing them. "You're not a policeman here. You can't arrest them!"

"I don't want to arrest them!" Sikes retorted, wiping blood off his chin with one hand. His hair and jacket were soaked with slush where he'd fallen. "Where's Cathy? Is she all right?"

"I'm fine, Matt. Just a little wet." Cathy stepped forward, out of Susan's steadying grip. There was an angry pink bruise across her temple, but no other marks of injury. The older *linnaum* with the scarred face hovered beside her, carefully shielding her from the hungry lenses of the TV cameras.

"Oh, shit," said Sikes, seeing the TV crews at last. He pushed at George's hand, trying in vain to dislodge it from his neck. "Let's get the hell out of here before we make the nightly news."

"Too late for that," said the cold voice of the former Overseer. The stocky *gannaum* paused beside his wife, glaring at George in disgust. "It's bad enough that we have to be taunted and attacked by humans. Did you have to grovel and lick up their abuse like the spineless *sansol* trash you used to be?" He snorted and grabbed his wife's arm, pulling her away from Susan and Cathy. George felt the skin around his eyes burn with frustrated anger as the Overseer's voice rose. "It will serve you right if the humans show your shameful actions to the rest of their species and decide that Newcomers should never be allowed out of Los Angeles again. Once a slave, always a slave!"

"Well, shit." Sikes stared after him resentfully, even though the insults hadn't been meant for him. "Who pissed in his coffee?"

George forced a deep breath past the cramping muscles of his throat. "No one had to," he said, tasting the bitterness of anger in his dry mouth. "Once an Overseer, always an Overseer."

CHAPTER 3

SIKES HAD TOLD Cathy he'd be sleeping. Instead, he lay in the dark of their hotel room and listened to the music of Cathy in the shower.

It wasn't just the smooth, subtle rhythm of her singing or the pleasantly alien sound of her words. It was the hollow thrum of the overheated pipes, the steady percussion of the water against the walls that kept him pleasantly awake. He liked the sound of her private industry, the little things she did when she was by herself and didn't know he was listening. It was like sharing his life with two different women—the public one and the private who complemented each other so beautifully that he couldn't help being in love with them both. He sighed a long sigh of the spicy, steam-laden air creeping out from under the bathroom door, and smiled a little in the darkness. This was almost as good as sleeping, he decided, and a hell of a lot more restful than the plane.

Three precise thumps on the hotel room door broke across the sound of Cathy's shower. Sikes pulled a pillow over his face and thought about ignoring it, but the knocks only sounded again—equally measured and firm—and he realized with a growl that it must be George with a bug up his butt about something.

His partner didn't even say hello when Sikes pulled open the door. "I hope you're happy."

Sikes squinted at him, tangling one hand in his hair as he propped his elbow against the doorjamb. "Delirious, George—I haven't slept in two days. What do you want?"

"The entire nation," George said with a deep breath of frustration, "now knows that you're an ass."

So what was new? "Excuse me?"

George stepped past him into the darkened hotel room, making a beeline for the television even as Sikes turned and tried to blink his eyes back into focus after the brighter hall. The door latched softly shut behind them. "Beatrice Zepeda just telephoned—"

"Zepeda?" Sikes followed his partner back into the room. "What? Is something wrong at the station?"

"No. In fact, she was absolutely delighted because she and Sergeant Dobbs just finished watching the cable news." The television screen sprang to grainy life while George played with the dial. The Newcomer's face looked angular and too white in the dim lighting. "Ah, here we are."

George stepped back with a flourish as a grim announcer's voice said, "—symposium in Pittsburgh

27

today when a Newcomer guest attacked a human protestor outside the convention housing." A video clip of a suited Newcomer throttling a snow-damp, struggling human monopolized the screen, and it took Sikes a moment to realize it was he and George from just a few hours ago. The grim Overseer's inset image scolded, "It will serve you right if the humans show your shameful actions to the rest of their species and decide that Newcomers should never be allowed out of Los Angeles."

"Gee," Sikes said, unimpressed, "they're right— you do look ten pounds heavier on TV."

George turned off the television with a slap of his hand. "It's not funny."

"I dunno, George." Sikes turned back to his bed with a shrug. "Our buddy the Overseer certainly seemed to be having a good time." He flopped amid the rucked-up covers and wished George would go away.

"That's exactly my point. What if humans who know nothing about Newcomers listen to him and believe the things he says? Confining us to Los Angeles would be just like making us slaves again."

Sikes opened one eye to peer up at his partner. "Nobody's gonna confine you to L.A. Most of us don't even wish that on each other."

George's nose was wrinkled with concern, and it occurred to Sikes with some surprise that the Newcomer really was afraid of all the things the Overseer suggested. He pushed up onto his elbows, nudging George with his toe.

"Hey, George, it's just five minutes of news."

"Five minutes of news," George said without looking at him, "that people will talk about for days." He slid an unhappy look at Sikes. "This kind of exposure is important to us. I thought it was important to you."

Sikes felt a little sting of embarrassment mixed with his resentment but wasn't sure why. "I'm just a guy who traveled cross-country with his girlfriend, George. I didn't come here to be anybody's good example."

"But you came here as my friend." A little of the tightness eased around his eyes, and George looked suddenly fragile and afraid. "I'm asking you as my friend. Please, don't give them any more reasons to hate us."

Sikes bit down on the back of his jaw. "In other words, behave."

"Please," George said again, and whatever little knot of dissension fueled most of Sikes's anger melted into regret.

"All right," he sighed, falling flat on the bed again. "I'll try." He halfheartedly tossed a pillow at George. "It's not gonna be easy."

George caught the pillow against his chest, and smiled. "If this was going to be easy, Matthew, I wouldn't even have had to ask."

An hour and a half of almost sleep helped a little, although eight or nine of the real thing would have been better. Still, in his line of work you learned to take what you could get, and Sikes was pretty sure he could function at least long enough to muddle through a press-sponsored dinner and the associated gushing.

Waiting with Cathy for the Franciscos, he stole a glance at himself in the mirrored panel between the elevator doors. He'd barely made eye contact with his image before having to clap both hands over his face in an effort to contain a monstrous yawn. Oh, yeah, he'd be fine.

Cathy slipped her arm inside his suit jacket and fitted herself beneath his shoulder. "You don't have to come," she told him, somehow making it sound just as sincere as the first time she'd said it twenty minutes ago. "Why don't you stay up in the room and sleep? I'll bring you something from dinner."

"Knowing what you guys eat, I'd rather not take my chances." Sikes let one arm fall across her shoulders while he scrubbed at his eyes with the other. "I wanna come," he said around another, smaller yawn. "I came here to be with you. I don't want to waste any of our time."

Cathy tipped her head and touched her cheek to his without commenting. Sikes knew that was as good as a kiss and a smile.

"Oh, good heavens, I can't believe what I see!"

Sikes felt a burn of annoyance start in his stomach, but kept himself from saying anything until he'd turned to face the *linnaum* approaching from behind. She tossed her smooth, spotted head, and flashed him a flawless, overly perfect smile. "Detective Sikes, isn't it? My goodness, but it *is* a small world!"

Sikes took her extended hand and shook it once, trying to seem pleased. "I guess there's no point in asking what you're doing all the way out here."

Emma Bovary laughed a polyester laugh, and Cathy

said stiffly into Sikes's ear, "Matt, who's your friend?" proving, perhaps, that women were women regardless of their species.

"Not a friend," Sikes said, releasing Emma's hand to reach for Cathy's, "just someone from a case about a year ago. Emma Bovary, this is my . . . friend, Dr. Cathy Frankel."

"A doctor! How charming." Emma exchanged a hand touch with Cathy so quickly that Sikes wasn't even sure if they'd made contact. "I've always loved the sciences," she said, quite earnestly. "But modeling just keeps me *so* busy that I don't know where I'd find the time."

"A model." Cathy rolled wise aqua eyes toward Sikes. "How charming."

"Business," he assured her.

"Mmm hmm." But she was smiling, which meant she was torturing him for the simple pleasure of it, not from any real uncertainty. "We can talk about this later."

Sikes smiled. "Promise?"

Then Emma Bovary declared, "Oh, you both are so *cute!*" and ruined the moment. Sikes went back to studying his reflection in the mirror while Emma told them all about the summer she'd spent counseling Chuck and Di in the south of France.

"Oh," Susan said, quite softly. "I had no idea there would be so many people."

Neither had Sikes.

People turned out like pigeons at a peanut stand for all kinds of human suffering—television reporters at big court trials, protestors and do-gooders at prisoner relocations, all kinds of idiots at every accident or shooting you could name. But stage something optimistic or intelligent, and you couldn't pay people to so much as poke their noses through the door. So when the elevator doors hushed open on the hotel's ballroom level, and the busy wall of white noise rolled over them, the Newcomers weren't the only ones who winced. Sikes felt suddenly a little sick to his stomach and wished he'd stayed upstairs to sleep after all.

"Well, come on, boys and girls." Emma Bovary patted a playful hand on Sikes's bottom, and he jumped. "We're not getting anywhere standing in the elevator. There's work to be done!"

Sikes crammed his hands in his pockets, but let the general pressure of everybody else's movement squeeze them all out into the vestibule. Emma made prissy faces in the elevator mirrors, checking her makeup, while George slipped up between Cathy and Susan to take Susan's hand in his own. "Is that actually a network news team?" he asked, watching a small group of humans, tied together by wires and equipment, scurry by. It encouraged Sikes a little that George sounded just as uncertain as he felt.

"You bet it is, hon." Emma didn't even turn to look at the bustling crews. Snapping closed her compact, she turned with expert smoothness and flashed a brilliant smile for anyone who happened to be watching. "Now, if you'll excuse me—it's show time." She slipped into the flow of cameras and people without even saying ta-ta. Sikes bid her a silent good riddance.

"Well, she was certainly a colorful girl." No doubt

Susan's way of doing the same. Sikes snorted a little laugh but didn't comment when Cathy glanced curiously over at him.

"Where do you suppose we're supposed to converge?" George asked, neatly deflecting the conversation to more practical concerns. He kept both hands very stiff and close to his sides, a sure sign he was nervous and trying to conceal it.

"I dunno." Sikes wondered what it was like to care this much about something you couldn't really have any control over. It probably sucked. "Can't you guys smell the food from here?"

Cathy wrinkled her nose. "I can't smell anything past all these humans." Then, apparently realizing what she'd said, her eyes flashed dark with embarrassment and she slipped her arm through Sikes's. "Oh, Matt, I'm sorry! You know what I mean."

"Unfortunately, I know *exactly* what you mean." He smiled, and laced his fingers with hers. "So where does that leave us? With—" He pantomimed shying away from the crowds with a gasp. *"—exploring?!"*

George only had time to peer at him like a grade school teacher before a woman's voice interrupted from behind, "Excuse me—Mr. Sikes?"

They turned as a unit, Sikes disentangling from Cathy as he did so. "Yeah?"

The elegant older woman behind them smiled, motioning her younger companion to follow as she stepped up and stretched out her hand. "I'm Nancy Thompson, the symposium organizer." She fidgeted one-handed with a long string of pearls around her neck. "This is Kathleen Westbeld, the program director for WQED." The dark-haired younger woman bobbed forward to shake down the line of hands while Thompson explained, "Ms. Westbeld's television station supplied most of the funding for the symposium and will be providing continuous coverage throughout the week, not to mention a feed to the cable news stations. That means a lot of good publicity for us all." Thompson beamed gratefully at Westbeld, who combed back a mass of shining brown hair with one hand and smiled.

"This is a pretty big coup for Pittsburgh all the way around," the executive admitted. "I'm happy to be a part of it."

"Kathleen, meet Matt Sikes and Dr. Cathy Frankel." Thompson let off toying with her necklace long enough to reach out and draw Susan a few steps forward. "And Susan and George Francisco."

George nodded in acknowledgment of Westbeld's bright "Pleased to meet you," looking, if anything, even more nervous. "I'm impressed, Ms. Thompson. I hadn't realized you were so familiar with your symposium attendees."

"Well, we try," Thompson said with a little blush. "Admittedly, your group is a little easier to pick out than some." She slid a shy, self-conscious glance at Sikes, and he knew what they were talking about even before she felt the need to tell Westbeld, "Mr. Sikes and Dr. Frankel are our only mixed couple at the symposium."

Westbeld's ears perked up like a K-9 over a kilo of cocaine. "Oh, really?" Never taking her eyes or her smile off their group, she backed up a few steps and motioned to someone around the corner whom Sikes couldn't see. "Are you just friends, or actually, you know, involved?"

Cathy's eyes widened a little with surprise, and Sikes stated bluntly, "None of your damn business."

Westbeld cocked her head in an obvious effort to show no malice of intent. "Come on," she cajoled as one of the roving camera crews rounded the vestibule to join her. "You know what I mean—"

Sikes resisted an impulse to shove Cathy behind him and cover her retreat. "I know exactly what you mean, and it's none of your damn business." He glowered at the technician who was busy mounting a camera on his shoulder. "Why don't you go talk to Emma Bovary? She'll tell you more about her than you'd ever want to hear."

"Look, Mr. Sikes," Westbeld said, "you really don't have to worry. I *like* Newcomers, I'm on your side."

"Then that's where you're wrong," Sikes told her, "'cause I'm not on anybody's side." The cameraman scooted a good three feet closer, and Sikes clapped a hand over the lens sharply enough to make the technician yelp. "You either put that thing away, or I'm gonna stuff it straight up your ass."

Westbeld locked stares with Sikes for nearly a minute, then looked away and sighed. "Do it, Adam."

The technician already had the lights turned off and the camera cradled against his chest. "Hey," he said, peering at Sikes, "aren't you the guy who got pounded by one of the Newcomers this morning?"

"Yes." George sounded particularly aggrieved. "I'm the one who was beating him."

"It happens all the time." Sikes, taking Cathy by the elbow, slipped back between the Franciscos to exit the other side of the vestibule. "We were fighting about a girl."

". . . and certainly you recognize the handsome fellow over there with Geraldo? That's Scott Free. He and his wife, Sandi, write together under the *nom de plume* L. A. Graf—the most *marvelous* science fiction novels about all the places they visited while on the spaceship and the significance of their experiences here on Earth. They're naming a character after me in their next book. A darling couple, just darling, and so *honest . . . !*"

Sikes wasn't sure about the Newcomer definition of darling, but the weedy *gannaum* with the vest and sweater looked more nerdy than darling to him. His wife was as unremarkable as pudding.

"Writers?" Susan pushed the remnants of what might have been lizards or squids or something equally grotesque to the edge of her plate and politely looked where Emma pointed. "Have you known them long?"

Oh, Susan, don't talk! Sikes silently groaned. *You'll just encourage her!* His own food didn't look a whole lot better than the Newcomers'. It was cooked, but he still wasn't sure what the gray mass in the middle was supposed to be. He'd actually started envying Cathy her salad plate.

"I sat with them in first class on the plane." Emma picked at her low-cal fungus with dramatically manicured nails. "They were the only Newcomers up there besides me. Well, me, and Ann Arbor." She made a little face, then seemed to think better of it and smoothed her features again. "That's her over there at the head table. She's such a butch, it's terrible."

Sikes stole a glance toward the front of the room and immediately focused on the *linnaum* at one end of the long head table. She looked unfortunately like a man in drag with her tasteful jewelry and well-cut dress, and she picked at her food almost as much as George. Thinking how he must look in his too-long hair and too-old tie, Sikes knew just how she felt.

"She's the Olympic gold medalist, isn't she?" At least Cathy had the brains to whisper the question to Sikes, rather than direct it at Emma.

Newcomer hearing did them in, though. Even as Sikes was opening his mouth to reply, Emma leaned around Susan and George to declare, "A decathlete, dear—gold medals in four or five things. Isn't it a shame?

Sikes threw his napkin across his plate like a sheet over a corpse. "Of course. Sports I can deal with. So they stick Superwoman with Peeping Westbeld and stick Supermodel with me."

"Oh, I'm sure you'll get your chance with her." Emma glanced around as though to make sure no one was listening, then leaned even further across Susan's plate. "They say she likes human guys."

Cathy caught Sikes's wrist under the table, but he was too tired of all the nonsense tonight to have thought of anything brutal to say, anyway. "It's all right," Cathy said, very close to his ear. "That just means she has good taste."

Sikes smiled at her, his face growing warm, and squeezed her hand without a word.

At the front of the room, a flurry of murmuring diners and popping flashes drew attention to Nancy Thompson as she stepped up to the speaker's platform. She and a handful of mixed Newcomers and humans had chatted at tables to either side of the podium all evening. Sikes recognized the sour-faced Overseer and his wife among them, but except for Ann Arbor, none of the other Newcomers looked familiar or interesting.

The dining room itself jutted from the side of the hotel like a huge, glassed-in balcony. Beyond the transparent walls, lights from both homes and trafficways etched twinkling paths up the tree-choked hills; the rivers moved past like slow, glossy ribbons less than a block away from the hotel's front door. Everything looked impossibly bright and clean in the brilliance of the still-deepening snow.

With an unexpected throb of discomfort, Sikes wanted ve y much to be back home in L.A.

"Ladies and gentlemen, humans and Tenctonese . . ." Nancy Thompson smiled across the roomful of symposium guests and reporters. "Welcome to the first annual Tenctonese Businesspersons Symposium. This convention has been established to foster human-Tenctonese relations across the United States by encouraging human-owned businesses to embrace the presence of successful Tenctonese in America's marketplace. We have with us today some of the country's most prestigious Tenctonese— businesspeople, police officers, athletes, and doctors—"

"—and models," Emma Bovary whispered huffily.

"What kind of publicity is she shooting for? Nobody's going to photograph a doctor over a model."

Sikes was surprised when Susan was the one to shush her.

"—especially grateful to Mr. Ross Vegas of Vegas Gengineering in La Jolla for his generous funding and organizational efforts on the symposium's behalf."

Applause swelled around them as Thompson stepped away from the microphone and the tall Overseer stood with an icy smile to replace her. Sikes snorted into his lukewarm coffee. Well, that explained that. Bring money into the picture, and you could probably get away with inviting a Nazi to a concentration camp reunion.

"Thank you, Ms. Thompson." The microphone popped when Vegas bent it to accommodate his larger height. "And thank you, Pittsburgh, for opening your arms to Tenctonese, *kleezantsun'* and *sansol* alike."

Two seats down from Sikes, George dropped his silverware onto his plate with a disgusted clatter.

"When we came to your planet six years ago, we had no idea what reception we would receive. It was not by choice, our landing. It was not by choice, our permanent exile here—"

"Is it by *choice* that you use your alien technology and alien brains to engineer monsters in your labs, *Mister* Vegas?"

Sikes twisted around to track down the strident voice at the back of the room. One of Protzberg's uniforms was already homing in on the guy even as various other reporters and news people tried to push him back out the door.

"Well, *Mister* Vegas?" The heckler caught himself on the doorjambs, bouncing up on his toes to see above the heads around him. "Isn't it true that your labs are being used to genetically engineer monsters for the military?"

Vegas's icy eyes grew even paler with anger. "That's absolutely absurd."

"Isn't it true you used fetal cells from your own *baby* to create test-tube slags for use—!"

"Enough!" Vegas's voice cracked through the room, almost drowned out by the microphone's protesting squeal. "I will not stand here and allow some slave-minded *tert* to vilify me." It didn't seem to matter to him that the shouting protestor was already gone. Vegas raked a lizardine stare across the assembled humans and former slaves. "You complain that we treat you like animals, yet this is the best you can do. You shame your race as much as you shame mine."

George hissed something Sikes assumed was impolite but made no effort to speak aloud or follow the Overseer when Vegas stormed away from the podium and into the murmuring crowd.

"So much for Ross's speech." Sikes downed the last of his coffee and kicked back in his chair. He grinned down the table at George. "Anybody for dessert?"

A shriek from the doorway behind him was his only answer. That, and the sticky, salt-sweet spatter of blood as a baby's mutilated corpse smacked to the tabletop between them.

CHAPTER 4

HUMAN SCREAMS AND stammering Tenctonese clicks exploded around the room as the symposium guests shrank back from the small bloody heap on the table. George scowled and dragged off his dinner jacket, flinging it over the pitiful body before the TV cameras could focus on it. In the night-dark reflections of the curving glass windows he saw Sikes vault through the double doors after the retreating protestors, Jen Protzberg and the hotel security guards at his heels.

"Oh, my God." Nancy Thompson stared down at the lump on the table as if she couldn't turn away, the fine dust of her makeup suddenly visible against her white cheeks. "Is that—" She swallowed hard. "—a *baby?*"

"No," George said flatly. "It's a monkey."

"A monkey?" Westbeld looked up and motioned the cameras to continue filming while they talked. She may have been a pro-Newcomer activist, George reflected dryly, but she was also a member of the press. News was news.

"How do you know that, Detective Francisco?" Westbeld asked, putting just a slight emphasis on his official title.

George put his hands on his hips, the Newcomer equivalent of a shrug. "Back during the Purist riots in L.A., this was a common Purist shock tactic. They'd buy a monkey from a pet store or steal one from a medical research lab, then kill it and skin it without draining the blood." He gestured at the dark stain spreading across the tablecloth. "As you can see, it makes a very effective mess."

"But it looked so *human*," protested Thompson, unconvinced. "Are you sure it's not a baby?"

"Bring in a curator from the Pittsburgh Zoo if you don't believe my husband." Susan's calm and sensible voice startled George by its nearness. He turned to see her standing just behind him, frowning at the bloodstains on his dinner jacket as if daring them to spread any further. "But even I know that human babies have much larger heads in proportion to their bodies than this poor thing does."

"Yes, that's true." Relief crept into Nancy Thompson's face with a rush of returning color. George saw the humans in the room glance thoughtfully at the silhouetted shape under the cloth, the horror fading from their faces. Not for the first time, he blessed his wife's talent for saying the right thing at the right time. "Thank you for pointing that out, Mrs. Francisco. You have no idea what it feels like—"

George felt his skin shake with sudden cold under

his thin silk shirt. None of the humans in the room, he realized, understood just what the Purists had done. He reached a long arm out and gathered Susan tight against his side, as much for his own comfort as for hers.

"My wife knows *exactly* how you feel," George told Thompson, trying to keep his voice from sounding too fierce. He felt Susan's shoulders tremble beneath his arm and knew it wasn't from the cold. "Ms. Thompson, this protest wasn't aimed at humans."

Thompson gave him an uncomprehending look. "It wasn't?"

"No." George heard the small whir of a camera lens refocusing and looked up to find the TV crews aiming their equipment at him. He met the camera's watchful eye steadily. "Compared to human babies, newborn Tenctonese have smaller heads, longer limbs, and darker eyes. They are also born with many of their teeth already formed." He glanced at the small wet bulge under his coat, remembering the gleam of teeth inside its bloody mouth. "That skinned animal wasn't meant to frighten you," he said grimly. "It was meant to frighten us."

"Do you *really* think they believed you?"

George looked across the elevator, startled by the salt-bitter edge in Lydia Vegas's voice. The Overseer's wife refused to meet his gaze, staring instead at the sliver of her own spotted head visible in the thin mirrored strip that accented one wall. The murmuring group of Tenctonese who had just entered the elevator fell silent, waiting for his reply.

"I believe Nancy Thompson did," George said

while the elevator doors slid closed. "She apologized several times to Susan for her comment. And I heard Kathleen Westbeld repeat my description of Tenctonese babies to several of the other reporters there."

"I don't mean them." Lydia untwined her tensely knotted hands and flung them outward, as if to encompass the entire city of Pittsburgh and beyond. "I mean *them*. All those humans who watched us on television—do you think *they* understood?"

"Not all of them did, I suppose," George admitted. "But surely some—"

"*Some* isn't enough," Lydia said fiercely. She turned away from the wall when the elevator slowed for their floor, and George was shocked to see red rims of grief around her pale eyes. "Don't fool yourself, Detective Francisco. You can't keep all humans from hating us, no matter how hard you try." Her mouth flattened into an expression bleaker than a frown, an expression George had seen too often among Tenctonese on the ship. *"Vots garsa ot aeb' blafta lon coke see 'ser la su rom heef,"* she added in flat Tenctonese. *Your struggle to change things only brings the rest of us more pain.*

George felt anger surge hotly up his throat. "That's a slave saying!" he snapped. "You only think that way because the Overseers trained—"

Susan thumped a sharp elbow into his chest, and George grunted in surprise. The blow kept him breathless long enough to remember that Lydia Vegas was married to an Overseer. No wonder she still talked like a slave, he thought grimly. A glance into

Susan's determined eyes told him that further comment on that subject wouldn't be welcome.

The elevator doors hissed open, breaking the painful silence that had fallen over the small crowd of Newcomers inside. They trickled out, breaking into ones and twos as they moved down the third-floor hall to their allotted hotel rooms. At last only George and Susan remained, blocked from leaving by Lydia Vegas's rigid figure. The Overseer's wife hadn't moved at all since her outburst, not even when the other Newcomers jostled past her. George had to reach out and flatten his palm across the elevator's retracted door to keep it from closing on her face.

"Come on." Susan pushed at Lydia's elbow, urging her gently out of the elevator. "You need to get back to your room now, Mrs. Vegas. You're upset."

"Upset." The thin, bitter laugh that jerked out from the older *linnaum* shocked George into adding his efforts to Susan's. Between the two of them, they managed to get Lydia Vegas out and walking slowly down the hall. She shuddered beneath their hands, her slight bones vibrating with the stress. "I suppose you could call it that. But you can't know how it felt to see that—thing—on the table. You've probably never lost a child—"

George stiffened, more in surprise than offense. "We *all* lost children on the ship," he reminded her sharply.

"I don't mean having a child taken away." Lydia gazed down the long, dimly lit hall, the bleak look back on her face. George wondered if she was thinking about her husband. "I mean lost in birth, lost while he

45

incubated in his father's pouch. Lost when he looked just like that—"

Susan reached out with her usual quick sympathy to press her palm against Lydia's scarred cheek. "You had a miscarriage."

"Yes." The older Newcomer's brittle voice cracked into a sob, but she kept walking. "It happened last year, just before the Days of Descent. Ross was never home, he was working so hard to get his business started, and he wouldn't listen when I told him—"

A door slammed open a few meters down the hall, spilling a fan of brighter light across the floor. The stocky figure of Ross Vegas stood silhouetted in the doorway, his shadowy face unreadable but his shoulders high with anger.

"Lydia." He strode forward to catch her by the arm and yank her toward him, as if Susan and George's touch had somehow contaminated her. "You shouldn't inflict your personal problems on strangers."

His wife fell silent, a blank wall of politeness slamming down across the pain in her face. Vegas turned toward George and Susan, his eyes clenched with anger. "I don't know what you said to upset my wife," he growled, "but from now on I want you both to stay away from her. Is that clear?"

Years of resentment rose inside George, making his own eyes narrow reflexively. He held Vegas's pale gaze for a long moment before he spoke, silently informing the Overseer that he wasn't intimidated. "Your wife was distressed by what happened at the press conference, *after* you stalked out and left her there," he said at last. "If you're looking to blame someone for that, I suggest you check a mirror."

Vegas scowled at him, anger and surprise mixing in his face. "You're *cha'dikav!*" he said, using the Tenctonese word that meant "too intractable to be trained." An insult among the Overseers, but not so among the slaves. "What are you doing here? Someone like you should have been sold off the ship long ago."

George smiled back at him, tightly and without humor. "I was," he agreed. "Several times. But I was *cha'dikav,* so they always sent me back."

The welcome kiss of warm air met them when they opened the door to their hotel room, and George felt some of the tension drain out of his feet. Beside him he heard Susan release a grateful sigh as she locked the door behind them. "You remembered to turn up the thermostat," she said, and turned to brush her temple against his. "Thank you, *neemu.* I don't think I could have stood the cold much longer."

"Neither could I." George leaned his cheek against the silken heat of hers. A little more worry seeped away. "We could get even warmer in bed."

Susan laughed and pushed him away. "I think you've spent too much time with Matt lately."

"I have," George agreed seriously. "We were on a stakeout together for most of last week."

"That's not what I meant." Susan kicked off her shoes and headed for the bathroom, her voice floating out past the half-open door. "You never used to feel the need to antagonize Overseers, George, no matter how much you disliked them."

George settled on the nearest flower-patterned bed, working his own shoes off and massaging his stiff ankles. "I never had an Overseer insult my wife after she had gone out of her way to be nice to his."

"Poor Lydia." Susan emerged from the bathroom with her face scrubbed clean and glowing. She unzipped her strapless blue dress and slid out of it, then folded it carefully away in a dresser drawer. George appreciatively eyed the translucent silk slip she wore under it, wondering what kept it in place. "That's a terrible thing to have gone through. I keep thinking about how close we came to losing Vessna—"

"Don't." George reached out and pulled her onto his lap, stroking a distracting hand down the nape of her neck. Susan sighed in surprise and delight. "I like this slip you almost have on. Is it new?"

His wife chuckled wickedly. "No. Cathy lent it to me."

"Oh." George paused, a little disturbed by the thought of Sikes seeing this same garment, even if it had been on a quite different female. "She didn't think Matthew would mind?"

"She didn't think he'd notice." Susan leaned over to run a knowing finger down the most sensitive line of his spots. "But if you're really worried about it, we can always take it off."

"Good idea," George said, and started to implement it. Unfortunately, the phone rang before he could finish. He groaned and reached for it.

"Matthew, if you need me to bail you out—"

"It's me, Dad." It was Buck's voice, unusually cheerful and as clear as if he were calling from the next room instead of from Los Angeles. "Bad time to call?"

"Not as bad as it could have been." George pulled Susan down onto the bed beside him and cradled the phone between their faces so that both of them could hear their son. "How are things at home?"

"All right so far. Albert took pretty good care of Vessna while Em and I were at school."

"Except for putting her diaper on backwards," Emily's indignant voice said from another phone. "I had to show him the right way to do it."

"I knew we could depend on you, Emily." Susan smiled at George over the phone. At thirteen, their daughter had eagerly adopted all the responsibilities of an adult and liked to be treated that way. "Thank you."

"Don't be too hard on Albert," George reminded her. "He's doing us a big favor by taking vacation to baby-sit Vessna." Then parental concern overrode his sense of duty. "Did you make yourselves a good dinner?"

"Fresh badger. And we saw you on TV while we were eating," Buck informed them. "Hey, was that skinned thing as gross as it looked under your coat?"

"Bu-uck!" Emily wailed, suddenly reverting to outraged childhood. *"Gross!* Don't remind me!"

George groaned again. "Oh, no. Don't tell me I was on national television!"

"All five channels," his son said cheerfully. "And your tie was crooked on all of them."

"It was?" George put a hand up to his throat and found the knot of his tie firmly wedged under his left shirt collar. He grunted, realizing that he must have twisted it to one side when he'd hauled off his jacket. "Sorry I embarrassed you."

Buck laughed. "No, Dad, you were great. You really told that stupid human woman off when you explained about the monkey. All the news commentators are talking about how the Purist movement made a big mistake in messing with dead Tenctonese babies."

"And the Newcomer station in L.A. has made you Tenctonese of the Month," added Emily with glee. "They called and told us just now. I can't wait to tell my friends at school."

George blinked across at Susan in astonishment. "But all I did was explain why the Purists used a monkey."

"I guess it doesn't take much to be a hero these days." Buck's voice reverted to its more familiar cynical tone. "Hey, don't argue about it, Dad. Maybe somebody will ask you to write a book, and we'll all be rich."

"Speaking of money—" In one of those dizzying shifts that George still wasn't used to, Emily sounded very adult again. "—this phone call must be running up a lot of it. We'd better hang up."

"Yes, dear," agreed Susan, her mouth quivering as if she was trying not to laugh. "Nuzzle Vessna for me and tell her we'll be home soon."

"I already did," said Emily proudly. "'Bye, Mom! 'Bye, Dad!"

"We'll be watching for you on TV," Buck added evilly just before the phone clicked.

George sighed and leaned over Susan to replace the phone in its cradle, then sank back into her warm embrace. She smiled and began loosening his crooked tie, then paused to look at him closely. George knew why—he could feel the odd way his mouth was twisting.

"Is something wrong, George?" Susan asked in concern.

"No, not wrong." He rubbed a finger reassuringly down the bridge of her nose. "It's just that I've never before done something that Buck has actively approved of. I'm not sure how to react."

She laughed and finished pulling off the tie. "Well, at least you can take comfort in the fact that he doesn't think much of you being named Tenctonese of the Month."

"No." Mild embarrassment prickled down the nape of his neck when he met her amused gaze. "What do you think of it?"

"I think it couldn't have happened to a more deserving *gannaum.*" Susan unbuttoned his shirt and slid both hands into it. "Come here and let me congratulate you."

Planet dreams. George hated planet dreams. The rank smells of alien vegetation, the slap and scratch of branches across his skin as he ran, the harsh rasp of humidity in his lungs, and the glare of bluish sunlight—

The *levpa* was chasing him, silent as it always was, nose to ground and nearly invisible against the forest floor. Somewhere behind it were the Overseers, or at least, George hoped they were. He kept glancing over his shoulder as he stumbled up each hill, waiting for the impact of the *levpa,* for the familiar whine of the aircar to arrive and haul him back to the ship. It had to come, he knew it had to come, he knew they'd never let him really escape . . . but in his nightmares, they always did. George ran until he staggered with thirst, ran until he went blind with exhaustion, ran until the bitter dismay of failure rose up in his throat and choked him.

A shrill buzzing ripped the alien forest away from him without warning. George jerked up in bed, aware of Susan's warmth beside him and the glittering, reflected glow of the river in their dark hotel room, not sure what had woken him. Then the buzzing shrilled again, and he recognized it as the phone. He reached out and yanked it off the bedside table.

"What?" he demanded, still fierce from his dream.

"Spongehead." The cold human voice on the other end of the line brought George completely awake. "You're going to get another chance to be on TV." The voice paused, then went on with a chuckle before George could speak. "In about a million pieces. There's a bomb in your hotel, and it's going to blow up in five minutes."

CHAPTER 5

BLUE AND RED police lights strobed across the roped-off snowfield in front of the hotel—a snowfield that in better weather served as some kind of park. The armored bomb-squad van had crunched over salt heaps and pack ice to park right against the hotel's revolving brass doors, almost out of sight beneath the entrance overhang and behind the doorman's elaborate booth. They'd brought far too many police types to the scene. Sikes figured that was to be expected. Not only were there also far too many yo-yos hanging around the edges, eager to see somebody, anybody get blown all to hell, but there were far too many news crews, as well, all equally unwilling to miss the East's first Newcomer flambé. Sikes jammed his fists more securely into his armpits and wondered why nobody ever held these symposiums in the summer.

"Matt, come here. You're going to freeze." Cathy moved up behind him to open the front of her borrowed peacoat and enfold him against her. "You know, human core body temperature only has to drop two degrees to cause serious biochemical problems."

What a cheerful thought. "Don't worry about me," Sikes said through chattering teeth. "The cold's the only thing keeping me awake right now." Still, he was glad for her steady warmth and the feel of her slim arms wrapped around his. "Where's Susan?"

"I'm here." She was almost invisible beneath two of the hotel's quilted comforters, dwarfed by George's greater build and height inside all that fabric. "I hope this isn't going to take too long."

"It depends on whether or not they actually find a bomb," George said. His nose and forehead were already pinkish with cold, but he hadn't taken his eyes off the third-floor windows since they'd come outside. "The sooner they find it, the sooner they'll leave."

"And if they don't find it," Sikes continued for him, "we could be out here all night while they search every room in the hotel."

"How do you know?" Another alien couple, swathed in heavy clothing as well as what looked like their hotel room draperies, skirted the edge of the sidewalk to shuffle closer. Sikes recognized Scott Free's snow-speckled wire rims beneath a haze of breathy steam. "You're not with the Purists?" The look he directed over Sikes's shoulder at Cathy as good as said, "You can't be."

"We're police officers," George told him. "This sort of thing doesn't change much from place to place."

Not that George would know, Sikes thought. But not

that he was wrong, either. He must have read it somewhere. "Besides, it's still humans doing the cop work. I know about humans, even if I don't want to some of the time. They're not gonna let us go back in until they're sure."

"That's good, I guess," Sandi Free said with a sigh. "It's just, it's so *cold.*"

"Yeah." Sikes wished he could somehow draw them all together in a big huddle or something to conserve what they could of their body heat. But he felt stupid for just thinking about how that would look, so he said nothing. "Try to keep moving—it'll raise your temperature."

Scott pulled his wife tighter and they shuffled away down the sidewalk. Although they didn't stop, Sikes heard the liquid click-clicking of their voices as they passed other knots of Newcomers, urging their peers to move around. As the rigid line of former slaves began to break apart, Cathy said from behind him, "Maybe you should take your own advice."

"I'm not the one in danger of freezing to death even inside a big blanket." Still, he started slowly down the sidewalk away from the direction taken by the Frees, thinking about Cathy and what his increased body heat could do for her.

Slow stepping with her directly behind him was a little awkward, but Cathy didn't protest and Sikes didn't mind. Snow encroached annoyingly close as shoveled-bare sidewalk gradually ran out, and the spidery latticework of a bridge reflected top and bottom against the river several yards ahead of them and the sky. It had stopped snowing hours ago, but the snow plowed up along the curb was waist high, the undisturbed blanket on the grass taller than Sikes's knees. Slowing to a stop just beside a row of sagging bushes, Sikes was suddenly awash in unwelcome memories of Detroit winters spent wielding a broken snow shovel in sweat-soaked woolens and secondhand boots. He shook the thoughts away with a shiver.

Cathy rested her chin on his shoulder. "What's the matter?"

"Nothing," he said automatically. Then, feeling guilty for the easy lie, "I dunno. Just getting fed up with the assholes, I guess."

"Hm." She slipped around in front of him, exposing his back to the frigid night, and locked her hands around his waist so they could face each other, eye to eye. "Anything in particular or just the usual Matt Sikes disgust with the whole world?"

He sighed, and his breath curled around them like smoke. "Is it that wrong?" Even he was surprised at how quietly he asked it.

Cathy frowned. "What?"

"Us. Being together like we are, you and me."

He wasn't sure how to interpret the subtle expression that flitted across her face, but he'd known her long enough now to recognize the calmness that replaced it as Cathy trying to protect him from her hurt. "Who says what we have is wrong?"

Sikes reached up to rub one finger against her brow. "You're not stupid, Cathy. Everybody! Every TV journalist who feels the need to point it out to the public, every Newcomer busybody who disapproves of it with her friends."

"We're not the only Newcomer and human couple

on the planet," Cathy told him, but Sikes shook his head.

"We are out here." He looked beyond her at the dirty snow and the passing cars full of morbid curiosity. "You don't know what it's like out here, how lucky we've been, living in L.A. Out here, seeing whites with blacks or Asians is a big deal. In some places, it used to be a crime. And here I am, getting seen nationwide with an alien." He pulled his attention back to her, and snuggled deeper into their coat for lack of any better way to express his regret. "I'm sorry . . . It's just, I don't want to be with you because it's some kind of statement, and I *hate* feeling like I'm getting forced to stand for things I never even thought about. It's like everybody's using us for whatever it is they want, and there's not even anybody I can punch out to make myself feel better."

Cathy laughed warmly in his ear, then pushed just far enough away to look at him squarely. "Do you love me?"

A swell of hot panic swept over him, quickly followed by confusion and a little fear. "I care about you a lot." It was as close as he was willing to say.

Cathy accepted it without pushing for more. "Do you love me because my sexual organs are in a different arrangement than a human woman's or because of who I am and what I feel for you?"

He reached up with both hands to stroke the sides of her face. "Cathy, no offense, but I don't love any sexual organs that make me take a night class for six weeks just to use them."

"Well, then—" She kissed him tenderly, something

she'd also learned within the past few months, just for him. "Our agenda is to care for each other and make each other happy. What difference does it make what everybody else wants from us?"

"Everybody else runs the world, hon," he explained with gentle regret.

Cathy smiled and kissed the end of his nose. "But you don't have to take them all to bed with you."

"True," he conceded. "Very true."

"Have you seen my husband?"

Sikes glanced away from his bored inspection of the cop silhouettes in the hotel room windows. An hour into their silly search and they'd turned up nothing. He wondered how long it would take them to figure out that the word *hoax* more than just a little applied to their situation.

Lydia Vegas, the spots on her scalp flushed dark with cold, stood just to their side of a blue historic landmark sign, apparently trying to use it for a windbreak. It wasn't working very well. The blanket she hugged around her snapped and fluttered in the stiff breeze, as though trying to grope around to the front and smother her. Without her husband there to help warm her, she looked particularly frail and tiny.

"You can't find Ross?" Sikes, casually balanced with his hips against the park's chain-link fence and Cathy all but sitting on his lap, silently urged her to stand as he straightened. "Did he come out with the rest of us?" A quick glance across the line of bare heads didn't reveal the tall Overseer among them.

"Yes." Lydia turned to look as well. Her scarred face flashed from red to blue to red in the passage of silent police lights. "We were here together until just a half hour ago. Then he went to talk with the human in charge about how much longer we'd have to stand out in this cold." Her eyes colored in a way Sikes couldn't read. "He hasn't come back."

Sikes's pulse began a little dance of anxiety, and he pushed himself clear of Cathy even as he craned to look around them for some sign of the errant Newcomer. "He probably got tied up bitching at the cops," he said, not believing it. He pulled the peacoat tight around Cathy, ignoring the bite of winter cold through his sweater, and fastened her first few buttons. "Go get George. I'm gonna go talk to the cops."

Her eyes darkened with worry. "Matt—"

"I'll be right back."

Except for the way the cold slipped into his lungs, the jog across the street was easy. No traffic to avoid, at least, and most of the bystanders had gotten tired of the cold and wandered back to bed. Sikes was glad when he made the sidewalk and could slip behind one of the cruisers to cut the wind. The nearest uniform saw him and waved imperiously back toward the police line. "Hey, back across the street, guy!"

Sikes reached instinctively for his badge, then realized it wasn't there when his hand closed instead on cold sweater hem. "I'm a cop," he said in his best crime-scene voice. "LAPD."

"LAPD?" The cop looked as if he was about to say more but stopped himself after glancing beyond the squad cars at the milling Newcomers. "You with them?" he asked with a jerk of his head. Sikes nodded, and the cop turned to bark at his partner, "Barb! Get this guy a jacket."

It was all Sikes could do to keep from jittering in place from the cold. "Oh, man, thanks! I've been *freezing* out here."

"All that L.A. sunshine thins your blood." But the cop smiled as he passed across a black padded police jacket. "Bosserman," he introduced himself.

"Sikes." They shook hands in between Sikes shoving his arms down the sleeves of the jacket. It was deliciously warm from the inside of somebody's car. "Look, have you seen one of the Newcomer men around here? Talking to your chief or anything?"

Bosserman frowned, glancing around as though he might have missed something. "You mean besides across the street? Nah. Why? You missing one?"

"Apparently." Sikes zipped up the jacket, chewing the inside of his lip. "Do me a favor—ask around your guys to see if somebody's seen him. His name's Ross Vegas, and he financed a lot of this convention." He backed up toward the street again. "I'm starting to wonder if maybe the bomb threat wasn't just a setup to get us outside where somebody could nab him."

While Bosserman collected his partner and hurried off to question the rest of the assembled cops, Sikes trotted back across the slushy street to meet George at the edge of the sidewalk. The Newcomer had left Susan and the blanket with Cathy; Sikes could see them hovering near Lydia Vegas just a few yards away. "Did Cathy tell you?" he asked George quietly as he joined him.

George nodded grimly. "He isn't with the police?"

"No." Sikes unzipped the jacket and started to strip out of it as he spoke. "Let's take a quick walk around the block, see if he's wandered off."

"Why would he? He knows the Purists must be somewhere nearby."

"George, I don't know! Maybe they suck Overseers' brains out their ears when they give them their tattoos. Here." He pushed the jacket into George's hands, then grabbed his elbow to start him walking. "Put this on. If we're gonna find Vegas dead on a street corner, the last thing I want is to lug both your frozen bodies back home."

George shouldered into the jacket without disguising his relief. "Thank you. Not just for this, but—"

"Stop it, George. I'm sick of qualifying for sainthood just because I put up with you people."

George cocked his head, all semblance of sentimentality gone. "Doesn't it seem like my people ought to be the ones gaining some blessed status for putting up with you?"

"Shut up, George. Just shut up."

Nothing. No sign of Vegas in the two-block area they scouted, not many people in evidence that they could even ask. The two homeless men they came across seemed too confused by their questions to be helpful, and even using George as an example didn't get any information out of them, meaning they most likely hadn't seen Vegas or anyone looking even remotely like him. Sikes dragged George away while the Newcomer was still digging through his pockets for change, ignoring George's protests in favor of devising their next course of action.

"I think we should go back to the hotel," George suggested. "For all we know, Vegas is already back there and everyone is back inside."

Somehow, Sikes thought it unlikely. "Come on, George, think. Where would a guy like Vegas go on a night like tonight?"

"I'm not *kleezantsun',*" George said stiffly.

"No," Sikes agreed, "but you are Tenctonese. Don't you think even a little bit alike?" He balled his fists up inside the cuffs of his sweater, trying to save what little heat he had left.

"Matthew, this would be like me asking you what Adolf Hitler would do lost on the streets of Pittsburgh." George's voice took on a mocking, frustrated tone. "You are human, after all. Surely you and Hitler must think something alike."

Tired, Sikes waved him into silence before he could really get going. "All right, all right, fine, I see your point. But where does that leave us?"

"With going back to the hotel," George stated plainly.

Sikes stuck a finger in his partner's face. "You're a real pain in the ass when it comes to advice, you know that?"

"Well," a coarse voice interrupted them, "look who we got here, two refugees from the slag-lover's convention." Sikes threw a startled look over George's shoulder, and the Newcomer spun around with a click of surprise when three dark figures materialized from the shadows of a building nearby. "We've got a message for you'ns."

They were none of them tall, Sikes noted, but all three wore gloves and heavy jackets. It was blows to the head and legs, or nothing at all.

"We're looking for a missing Newcomer." Something about George's excruciating calmness made Sikes hold his breath. "We don't want any trouble."

"What you want's got nothing to do with it." The leader jammed his hand into one coat pocket, eying George. "They say slags got different body types than humans. Are you'ns different enough? Or do you'ns feel pain just like everybody else?" Sikes glimpsed a flash of black metal as the man's hand pulled clear of his pocket. "I guess we get to find out."

He heard the click of something stiff being pulled back into place and charged past George to tackle the man before his brain could warn him not to.

"Matthew, no!"

They hit the ground with Sikes on top. Sikes levered himself up with an elbow on the Purist's chest and hit him once across the face. The recoil from the blow nearly threw Sikes off balance, but he caught himself by falling forward and cramming a forearm against the attacker's throat. "Hell of a message," he grated in the Purist's face. "Wanna try delivering it to me?"

The Purist twisted with a growl. "You got it, guy." And he jammed his hand upward in a hard, awkward frontal blow.

The pain came as a surprise. Sikes barked a startled cry, jerking up and away as every muscle in his torso convulsed into a rigid knot. He wanted to fight back—wanted to do just about anything besides curl into a shuddering huddle in the snow—but couldn't even convince his lungs to draw in air, much less do anything to stop the Purist from scrabbling out from under him and taking off down the street at a run. Vaguely, Sikes was aware that the guy's friends were running with him, and he was suddenly very afraid for George.

"George . . . ?"

He only got as far as struggling to knees and elbows before someone's hand closed firmly on his arm to help him stand. "That was incredibly stupid," George scolded, pulling him onto the sidewalk.

Sikes stumbled to a stop beside his partner, pain receding to nothing but a twitching memory along his nerves. "I thought the guy was gonna shoot you." He tugged the hem of his sweater outward in search of some sign of blood or damage. A gallon of oily street slush and two holes the size and shape of cigarette burns were all he found. "What the hell happened?"

"A stun gun," George told him. He helped swipe the worst of the slush away. "He couldn't possibly have gotten close enough to me to use it. He was just trying to scare us."

"Worked, didn't it?" Sikes hugged himself with both arms, shivering from more than the cold now. "We've got to head back to the hotel now. If I don't get dry clothes, I'm gonna freeze. Damn." He vented the edge of his frustration on a snowplowed ridge. "When we find Vegas, I'm gonna kick his ass. Doesn't he have the faintest idea how much trouble he's caused?"

"I don't think he had any choice."

Sikes turned, stilled by the odd tone in George's voice, and saw his partner stopped in the middle of the sidewalk, staring downward. "What?" He hurried back to him. "George, what are you talking about?"

George stooped and peeled a scrap of muddy paper off the pavement. It was almost transparent with meltwater, the jagged tread mark of one of the Purists' shoes obscuring the pasted-together words in one corner. What it said was easily readable, though, and made Sikes itch with anger even as he thought about the three Purists who had gotten away.

We have the slag Ross Vegas. Do like we tell you or everybody dies.

CHAPTER 6

BREAKFAST WAS RAW marinated weasel, artfully draped over a wedge of cantaloupe and garnished with tender young grasshoppers. George eyed the combination doubtfully as he settled at the linen-draped table in the smaller of the hotel's two ballrooms.

"Who ever heard of serving weasel with cantaloupe?" he demanded of Susan. He was still slightly irritable from lack of sleep, and the absence of real sunlight in this enclosed ballroom wasn't helping his mood. Around him, other Tenctonese filed in and found their places, conversing in subdued murmurs and softened clicks about the events of the previous night. Security guards at the door scrutinized each incoming guest for a name badge. After the incident at the press conference, the symposium organizers had decided to bypass the hotel's public dining rooms. The policeman in George approved of the additional

66

security, but he couldn't help being saddened by its necessity.

"I think it's refreshing." As usual, Susan didn't pay much attention to his morning complaints. She smiled up at the polite human server offering her a choice of juice or tea. "We'll both have decaffeinated tea, please, with rice vinegar."

George waited until the young man had poured the tea and left. "Well, if you ask me, I think it's some silly human's idea of Tenctonese food." He lifted his cup and let the warm tang of acetic acid soothe his throat.

"No, it's some silly human's idea of hotel food." Across the table, Sikes glowered at his own plate, on which two eggs, a sausage link, and a strip of bacon had been combined into a vacuously smiling face. "Be grateful. At least you didn't get the rugrat special."

Susan looked up from her breakfast in surprise. "Matt, you never told us you liked rat."

The human groaned and buried his face in a cup of coffee, as if the effort of explaining had just exceeded his sleep-deprived capability. George kindly did it for him. "I believe Matthew was referring to the intended consumers of the dish, and not its contents," he told his wife. "Rugrat is one of the terms of affection human males use toward their offspring. They also call them toenail biters."

"Ankle biters, George." Sikes looked up as human voices rose flatly above the Tenctonese murmur of the crowd. He groaned again and cuffed George on the shoulder, swinging him around to see two gray-suited men enter the ballroom doorway. The taller of the pair had just flipped a badge open for the hotel guards to inspect. "Here come the feds."

Cathy looked up from her fruit plate, casting a surprised look at the door. "How do you know those are FBI agents? They could be Pittsburgh police detectives."

Sikes snorted. "Not with tailoring like that. What do you want to bet they're here to talk to us?"

"I don't see why they should be." George frowned, watching the pair cross the room. "They probably want to question Lydia Vegas about her husband's kidnapping."

"Lydia Vegas wasn't on TV yesterday. We were."

"Humph." George absently ate some weasel, watching the men stop at another mixed table of humans and Newcomers. With some surprise, he realized that the casually dressed woman he had taken for one of the television stagehands was actually Jen Protzberg, the Pittsburgh detective who had escorted them to the hotel. She rose to speak to the suited men, then nodded and glanced around the room until she spotted George. The two men turned and followed her through the maze of tables toward them.

"Told you." Sikes finished cramming the last of his bacon into his mouth, then grinned maliciously at George. "They want to see what kind of troublemakers we are."

Soothed now by tea and food, George refused to take the bait. "Really, Matthew, you ought to chew your food before you swallow." He looked up as the trio approached. "Good morning, gentlemen. Can we help you?"

The taller man brought out his badge again and showed it to George. "Agent David Jordan, FBI. This is my colleague, Agent Steve Golitko. You're Detective George Francisco of the LAPD, correct?" George nodded and Jordan turned to glance across the table. "And you're his partner, Matthew Sikes?"

"That's right." Sikes grinned mirthlessly. "When I'm not an innocent human bystander, that is."

The FBI agents looked puzzled by the comment, but Jen Protzberg laughed. "The media mistook him for the victim in a fight yesterday," she explained, then cast a sardonic glance at Sikes. "They weren't too happy to find out he was actually the instigator."

Sikes scowled. "You didn't tell them that, did you?"

"No," admitted Protzberg. "Your captain back in L.A. did."

Jordan cleared his throat diffidently. "If you don't mind," he said to George, "we'd like to ask you a few questions about the Vegas kidnapping."

"Of course." George pulled out the empty seat beside him. "Won't you join us for breakfast?"

Golitko cast an appalled look at the weasel left on Susan's plate and took an involuntary step back. Jordan smiled, though, and settled into the chair George offered him. At close hand, the federal agent looked lanky and unpretentious despite the neat creases of his suit.

"Thanks," he said, reaching gratefully for the carafe of coffee. "They assigned us to this case at four this morning, and we caught a flight from Washington an hour later. Right now I'd just about kill someone for a doughnut."

"Have some of my toast." Sikes pushed his plate across the table, eying Jordan more sympathetically. Cathy pulled out another chair for the still-silent Golitko, and he took it after a wary glance at her fruit plate. Protzberg leaned a hip against the table beside him and waited, wearing the slightly skeptical expression that federal agents always brought out in local police.

"What we're concerned about," said Jordan around a slice of toast, "is the Purist angle in this case." He pulled a dark gray palmtop computer out of his suit jacket and punched up a display of notes. "Our records show almost no evidence of Purist activity in the city of Pittsburgh over the last five years, but you guys say you're sure it was Purists you ran into last night. We'd like to know if the circumstances surrounding this case seem consistent with the Purist activity you've dealt with back in L.A."

George exchanged a thoughtful glance with his partner. "In some ways it does. For example, the street demonstrations were a common Purist tactic during the early years of Tenctonese integration in L.A. And bomb threats were used quite often as well, although I can only recall one instance where a bomb was actually planted."

"But," prompted Jordan, quick to pick up the unspoken reservation in George's voice. Sikes answered for him.

"But only one kidnapping," the human detective said flatly. "And that was kind of special circumstances."

George nodded, sipping tea. "Purists in L.A. mostly preferred to vandalize Newcomer property. There were many gang beatings and even some scattered sniper shootings, but I can't recall them ever holding a Tenctonese for ransom." He cocked his head intelligently at Jordan. "Since the FBI is concerned with the case, I assume there has been a specific ransom demand?"

The tall human shot a questioning glance at his colleague and got a silent nod in return. "Someone phoned Nancy Thompson last night at her home. They told her to turn on her answering machine, then forced Ross Vegas to read a statement from his kidnappers." Jordan poked a button on the palmtop, then handed it to George. "I have the transcription here. See what you think."

Sikes scooted his chair around the table, squinting over George's shoulder as he scrolled the message up the small computer screen. "I am being held by the Society for a Clean Earth, Pittsburgh Brotherhood," said the colorless gray words. "They demand the immediate return of the thirty-nine slags in the city of Pittsburgh to Los Angeles, followed by evacuation of all spongeheads to the Mojave Desert, to be held in permanent quarantine and isolation. In order to eliminate all alien viruses and parasites, the contaminated area known as Slagtown is to be firebombed and the desert must be permanently sealed and guarded from any further human contact. (Pause on tape.) You have until noon tomorrow to send the slags in Pittsburgh home and begin preparations for permanent quarantine. If you don't, we will kill one Newcomer a day until our demands are met."

George swallowed, feeling the fierce double thumping of his hearts as they reacted to the threat. His brain knew the demands were ridiculous and that the human authorities would never accede to them, but his chest still ached with rage. Susan sensed his distress and slid a hand to cover his. He turned his hand over and clasped hers, grateful for the small blessing of warmth.

"The tape seems authentic," he said, strengthened by the silent contact. "Purists have always spread rumors about alien diseases, and they've demanded a permanent quarantine in the Mojave since the day we landed there."

"A hell of a demand, given the number of Newcomers in L.A." Sikes's voice sounded casual, but George noticed he had to clear his throat before he could speak. "The government will never do it."

"They did it to the Japanese during the Second World War," Protzberg pointed out soberly. "And if they could say it was for your own safety—"

George's hand tightened on Susan's, but he kept his voice steady with an effort. "That's a clever twist," he agreed. "I'm not sure how it will affect public opinion."

Jordan sighed and retrieved his computer. "Well, I know how it's affected my opinion. It makes me very worried about Mr. Vegas. Since his kidnappers don't want money or any material ransom, we have no way to contact them. All we could do to protect him is cancel the symposium—"

"No!" said George, Cathy, and Susan in unison. The FBI agent blinked in surprise, and even Sikes looked a little taken aback by their vehemence. "That would be a grave mistake," George continued, more quietly. "If kidnapping has become a new Purist tactic, the last thing we should do is encourage it by giving in. The life of a single Tenctonese would be well bought if it prevented the kidnapping of hundreds more."

"Hmm." Jordan rubbed his chin, exchanging thoughtful looks with his colleague. "The federal government's official policy is not to negotiate with terrorists, and I suppose that by the nature of their demands, the Purists here might qualify. I'll talk to the symposium organizers and see how they feel." He got to his feet with sudden decision, Golitko rising with him. "In the meantime, would you two mind keeping an eye out for anything suspicious during the rehearsals today? I'd appreciate it if you'd keep me informed via Detective Protzberg. She'll be spending the day here, managing on-site security while we investigate the kidnapping."

"No problem," said Sikes, and George nodded. They watched Jen Protzberg escort the men over to the table where Lydia Vegas sat, listlessly picking at her breakfast. She looked up with stoic resignation at their approach.

"They're not as bad as they could be, for feds." Sikes stole a strawberry from Cathy's unfinished plate and popped it in his mouth, then turned to lift an inquiring eyebrow at George. "I don't suppose your willingness to sacrifice Ross Vegas to the Purists has anything to do with him being *kleezantsun'?*"

George felt his eyes sting with embarrassment. "Of course not!" he snapped. "I would have done the same if he'd been *sansol.*"

"Oh, yeah?" His human partner tilted his head, looking at George with disturbing perception. "And what if he'd been Susan?"

The room's winter chill suddenly penetrated into

George's blood and made him shiver. "It's cold in here," he said, jumping to his feet so he wouldn't have to meet Sikes's gaze. "Let's go next door so I can practice my speech for the rehearsal."

"Dammit, I stuttered!"

George sank into one of the folding chairs at the back of the ballroom. He could still feel the jittery shaking under his armpits from the stress of staring into too bright lights, with his mike squealing a mortifying whine of feedback whenever he moved too close to the amplifier pickup. George hated microphones anyway. When pitched for human comfort, they were always far too loud for Tenctonese ears.

Susan made a sympathetic noise and patted his hand. "It wasn't very noticeable, dear. And at least your talk didn't run forty minutes long this time."

"Only because I skipped a page of notes." George irritably slapped his sheaf of printed pages back into his briefcase. "And didn't even realize it!"

Three seats down the row, Sikes opened his eyes and blinked at George. "Oh, good," he said drowsily. "I thought I'd nodded off and missed something while I was supposed to be keeping an eye on things."

"You did." Cathy ruffled his hair affectionately. "But don't worry. I kept an eye on things for you."

"Did you see anything unusual?" George's self-disgust vanished under a surge of professional concern as he scanned the ballroom. Since today was merely the dress rehearsal for the televised symposium tomorrow, only a fraction of the folding chairs were filled with people watching the next speaker practice. George ignored the dark human heads he could see and carefully counted the spotted ones. "I only see thirty-six Newcomers here. Who's missing?"

Sikes snorted. "Ross Vegas, for one."

George gave his partner an exasperated look. "I was aware of that, Matthew, thank you. Who else is gone?"

"Ann Arbor is outside on the balcony, signing autographs." Cathy pointed through the guarded door at the crowd of human children and adults clustered around the tall decathlon winner. "Detective Protzberg went out to keep an eye on her."

"And Sandi Free went up to her hotel room an hour ago," added Susan. "She said her feet hurt from all the noise, and she was going to lie down. Lydia Vegas went up to give her some herbal tea for the pain, but I think she's back now."

"Yes, I see Lydia in front of us." George frowned and reached into his briefcase for the schedule of talks. He scanned the page closely until he found the name he was looking for. "That's what I thought. Scott and Sandi Free's talk is coming up right after this one." He gave his wife a concerned glance. "Surely Sandi would come down for that, even if she was still in pain."

Susan's smoothly spotted forehead creased into worried lines. "Well, I would."

George looked around the darkened ballroom until he spotted a slender young Tenctonese *gannaum* craning his head beside the speaker's platform. "There's Scott Free. He seems to be looking for her, too." He looked over at his partner, now fully awake and scowling. "That means he expected her to be down here."

"I don't have a very good feeling about this." Sikes

stood, squeezing past Cathy in the narrow row of seats and tapping George on the shoulder as he went. "Come on. Let's ask Protzberg if she sent an escort up with Sandi."

George nodded and followed him out of the room. They found the Pittsburgh police detective standing near the front stairs that led down from the ballroom balcony to the elegant main lobby below. A velvet cord discreetly closed off access at the bottom of the marble steps, with a security guard beside it to admit official visitors. Outside the facing wall of windows, George could see the flashing lights of two on-duty police cars stationed on either side of the hotel's freestanding portico. Given the bomb threat last night, he approved of the precaution.

"Protzberg." Sikes hailed her with the casual abruptness of a colleague, and the short, wiry woman nodded back at him in acknowledgment. "Did you send someone up with Mrs. Free to her hotel room?"

"Damn straight," she said without rancor. "I told him to go in and check the room before she entered, too. Why? Is something wrong?"

"She's about to miss her presentation," George explained. "We expected her to be here. She could simply be sleeping through it, but I'd rather not take the chance."

"Neither would I." Protzberg motioned another policeman from across the balcony to take her place, then led them toward the hidden bank of elevators. "Let's go give her a wake-up call."

The silently efficient elevator delivered them to the third floor in seconds, and George stepped out first into the deserted hall. His nostrils flared with the faintest hint of a familiar musky smell, and he jerked to a stop.

"Trouble?" demanded Sikes, pausing beside him.

"I smell blood. Tenctonese blood." George swung his head slowly and located the hall with the strongest scent. He strode down it, pausing by each oak hotel door to see if it was the source of the odor. Protzberg followed, watching him with mingled amazement and respect.

"I didn't know these guys could follow scents," she muttered at Sikes, respectfully quiet but not so quiet that George mistook it for a slur.

"Yeah, and they hear better than we do, too." Sikes nearly ran into George when he froze beside a hotel room door. "Christ, George, could you give us a little warning?"

George took a deep breath, tasting the reek of fresh Tenctonese blood strong in his throat. "This is it."

Sikes rapped on the door and got only silence in return. "Sandi Free's room?" he asked Protzberg.

She nodded, fishing in her oversize linen jacket for a hotel passkey. Her fingers shook, just a little, as she fitted it into the lock. "Dammit, I told her not to open the door to anyone but her husband! I don't know why—" The door opened, letting out a wave of mixed blood and torn-gut smell so strong that even the humans must have been able to detect it. George blinked rapidly in response, while Protzberg and Sikes cursed in unison. "Oh, shit."

Smears of blood and darker clots of ripped intestine patterned the tasteful beige carpet, coalescing into a frantic gray and pink swirl where something had been dragged in a bloody semicircle between the beds.

George closed his throat firmly against a stab of sickness, hearing Sikes choke and turn away behind him. For once, he didn't blame his partner for his queasiness.

Dismembered parts of Sandi Free's corpse lay everywhere in the room, scattered from dresser to bed to floor as if she had been torn apart by demons.

CHAPTER 7

THE FORENSICS GUYS had brought out all the towels from the bathroom to cover what they could of the body, and that helped a little. Sikes had also vomited in the hallway two doors down from the scene, and that helped a little, too. At least now when his stomach heaved, there was nothing left of breakfast to bring up, so a fit of halfhearted coughing usually drove the feeling away. The inside of his sinuses still burned, though. He clung to a tattered wad of bathroom tissue so he could continually clear his nose without having to leave the crime scene. It was bad enough that he had forensics teams on both coasts sneering at his uneven stomach, he didn't need them talking behind his back about how he wasn't man enough to stick it out until the work was done.

"Jesus," Jordan kept saying from beside Sikes in the doorway. "*Je*sus, I never expected anything like this!"

Who could have? It seemed kind of pointless to comment on that, though.

Jordan kept wiping his handkerchief across his mouth, although he hadn't succumbed to sickness quite yet. Sikes was tempted to tell him to give it a try. Jordan's face was as gray as his suit, and his eyes were very red-rimmed, as though holding back tears. "Have your Purists ever done anything like this before?"

Sikes almost laughed at the suggestion. "Oh, no."

"Then why now? And *how?*" Jordan waved unsteadily at the room in general. "Christ, I can't even tell you how to dismember a human like this, much less a Tenctonese. What could you use to do something like this?"

Sikes's eyes made a critical sweep of the room while his brain droned unconvincingly, *It's not blood, it is not blood, it's stomach medicine, that's all, not blood.* "A knife, maybe," he heard himself say. "A cleaver, that sort of thing. The guy probably whacked her over the head, then had at her while she was still too stunned to stop him." He blew his nose again, a good excuse for turning away from the room. "Guys on jack, they can do this kind of thing."

"No one used a cleaver on this woman."

The narrow little man with the coroner's badge lifted his head from behind one of the soiled beds. His tie had been twisted around to tuck down the back of his suit, and rubber gloves made his hands look yellow-white and hairless. He had a face like an earnest chihuahua's, with thinning gray hair and an accent thick enough to taste. "I can't go on record until I've run some tests, but I can tell you that I see no signs of edged weapon use on this cadaver."

Sikes was glad when the coroner stepped around the bed to come to them, instead of insisting they leave the doorway and join him. "You've got to be kidding. Nobody takes somebody apart like this without, you know, tools or something to help them. Like a chain saw."

The coroner shrugged, apparently not as confounded by the situation as Sikes. He wondered what sort of things went on in Pittsburgh that the guy could take this so calmly. "I haven't had a chance to examine all the body parts yet. Those I've seen exhibit clear evidence of rending damage, as opposed to cutting." At Sikes's questioning frown, he clarified, "The tissues are misshapen and ragged, the ligaments stretched and retreated into the musculature in a manner consistent with limbs that have been forcibly torn from the body. And the bones are generally intact, which also negates use of a cutting device." He angled a look up at Sikes. "Chain saw or otherwise."

Sikes heard Jordan unsteadily clear his throat from behind him. "What you're saying," the federal agent said carefully, "is that someone actually pulled Mrs. Free limb from limb?"

"Essentially, yes."

Suddenly overwhelmed with nausea again, Sikes transferred his gaze from the coroner's dispassionate face to the open window across the room. He was glad for the trickle of fresh air but wished he could better feel the icy breeze from the door. Cold air always helped his sickness go away. "What about cause of death?" he asked when he felt safe in talking again. "Any guesses as to what exactly killed her?"

The coroner hesitated, making Sikes shift attention

back to him. "What do you mean?" the little man asked. "Either shock or blood loss from the trauma, but I can't tell you exactly which yet."

"What?" The thought alone made Sikes's head spin. "You're telling me somebody pulled her apart like this while she was still *alive?*"

The coroner blinked. "Judging from both the tissue damage and the extent of blood loss—"

He didn't wait for the disclaimer to finish. "Do you have any idea how strong a Newcomer is? Hell, we have to carry special handcuffs just to book them in L.A., and you expect me to believe that somebody came in here, overpowered her, tied her to some kind of winch or something—"

"Oh, no, there's no evidence she was ever restrained or—"

"Whatever!" He ran both hands through his hair, feeling uncomfortably close to rude laughter. "This is nuts! Nobody tears up anybody with their bare hands, much less a Newcomer anybody."

"Could another Tenctonese do it?"

Jordan's calm question sliced through Sikes like the cold air outside. He turned to face the fed, wanting very much to seem unconcerned despite his sudden chill. "No." Then, feeling guilty about what he suspected was a lie, "To a human, maybe. But not to another Tenctonese."

Jordan nodded, but something about the guarded look on his face told Sikes the fed didn't believe a word of it.

"Matthew, Agent Jordan . . ."

Sikes and Jordan turned, bumping shoulders in the narrow doorway and unintentionally blocking both entrance and view into the bloodied room. Seeing George waiting in the hallway behind them, Sikes was glad for that accidental service—with a wife to worry about protecting from Purists, George didn't need any more reminders of what failure could mean.

"Mr. Free says he's ready to speak with you now," George told Jordan, half avoiding Sikes's eyes as though reading his partner's thoughts. "He is with my wife and Agent Golitko in Room 301."

"Go with him," Sikes urged George while Jordan moved into the hall. "It might be handy to have a translator around during the questioning."

"Susan is there—" George began, but Sikes caught his arm and pushed him away from the doorway when he tried to join Sikes there.

"Then go be with Susan," he said in a very low voice. "She's not used to this stuff like we are, and I don't want you hanging around here watching me get sick."

George's hand tightened on his partner's arm, and Sikes found himself caught in one of those inexplicable moments when George seemed to lay bare his soul with a single look. Just as always, the Newcomer broke the contact an instant before Sikes's own discomfort would force him to squirm away and said only, "Thank you," for all that the words seemed to carry a hundred more meanings than Sikes was willing to understand. He just nodded shortly and pushed George off down the hall. "Go on."

Being a cop had been a whole lot easier when the only differences he'd had to worry about in a partner were religion and the color of his skin.

Left alone with half a dozen forensics specialists

and at least a dozen body parts, Sikes found it increasingly harder to think about things not related to the mess spread out before him. "Look, do you guys really need me?" he asked at last.

One of the forensics guys looked up from dropping something too small to identify into a paper bag. "You the alien expert from L.A.?"

Sikes thought about disputing that, then decided it didn't really matter. As far as Pittsburgh was concerned, he was the closest thing to an expert they were going to get. "Yeah, I guess so."

The guy brightened as if this were the best news he'd heard all day. "It would be a big help if you could verify that we've got an entire body here." He passed the paper bag to an associate, then reached for another. "You know, just to make sure the perp didn't run off with any parts we're not aware of."

"Everything looks swell from here."

The forensics guy made a face at him. "I'm serious."

"So am I." Sikes did his damnedest to look cool instead of horrified. "They've got two arms, two legs, and a really big head. Other than that, you guys know as much as I do."

"Do they have fingerprints?" one of the other guys asked from just below the open window.

Sikes wondered if he was dusting. And, if so, what in all this blood he hoped to find. "No. We file their rap sheets with DNA prints instead." He hoped they wouldn't want a huge explanation of that, since he only understood enough to check the typing and verify a match.

Instead, the forensics guy closest to the window

climbed to his feet and headed toward Sikes, his head bent over a sheet of white hotel stationery. "You got any way to match handprints at all, then?" he asked. "Besides just fitting a hand against an impression?" He grimaced and handed the paper to Sikes. "I really don't want to have to haul this lady's hand around seeing if it fits up with every print in the room."

Frowning, Sikes took the sheet and stepped far enough into the room to catch the brighter light streaming out from the bathroom. Neatly printed in one corner, just below the burgundy red Hilton logo, was the upper third of a neat, long-fingered handprint. They probably couldn't have lifted a better impression with an ink pad. Milky pink fluid had dried to a crusty peach, but it was easy enough to see that no lines or creases had crisscrossed the print even when it was fresh. "Where did you get this?"

The forensics guy nodded over his shoulder. "Just under the window. But they're all over the room, even on the walls. I don't know if this means somebody played finger paints with our D.B. after the fact or if this lady fought like hell before they killed her." He shook his head sadly. "Not a footprint in the place, though, so I think it must have happened after, when the guy had time to be careful. Yuck."

Yuck, indeed. Sikes handed him back the paper and stepped into the hall. His nose was too numbed by gut smell and vomiting to notice the change in venue. All he knew was that he wanted very much to wash his hands, and if he stayed here any longer he'd be throwing up again. "Look, you guys have got everything you need from me. Get somebody from Pittsburgh P.D. to stay here with you."

"That's okay—we're mostly done." The forensics guy didn't seem to care much as he turned to the men behind him and called out, "All right, guys, bag her."

The image of the Newcomer being shoveled into a black plastic bag, piece by piece, made Sikes think unwillingly about how these people had been born into a world of dark alcoves and sleeping holes no bigger than this stretcher. What a pisser to finally win your freedom on a planet so far from home just to end up locked in the dark against your will, the very same way you started.

"Don't put her in a room with cut flowers," he heard himself saying. "And if you have to do an autopsy, don't cut her hearts loose from her chest. They don't like that, and it matters to them."

The forensics team all stared at him in a way Sikes couldn't quite identify, so he turned away from them to retreat to his room and his own quiet darkness. The zipper on the body bag purred shut behind him.

CHAPTER 8

GEORGE LEANED HIS forehead against the dark window of his hotel room, deliberately letting the chill of the glass burn against his skin. By day, the window framed a view of the long snowy lawns marking the point where Pittsburgh's rivers met, but none of that was visible now. A thin winter fog had risen from the melting snow and drifted across the city, dimming its illuminated bridges to faint blurs. The mist restricted George's view to the asphalt top of the hotel's portico and the balefully spiraling glare of the police cars parked below it. He reached down and opened the small casement pane at the bottom of the window as far as its hinges allowed. A cold wet wind flowed through the handspan of space and nosed at him like a curious wild beast.

"George!" Susan poked her head around the bathroom door, one earring on and the other clutched in her hand. "What on earth are you doing? I can feel that draft all the way in here!"

"Sorry." He pushed the window shut again. "Matthew is always talking about how cold air clears his head. I thought I'd try it." He gave her a tight, rueful smile. "All it did was make my feet hurt."

Susan clicked in wordless concern and came across the room to join him. Her dark green dinner dress shimmered in the misty light from outside. "You're thinking about those Purists again."

"Yes." George ran a hand back and forth across the thick velvet of her sleeve, warming his fingers with the friction. "Yes, I'm thinking about them. For all the killings they did back in L.A., the Purists there were never quite this brutal. I just don't see why they should be more fanatical in Pittsburgh than in Los Angeles."

"George—"

He waved an impatient hand at the winter night outside. "I mean, look at this climate. What can Purists have to fear when it would be nearly impossible for a Tenctonese to live here?" He frowned at his dark reflection in the window. "Yet the way they killed Sandi Free implies an almost psychotic rage."

"George—"

"In fact, if it weren't for the fact that the Purists had already issued a death threat in this case, I would have said all the signs pointed to a serial killer rather than a terrorist group. I wonder if—"

"George!" Susan framed her hands around his face and forcibly swung his attention away from the darkness outside. Her eyes met his, shining blue and intent. "George, stop obsessing on this case! You're

not a policeman here. You're not the one responsible for solving Sandi Free's murder."

He sighed. "But I am responsible for your safety, *neemu,* and mine. I want us both to get back to L.A." He felt her fingers tremble, perhaps with cold or perhaps with fear. He pulled them down to his chest, cradling them between his scarcely warmer hands. "I'm the only Tenctonese policeman within three thousand miles, Susan. If I can help the police and the FBI solve this case, I must."

Susan released a breath of mixed frustration and amusement. "George, why do you always have such perfectly reasonable explanations for being so single-minded about your work?"

He managed a smile for her. "Because that's the kind of work it is."

An urgent fist thudded against the door before Susan could reply. She cast a quizzical look at George. "Were you expecting Matt tonight?"

"Not particularly." George strode across the room, remembering just in time to check the peephole before he slid the door chain off. The subdued lighting of the hallway glanced off wire-rimmed glasses, throwing haggard shadows down the Newcomer face below them. He recognized Scott Free and opened the door at once. "Mr. Free, please come in."

"No, thank you." The novelist paused in the doorway, his gaze dropping to the carpet and then lifting hurriedly again, as if he remembered how it had looked spattered with his wife's blood. "Mrs. Thompson sent me to ask if you'd come down to dinner a little early. She has something she wants to talk to you about."

George glanced back over his shoulder at Susan, who hadn't yet put on her shoes or—more importantly—her makeup. He shook his head. "I'm afraid she'll have to wait until I can escort my wife down. I don't want her to go alone."

"Don't worry about me, George." Susan clipped on her other earring and smiled at him. "I'll call Cathy and Matt and have them stop by before I leave the room. I promise."

He frowned, a little startled by his own reluctance to leave her. "Remember to use the peephole," he reminded her, coming back to the dresser for his name badge. "And don't open the door for anyone but Matthew."

"Yes, George." She followed him to the door, touching his elbow just before he left. "You'll be careful, too, won't you?"

"Of course." George closed the door behind him and heard the reassuring scrape of the chain lock and the click of the bolt. He turned to meet Scott Free's bitter gaze and guessed the other male must be recalling the trustful way Sandi had left their own hotel room door unbolted and unbarred.

"You couldn't have known," George said softly, responding to the other *gannaum*'s distress with automatic concern. "You couldn't have prevented your wife's murder."

Scott Free's mouth jerked with pain. "I could have flown home with her yesterday morning," he retorted. *"If* the FBI had seen fit to tell us what the Purists' ransom demands were." He turned away abruptly. "Let's take the stairs. It's faster."

Inside the fire stairs, the air was chilly and dank

enough to make George wish he'd worn his camel hair coat over his suit. Free didn't seem to notice. He led George down to the ballroom level, then across the empty balcony to the room they used for meals. Human hotel workers went from one empty table to another, laying out place settings on linen cloths. At the far end, three women stood near a tangle of TV lights. Nancy Thompson, elegant and worried in gold brocade and pearls, watched as Kathleen Westbeld talked earnestly into a palm-size cellular phone. Jen Protzberg leaned against a wall beside them in the same rumpled linen jacket she'd had on earlier that afternoon. She looked up as George approached and nodded, the wordless greeting of one police officer to another.

"Who's your wife coming down to dinner with?" she asked brusquely. "Sikes?"

"Yes." George nodded his head politely toward the other women. "Ms. Westbeld, Ms. Thompson. How can I help you?"

Nancy Thompson sighed and rubbed at her high forehead. The worried creases didn't go away. "We'd like your input, Mr. Francisco, for a crucial decision we have to make tonight. Captain Protzberg thought you'd be the best person to ask." She glanced over at the silent novelist beside George and took a deep breath. "Mr. Free has asked us to cancel the symposium tomorrow. Do you think we should?"

George blinked rapidly, taken aback by the sudden thump of responsibility landing on his shoulders. "Surely the FBI should be the ones to decide—"

Westbeld shook her head, folding her phone to break the connection. "They say it would look too much like government censorship if they canceled it," she said in disgust. "But they won't take the liability of guaranteeing our safety either. It's up to us and the Pittsburgh police to make the call."

"I can't guarantee your safety either," Protzberg warned. "But if need be, I'll assign a policeman to cover every hall on your hotel floor. I'm not going to get caught with my pants down again, not if I can help it."

A big if, George thought, but didn't say so aloud. He turned his gaze back on Nancy Thompson. "Do you want my opinion on this as a police officer or as a Newcomer?" he asked bluntly.

The older woman blinked at him in bewilderment. "Are those opinions different?"

George nodded. "As a policeman, I agree with the FBI. There is no way to completely guarantee the safety of every Tenctonese guest at the symposium at all times." He gave them a mirthless smile. "Even if you escorted us to our rooms and watched us at the conference, we still need to use restrooms, as humans do. Purists as fanatical as these would find some way to attack us." He sighed. "As a policeman, I would say the safest course would be to cancel the symposium."

Scott Free took a deep breath of mingled relief and self-righteousness. "I told you—"

"I'm not done, Mr. Free." George silenced him with a frown, then swung back to Nancy Thompson. "I have another opinion as a Newcomer, and that has more to do with the method of your decision than its outcome." He paused. "Why are you making this choice for us as if we were children?"

Nancy Thompson gasped, her fingers tightening on

her strand of pearls. "We didn't think—we weren't trying to insult—"

"I know you weren't." George relented slightly, seeing genuine dismay in her gray eyes. "But we Tenctonese are the ones who are being threatened by the Purists. If you decide to continue the conference, our lives are the ones at stake. Can you truly make a decision like that for us and then live with the consequences?"

Nancy Thompson shook her head wordlessly. Westbeld glanced over at her, then back at George. "So what do you suggest?" she asked bluntly. "How *should* we make this decision?"

"In the traditional American way." George smiled at their puzzled looks. "Let's put the issue to a vote."

"I can't believe you guys voted to stay here." Sikes slammed a hand against the Door Close button as soon as he entered the elevator, as if the doors could not slide shut fast enough for him. He sounded merely disgusted, but the white-knuckled way he held Cathy's hand suggested that other emotions fueled his anger. "I can't even believe you suggested it, George!"

George frowned at him. "Would you rather I had made the decision for Nancy Thompson myself without consulting the other Tenctonese?"

"Hell, yes!" Sikes's voice bounced off the elevator walls, making both Cathy and Susan wince. George didn't. He was used to his partner's volume. "You can't ask a bunch of goddammed Newcomer overachievers if they want to pack up their bags and go home! Of course they'll say no. They think the future of their race depends on how well they talk at this fucking symposium." He glowered at George. "And that includes you!"

"Then it wouldn't have been any different if I'd made the decision by myself, would it?"

Sikes growled in frustration. "Dammit, George! You know better than the rest of them how much danger we're in here. They all think the FBI will track down the Purists who kidnapped Ross Vegas any minute now, and that the Pittsburgh police will protect them in the meantime."

"Won't they?" asked Cathy in a startled voice. "They said they would."

"They said they'd *try.*" Sikes hit the Door Open button as the elevator slowed for their floor, ignoring the fact that the doors were already opening. He stepped out and cursed as two riot-suited policemen grabbed his arms. "What the *hell—!*"

"Sorry." The policemen stepped back as soon as they saw Cathy come out behind him. "You must be Sikes. We're not supposed to let any humans onto this floor except for you." They nodded politely at George and Susan, then returned to the folding chairs and doughnut box that marked their guard post at the end of the elevator lobby.

"There, see?" Cathy joggled at Sikes's elbow, smiling. "The police are trying very hard to protect us."

"Yeah, right." He came to a stop beside their door and stabbed the key into the lock with barely repressed violence. "They can try as hard as they like, but when it comes to murder, you don't get an E for effort."

"Matthew." George caught his partner by the elbow

as the door clicked, to keep him from yanking it open. "Matthew, do you remember the ala mode?"

"Remember the *what?*" Sikes scowled at him for a moment, then his mouth twisted with recognition and disbelief. "George, what the hell does the Alamo have to do with anything?"

George put his hands on his hips. "Well, it's the best human analogy I can think of." He saw Susan and Cathy's puzzled looks and explained, "The Alamo was a walled encampment where a small band of humans was threatened by a large opposing force. They refused to surrender."

Sikes snorted. "And they were killed to a man."

"But the cause they cared about gained as a result," George reminded him. "'Remember the Alamo' became a rallying cry, and the slain men's comrades eventually won despite overwhelming odds. If they had surrendered, do you think the result would have been the same?" He paused, seeing from his partner's narrowed eyes that Sikes knew the answer but wasn't going to admit it. "Wouldn't you say the risk taken by those humans at the Alamo was justified?"

"But that was a war!" Sikes argued stubbornly. "Those men knew they might die when they signed up to be soldiers."

George gave him a searching look. "And do you think we Tenctonese didn't know that when we decided to try and live in your society?"

Sikes froze, his gaze sliding from George to Susan to Cathy. Whatever he saw in their faces, it was strong enough to make him curse and jerk free of George's grip.

"All right, fine!" He stepped backward, shaking his head. "You want to be the Sam Houston of Little Tencton, George, don't let me stop you. But I'll be damned if I'm gonna play Davy Crockett!"

Cathy cleared her throat, her voice pitched to a carefully neutral tone. "Does that mean you're going back to L.A., Matt?"

"No!" Sikes glared at George. "It means I'm not going to sit back and let us all get killed just so people can say 'Remember the Hilton!'"

He flung open the unlocked door, evidently trusting Newcomer reflexes to get George's hand away from the jamb before he slammed the door inward. Only partly to retaliate, George slapped his hand against the door and held it pinned open despite his partner's fierce tug. He scanned the room and found it secure and empty, then stepped back to let them enter. The door crashed shut behind them.

Susan glanced up at George curiously. "Do you two always argue like this when you're working?"

"Most of the time," he admitted, starting down the hall toward their own room. "Although not often so violently."

"He's worried about Cathy." A few moments later, Susan frowned. "George, hurry. I think I hear the phone ringing in our room."

George lengthened his steps, hearing it, too. He unlocked the door, reaching out an arm to catch Susan and hold her back as it swung open. She pressed against him urgently but knew enough to wait until he'd switched on the light and scanned the room before she pushed past and grabbed the phone.

"Emily!" She sank down on the bed, cradling the

phone against her cheek as tenderly as if it were her daughter's face. "Emily, don't cry! We're all right, we're both all right, they would have called you if we weren't . . . no, we weren't anywhere close when it happened . . . no, nobody's done anything to us at all." There was a long pause, and then Susan's voice rippled with distress. "Oh, Emily, I know you want us to come home, but we can't right now. You'll just have to be brave, like we were on the ship when they took your father away—"

George felt a familiar wrench of anguish in his chest, the fierce jerk of his heartsbeat as Susan's quivering voice brought unwelcome memories back. He dropped down on the bed and wrapped his arms tightly around his wife, trying to still the flooding panic with her nearness. He could hear the echoes of his dread in Susan's voice while she tried to reassure their daughter, tried to make her believe that she wasn't in danger of losing both her parents. He could tell it was only marginally successful.

"I was wrong," George burst out when Susan finally put the phone down and turned to huddle into his embrace. "I was wrong, Susan, and Matthew was right. We should have gone back to L.A."

"And lived for the rest of our lives with you thinking you were a failure?" Despite the film of tears turning her blue eyes nearly black, Susan managed to smile at him. "I'd rather risk being killed by Purists than face that kind of misery." She bit her lip, the smile fading into fierceness. "But promise me— promise me, *neemu,* that I didn't survive all those sale times on the ship just to lose you now. *Promise me.*"

"I promise," George said, then held her tight while

she cried in her silent, ship-trained way. It was the threat to her and the children that unnerved him, as intensely now as it had on the ship. Then it had been the *kleezantsun'*, trying to rid themselves of an untrainable slave by selling him off to the planetary installations they serviced. They had tried three times, and three times George had canceled the sale by running away from his new masters before the ship even left port. It had been a risky tactic, and the fear of failure, the horror of losing his family forever still burned along his nerves each time he thought of it. It burned in him now, a fear that clung to him like mist and followed him relentlessly into sleep.

The shrill buzzing of the phone woke George to instant readiness, aware even before his eyes opened that it was too dark in the room for this to be his wake-up call. *Not another bomb threat,* he thought in alarm, but the voice that answered his curt "Yes" spoke in frantic Tenctonese. For a moment, prepared as he was for another threat from the Purists, the clicking murmur of his native tongue rolled over George as meaninglessly as the rush of water. He blinked and forced himself to listen.

"—and I'm sure they're out there," said the light, breathless male voice. "I can hear them throwing something at the window, something sharp like pieces of metal—"

"Mr. Free?" George sat bolt upright as he recognized the voice. He heard Susan wake with a gasp beside him, then reach to turn on the light. "Mr. Free, what are you talking about?"

"Purists," said the novelist, speaking suddenly and

bitterly in English. "There are Purists outside my window trying to scare me."

"I see." George took a deep, steadying breath. "What room are you in?"

"Three seventeen."

All the way down the hall from here, but only three doors down from Sikes. And not much farther, George suddenly remembered, from the policemen guarding the elevator. "Mr. Free, listen to me," he said firmly. "I want you to get out of your room and head for the elevator."

"But I want to see them," said the other *gannaum*, lapsing into Tenctonese again. "I want to see them and know them, so I can make them pay for what they—"

The phone connection shrieked, then fell into a painful, distant buzzing, as if the line had suddenly been disconnected. George felt the quick double thud of panic in his chest. He tossed the phone at Susan while he scrambled out of bed and dove for his suitcase.

"Call Matthew," he ordered her, grabbing up the first pair of pants he found. "Tell him something's happened to Scott Free, Room 317. Tell him to get there, fast!"

"Scott Free, Room 317." Susan was dialing even as she memorized it. George struggled into his pants, blessing her cool competence, then yanked off the door chain and hurtled through the door. Behind him, he could hear her passing the message to Sikes.

The hall was a silent tunnel at this hour, swallowing even the sound of George's rapid footsteps. The sensation of running without shoes was eerily familiar

—it was the way he always ran in his planet dreams, the way he had been forced to run when he'd been sold. The memory was so sharp-edged that he almost didn't recognize the rangy form that shot from a doorway ahead of him. He skidded to a stop, his blood shivering in expectation of the *levpa*.

"George!" A rough hand slapped at his shoulder while the sound of Sikes's familiar voice dragged him back into the here and now. "What the hell was that room number?"

"Three seventeen." George shook himself to clear the last traces of nightmare and started running again. One door, two . . . and the smell of Tenctonese blood roiled up the hall to meet him, warm and metallic and fresh. He caught his breath in dismay.

"Oh, hell." Sikes must have smelled it, too, and realized what it meant. He stopped beside George when they reached Scott Free's room, both of them listening to the ominous blank silence within. In the rooms to either side, the muffled sound of voices showed that this time the attack hadn't gone unnoticed.

"I'll get one of the policemen at the elevator," said Sikes, and disappeared. He came back a moment later with a trim black woman, sharp-eyed and alert despite the hour.

"Did anyone come past you up the elevator or the stairs?" George asked her, although he was already sure what her answer would be.

"No one." She reached for her passkey, frowning when she caught the smell seeping under the door. "And I didn't doze off either—Bosserman and I played cards to stay awake." The key turned in the lock, but the door only swung a few inches before it stopped, caught by the length of security chain. George exchanged glances with Sikes, then reached out and caught the chain in one fist, ripping it out of the wall with one easy shove. He heard the policewoman's breath suck in behind him, but he knew it wasn't the display of strength that had startled her.

Like his wife before him, Scott Free had left most of his blood upon the carpet. Unlike his wife, the rest of his body wasn't visible. But the shattered frame of the casement window and the clear pink stains dribbling down the glass showed where he had gone.

CHAPTER 9

"Oh, man, this is so *bogus!* I didn't do *nothing!*"

Sikes sat on the tabletop, his tennis shoes wedged between the slats in the chair back in front of him, and the chair itself tipped until it balanced on two legs beneath the table. The police observation room was darkened and smelled acridly of smoke; more than a pack of cigarettes lay stubbed out around an overcrowded ashtray, the pitiful glow of the last four butts burning the stale ash orange-gray. Sikes had been watching the questioning long enough for the cop with him to puff through every one of those lousy cigarettes. It was enough to make Sikes wish he'd never quit smoking in the first place.

"What if I told you your buddy already admitted to getting you into the hotel?" the cop on the other side of the window snarled. "He's gonna roll over and tell us everything about you."

The Purist seated at the dirty, scarred-up table shook his head, but Sikes could see the beginning of desperate tears in his eyes despite the two-way glass between them. "Man, he's lying. I wasn't even with him when he delivered that message, you know? It ain't fair." The cops had given him a cigarette, too, and he lifted it now with shaking fingers and tried unsteadily to fit it between his lips. "We just go to his house every Friday and talk about hating slags, that's all . . . that's all . . ."

Sikes sensed more than saw someone move up beside him in the dark room. "And Hitler just wanted to improve the economy," Protzberg commented dryly. A slim white hand slipped into Sikes's line of sight, offering an unlit cigarette between two fingers.

He took it from her without looking away from the glass. "Thanks." The chair seat beneath him was already littered with the guts of a half dozen other unsmoked cigarettes. He started in on this one by snapping it in half with one hand, prying out the filter and flicking it at the glass. "How much longer you gonna grill this guy?"

Protzberg's face flashed into being in the glow of her lighter flame. "Until he tells us something useful." She went dark again, and Sikes heard her breathe a stream of smoke past the cigarette's crimson end.

"You're gonna be here all week then," he told her, crumbling up the last of his own unlit smoke. "This guy doesn't know shit." He turned away from the observation glass at last, trying to adjust his eyes to the darkened room behind him.

Protzberg snorted an unhappy laugh. "Working with Newcomers makes you psychic, too?" she asked.

"Or have you just got a low opinion of Purist incentive?"

"A little of both." He pulled closed the curtains between them and the questioning room, then groped his way toward the light switch by the door. "I don't think that guy could find his ass with both hands. He's scared shitless of your boy in there, he doesn't have so much as his mother for an alibi, and he hasn't contradicted his story even once in the four hours you've had him in there." The lights bloomed before he reached the switch, and he blinked at Protzberg through stinging eyes while she toed open the door to let in air from the hallway. "This guy could have watched a TV show and had a better idea how to cover himself on a murder charge. I don't think he did it."

Protzberg took another drag on her cigarette, then crushed it out amidst all the others despite having smoked less than an inch of it. "Then I guess it's a good thing you don't work for this department, isn't it?"

Sikes resisted an urge to kick the closest chair across the room. "Hey, lady, I'm the one who has to deal with these jack-offs every day, remember? I'm trying to help you here."

"You don't deal with these jack-offs," Protzberg said, leaning her shoulder against the doorjamb. "You deal with jack-offs from L.A. Don't make the mistake of thinking those two populations have anything to do with each other."

"They have to," Sikes told her. "Whoever tore up Scott and Sandi Free knew enough about Newcomers to do them in without leaving so much as a drop of human blood on the scene. That means experience with the real thing, not just reading about them in books. Newcomers would have creamed any human who wasn't completely prepared." He shook his head, jamming both hands into the pockets of his leather jacket. "Somebody from the L.A. Purist crowd is using your locals for a front. They're involved, sure, but they aren't doing it."

Protzberg toyed with the badge on the waistband of her jeans while she thought. Sikes waited for her, respecting the brainwork of another officer. "You know what I'm thinking?"

He made an interrogatory noise.

"I'm thinking maybe Ross Vegas's kidnapping is just a setup for the rest of this."

Sikes frowned. "Of course it is. You saw the ransom demand."

"I don't mean killing Newcomers in place of a ransom. I mean keeping us distracted about what's really up, what we're really after." She pursed her lips in grim annoyance, focusing again on Sikes. "Five'll get you ten Vegas is already dead. They're just hoping we waste our time trying to figure out how to save him while they pick off your buddies, one by one."

"Why bother kidnapping him, then?" Sikes wanted to know. "Why not just bump him off in his sleep to begin with?"

Protzberg shrugged. "Because then it's just a murder. With him kidnapped, it's a puzzle. Murders, you react to—puzzles, you solve."

Sikes grumbled to himself and started pacing. "I dunno." Good as it sounded, something about Protzberg's theory didn't sit quite right with him. "I think there's some piece we're missing, something that explains what Vegas has to do with all this. We just don't know what it is yet."

"More Newcomer ESP?" Protzberg asked, obviously skeptical.

Sikes grinned at her. "Twenty years of cop intuition." He sidled past her and into the hall. "Which isn't worth the doughnuts I spent on it if I don't listen to it every once in a while."

Protzberg let him get almost to the outside door before calling, "So where the hell are you going now?"

Sikes zipped up his jacket as he backed out the door. "To see if I can't dig up the missing Purist in our equation."

The Purists had printed their flyers in bright Day-Glo magenta. Sikes wasn't sure if they meant the color to entice people to puke, but it certainly had that effect on him. Maybe it was supposed to attach bad connotations to the words *slag, spongehead,* and *ordained by God.* All Sikes knew was that the verbiage, layout, and mental garbage were almost identical to the flyers fluttering around half of L.A.'s Slagtown. Maybe the Purist Party would be making more headway if they bothered to pay a real advertising agency to produce their racist PR.

Sikes folded the flyer in half again to keep his eyes from continually glancing over the hateful words. He'd been handed the Purist tract by a mittened teenage girl when he left the police station three hours ago. She'd reminded him of his daughter, whom he hadn't seen in more than a year now, so he'd smiled warmly and thanked her for the paper before stopping to consider what it was. When it finally occurred to him, he'd smashed the flyer into a magenta wad between both hands. Then he stopped himself from throwing it away when he realized the opportunity it gave him.

There were more copy services in downtown Pittsburgh than Sikes would ever have guessed. He started from the cop shop and worked his way out and riverward, stopping only once to check a pay phone for a directory or yellow pages. No luck. Apparently social miscreants in Pittsburgh were as evil on phone books as they were in the West. After that, it turned into solid legwork, simply walking each street, then turning the corner and coming back from a block further down, reading the store signs and taking his bearings from the tall downtown Hilton by the rivers.

He was surprised how happy the tedious activity made him. It certainly wasn't the weather—the damp overcast and chill gusts cut through his leather jacket the way winter weather in L.A. never could. The temperature had soared to nearly forty today, which meant puddles instead of ice on the streets and lots of drizzling rooftops and signs to avoid. Still, something about canvassing an alien downtown armed with nothing but his intellect and a flyer appealed to the displaced cop in him. *That's been my problem,* he thought. *I'm the only Angeleno in Pittsburgh with nothing to do.* God knew there were plenty of problems needing attention just now. It felt good to be useful again while the Newcomers promoted their race and the Pittsburgh PD kept an eye on Newcomer safety. If nothing else, it gave him something more constructive to do than lie awake in their hotel room worrying about how to protect Cathy from going the way of the Frees.

He stopped beneath a red-and-white copy shop sign, reading over the ads in their windows. All kinds of copy, faxing, and computer services available, and all of it twenty-four-hour. Shaking out the crumpled flyer, Sikes pushed open the door to a welcome rush of heat and dry air.

The copy places all smelled the same—crisp paper scent, overhot machine oil, and a bright, chemical smell that Sikes assumed must be copy-machine toner or some such. It wasn't the greatest collection of smells ever invented to begin with; after being in six or seven stores of it in the same morning, it was all Sikes could do not to grimace upon setting foot in the shop.

The woman behind the counter glanced up when he came through the door. She was tall and attractive enough, although close inspection revealed her as older than her artfully placed makeup proclaimed. She frowned a little upon seeing him. Sikes stopped just short of the counter, all his instincts flaring to full alert. Her frown was one he associated with people who could somehow sense a cop in their presence, and it usually meant trouble if he slipped up in their talking. And him without even a badge or a gun. Sikes smiled at her, keeping a peripheral awareness of his distance from the door in case something went sour and he found he had to cut and run.

"Morning!" He displayed the wrinkled flyer with his most disarming smile. "I don't suppose this is a print job your shop did in the last couple days?"

Her eyes stayed on him for a little longer than was comfortable before she flicked them away to look at the paper. "Yeah," she said, relaxing a little. "We've done two runs for them now. Are you here to order another?"

"Not exactly." He stuffed the flyer into one jacket pocket. "I'm looking for the guys who placed this order with you."

"I don't have to give out that kind of information," she said before he'd even stopped to take a breath.

Sikes clenched his fists inside his pockets in an effort to keep his irritation out of his voice. "I just want to talk with them," he said, exceedingly even.

She squinted again, and his nerves stung with renewed warning. "What for?"

"Personal reasons." That wasn't even a lie, really.

"Are you with Pittsburgh Public Safety?"

Amazing how far you could get without actually stretching the truth. "I don't even live in Pittsburgh."

She peered at him unhappily for a few more minutes, and Sikes ended up drumming his fingers inside his jacket pockets to keep from jittering with impatience. He tried hard to look honest and innocent (a bad combination for him), and was just about ready to launch into a whole new round of coercion when she asked suddenly, "You're that guy those Newcomers were beating up on TV the other day, aren't you?"

Sikes was beginning to wonder if there was a Pittsburgher anywhere who didn't spend half their time watching news clips on television. "Yeah, I guess I am," he sighed.

She nodded thoughtfully, holding out her hand, palm up. "Give me that flyer."

Sikes fished it out of his pocket and let her take it. She smoothed it against the counter with the side of her hand, then scribbled across the back of it in neat, tiny script. "I didn't know you wanted to talk to them for real," she said as she wrote, "or I wouldn't of held back on you. The cops are just being kind of pissy with us right now, you know? I didn't want to get into anything."

Sikes swallowed dryly against a sudden bad taste in his throat. "I can imagine," he said, as coolly as he could manage. "Murder's pretty serious to get caught up in."

She pushed the flyer back at him with a neat, understanding little smile. "Depends on how you look at it. The only good slag's a dead one, right?"

He took the hideously colored sheet without answering her, couldn't even bring himself to plaster on a sick smile for her benefit. When he got outside, the frigid wind blasted away what little heat he retained. It felt good and clean and right to be shivering and unprotected in this uncaring weather.

Wanting only to put distance between himself and her racist sympathy, Sikes walked nearly four blocks in the bitter cold before he even thought to read the address she'd written on the flyer and figure out where he needed to go next.

CHAPTER 10

THE MIXED SOUNDS of human and Tenctonese applause jerked George awake from a dream of being chased. He blinked and looked fuzzily at Susan, seeing her warm smile emerge from the darkness when the ballroom lights came up. "Was that the last talk?"

"For the morning session." She touched her forehead affectionately to his cheek. "You slept for an hour. Do you feel any better?"

"Not much." From the ceiling, he could-hear the elegant echoes of Nancy Thompson's amplified voice, thanking the final speaker for his presentation and summarizing the afternoon schedule for the benefit of the television viewers. Partway through the list of talks, George woke up enough to count spotted heads in the audience before him.

"Thirty-four." He cursed and surged to his feet,

feeling a wave of what humans called déjà vu. "There are two of us missing."

"Maybe they're in the restroom." Susan followed him when he pushed out from the row of chairs and headed toward the empty balcony. A sprinkling of hotel guards walled off the stairs, but otherwise the long sunlit stretch was empty. "Do you want me to check the ladies' room for you?"

George frowned at the public restrooms, not sure he wanted to send Susan into possible danger. While he watched, however, a pair of TV camera operators emerged from the ladies' room and headed for the water fountain. He pointed them out to Susan. "Just ask them if they saw a Tenctonese inside. I'll check the men's room."

"All right." Never shy about talking to strangers, his wife approached the two humans without hesitation. George allowed himself one reassuring look to be sure they didn't pull out any weapons they might have cleverly hidden in their camera bags, then headed for the men's room.

A darkly bearded human in a trim suit looked up from the sink when he entered, his knife-sharp gaze familiar from many hours of cable news. "Detective Francisco, isn't it? Can I just ask you a few questions—?"

"Sorry, I'm looking for someone." George scanned the rest of the room and found it empty, then ducked out again to see Susan shaking her head at him from across the lobby. His stomach muscles winched themselves a little tighter with apprehension.

"They didn't see anyone at all in there," Susan reported when he came to join her at the balcony's edge. The rumpled quilt of snow outside glittered fiercely, melting in the midday heat. Even stripped of its ultraviolet by the window glass, the reflected sunlight felt good on George's face. "But they thought they heard someone talking in the dining room."

"Let's go look." George strode past the main ballroom, hearing the scraping of chairs and rising hum of conversation that meant the symposium had just broken for lunch. He quickened his step, not wanting to be distracted by Newcomers he had already counted. Even before he stepped into the dining room, however, the rising and falling cadence of a familiar voice told him he'd found one of his missing Tenctonese.

"Emma Bovary." Susan made an exasperated noise when she saw the beautifully spotted *linnaum* seated at a table directly in front of the camera stand. A gaggle of starstruck human girls clustered around her, breathlessly hanging on her endless stream of anecdotes. "I bet she left the symposium early just to get that seat."

"It doesn't matter, as long as we have her accounted for." The grinding in George's stomach didn't stop, however. He knew enough by now to know that the Purists were taking them one at a time. "Let's go up and check the hotel rooms."

"All of them?" Susan turned to look up at him, dismayed. "George, we're going to miss lunch, and you don't even know if anything is wrong!"

Common sense warred with his overwhelming need to be sure that all the Tenctonese were safe—and lost. The concern in Susan's face, however, prompted him to find a compromise. "I won't miss lunch if you stay

113

down here and save it for me." He saw her eyes darken with incipient protest and added, "That way, if you count thirty-five of us in the room, you can have the hotel page me, and I'll know to come back down."

"Oh, all right." Susan sighed and gave him a little push toward the elevators. "Go do your policeman stuff if you have to."

"I'll be back before the next session starts." Once again, he found himself watching protectively after her while she turned into the room, uneasy at the way the emerging symposium crowd swirled around her. It wasn't until he saw her find a seat beside Cathy that he finally felt his feet loosen themselves from the carpet and take him toward the elevators.

Rounding the corner, George was startled to see a brand new line of red velvet rope fencing off part of the vestibule. Three gray-suited humans stood near the isolated elevator, carefully guarding its open doors. As soon as they caught sight of him, one of the males pulled out a pocket radio and spoke into it while the female started toward him.

George frowned, recognizing the clean-cut efficiency of the maneuver. *If I were Matthew,* he thought, *I'd say those looked like FBI agents.* The woman reached him and nodded politely, but when her eyes scanned the balcony behind him rather than meeting his, George was sure of his guess.

"If you're going up to your room, you need to use this elevator now," she informed him, professionally brisk. "Name, please."

"George Francisco." George wondered why she couldn't read it from his badge, then saw she had pulled out a pocket computer with a microphone attached. Checking his voice prints, he guessed. Was the FBI afraid that Purists were disguising themselves as Newcomers?

The computer beeped and the young woman stepped back, allowing him access to the roped-off area. "All right, you're clear to go up." She walked him toward the waiting elevator. "You don't have to worry about hitting any buttons now. It's programmed to stop at your floor."

And nowhere else, George guessed, disturbed by this sudden control over his movements. It reminded him too much of the ship, of cages and locked doors and *kleezantsun'* telling him where to go. He was so busy trying to dismiss the ugly images in his mind that he barely watched the elevator display. The efficient hiss of the lifting motors seemed to take longer than usual, but it wasn't until the doors opened on a sunlit and completely unfamiliar vestibule that George realized what the FBI had done.

"Francisco." David Jordan greeted him from inside an elaborate nest of communications equipment spread over what must have been a concierge's desk. Behind him, the windows of the penthouse lounge opened onto a spectacular sixteenth-floor view of rivers and distant traffic. "I'm glad you came up. We're trying to decide where to put our surveillance cameras." He gestured down the hall to a group of men armed with ladders and coils of wire. "Should we scan all the room doors or just concentrate on the fire exits?"

It was a transparent attempt to make George feel

like they were all part of one big team, and that only made it harder for the *gannaum* to take a deep breath with the scalding bite of anger in his throat. "That depends on whether you think one of us is going to get killed," George said acidly, "or is going to be the killer."

"If we do our jobs right, there won't be any more killings." Jordan scowled at him. "What's your problem? All I'm trying to do is get as much advance warning as I can."

"Advance warning." George strode over from the elevator, unable to contain his anger any longer. "Why didn't *you* give us some advance warning before you moved us all up to this floor? Who gave you the right to do that?"

"I couldn't take the chance that the news would leak out before we had secured all the rooms up here." Jordan leaned back in his chair, crossing his arms and tucking his hands in his armpits. The posture signified defensiveness to a Tenctonese. George wasn't sure why it meant the same thing to humans, who didn't have sensitive glands to protect in those areas, but apparently it did. "I couldn't risk that. My orders from D.C. were very clear on that point."

"Orders from D.C.?" Awareness flooded through George. "Then this isn't a cooperative operation with the Pittsburgh police?"

Jordan shook his head. "Not any more. I spoke to my department chief in D.C. this morning, and he told me that the bureau has agreed to cover security at this symposium. As of now, you can consider us officially in charge."

Silence fell while George considered this sudden about-face from yesterday. Only one explanation made sense. "There's pressure coming down from the legislature?"

Jordan had the grace to redden slightly. "Representative MacLaine is upset about the murders, and she's influential with the press." His mouth quirked. "She's also grateful to the Tenctonese voters who supported her in the last election."

"So she convinced someone in the bureau to protect us." George gave the human a sharp look. "Well, what is the FBI going to do to protect us that the Pittsburgh police haven't already done? Besides moving us to the sixteenth floor without telling us?"

Jordan took a deep breath, as if this was the question he'd been waiting for. "The move is the main protection. Putting everyone up here will eliminate window access from that roofed portico just below the third floor." Despite his defensive posture, the federal agent managed to sound confident and completely in charge. George wondered if Sikes was right when he claimed they taught them how to talk like that at the FBI Academy. "We've also reprogrammed the elevator you came up on so it's the only one that can reach this floor. It can't stop to pick up passengers anywhere except the ballroom floor, and we've got that access guarded."

"What about the fire stairs?" George demanded.

"That's a bit of a problem," Jordan admitted sheepishly. He cast a disgruntled look down the hall, where men hammered camera mounts into the ceiling. "We can't block them off for safety reasons, but we'll post guards at all of them and keep the whole floor monitored for intruders. That should be good enough."

"Good enough for government work!" George put his hands on his hips in exasperation. "Jordan, did it ever occur to you that we Tenctonese might like to be consulted on this move before you made it? That we might not be willing to just take your word that security here will be 'good enough'?"

"Hey, it was your congresswoman who pulled the strings that got me here!" Jordan retorted. "If you don't like the way we're handling things—"

He broke off when a deep voice rang down the hallway, a staccato shout of rage. George recognized a familiar Tenctonese curse and relaxed so suddenly he felt his stomach muscles ripple. He'd almost forgotten about his missing Newcomer during the argument with Jordan, but his body obviously hadn't. More shouts came down the hallway, human yelps of shock and indignation.

"Oh, hell!" Jordan vaulted out from behind the desk and ran for the hall. "Goddammit, nothing showed on the monitors!"

"They aren't all hooked up yet." George sprinted after him, not waiting for permission to follow. "Which Tenctonese came up before me?"

"That Olympic runner, or whatever she is—Ann Arbor." At the end of the corridor something crashed against a wall, and George heard the sound of moaning. Jordan must have heard it, too. He cursed again and dove recklessly into the alcove at the end of the hall. A few seconds later, he staggered out of it again, flung backwards by the force of another body hitting his. Both men went down in a tangle of flailing arms and curses.

"Golitko!" Jordan struggled with his blindly thrashing colleague until George reached in and lifted the smaller man away. Golitko tried to wrestle free, then seemed to realize he wasn't fighting anyone anymore. He subsided into the desperate, whooping gasps of someone who's been thoroughly winded.

"Who hit you?" demanded Jordan. Golitko pointed wordlessly at the half-open door of Room 1612. Inside, George could hear the raspy breathing of another human, probably unconscious. Then cloth scuffed along the rug, loud enough even for the humans to hear.

George threw a glance at Jordan and saw him nod, then edged in toward the narrow opening. The FBI agent paralleled his course on the other side of the door, pulling his gun from its holster as he went. He paused when George held up a warning hand. The scraping sound got louder, then turned abruptly into a thump. The door swung open without either of them touching it, and a limp form in a torn suit fell through it.

"You!" Ann Arbor lifted one strongly muscled arm and pointed an accusing finger at David Jordan. The athlete's big-boned face wore an expression of disgust. "You stole my medals!"

"What?" Jordan stared back at her, so startled that he forgot to reholster his gun. "What medals?"

"My Olympic medals." Arbor accusingly showed him a handful of empty satin ribbons. "Your agents took them when they moved my luggage up here!"

George glanced down at the unconscious man at his feet, still hearing Golitko's gasps behind him. "Did you catch them in the act, Ms. Arbor?"

"No," she admitted grudgingly. "But who else could have done it? They're the ones who broke into our rooms without permission and moved all our things!"

Jordan finally remembered to put his gun away, then pushed his mop of tousled hair out of his face. "We had a legal warrant to enter your room, Ms. Arbor," he pointed out with some dignity. "And it was a hotel employee with a passkey who let us in, in groups of three at a time. I doubt if anyone could have stolen anything without one of the other agents noticing."

"You could have all been in collusion," the tall *linnaum* said stubbornly. "These two were trying to break into my room again just now, looking for something else to steal!"

George thought it best to intervene. "Ms. Arbor." He reached forward, tugging her gently around to see the ladder in the alcove behind him. "These men were installing a security camera above the fire door. The noise you heard was them hammering on the ceiling, not on your door."

"Oh." Ann Arbor's face stayed stiffly indignant for another moment then melted into a smile of completely unexpected charm. "Oh, dear. Did I beat them up for nothing?"

"No, I wouldn't say that." George bent to help the groaning young man to his feet, dusting off his well-tailored suit. "After all, they *did* move all our belongings up here without even telling us. I think they deserve to be shot-putted through a few doors for that." He aimed an exasperated look at Jordan, who had the grace to redden in response. "And I suspect I won't be the only Tenctonese who thinks so."

CHAPTER 11

THE ADDRESS SIKES had gotten from the woman at the copy shop was for someplace in a suburb half an hour's bus ride from downtown. He figured out how to get there by waiting at various street corners, showing the address to bus drivers who stopped, and asking if they could take him there. The sixth driver said yes, and Sikes dropped $2.50 on the loudest, roughest, smelliest transportation this side of the L.A. Freeway. The man next to him talked softly and incessantly about God's fears for incestuous sinners, and Sikes was working on a headache long before the bus dropped him off in a cheap hotel's age-cratered parking lot.

Squinting against a spitting snow, he waited for the bus to pull away before digging the ugly flyer out of his pocket and checking the address again. It said

Chuck's. The hotel marquee read Chez Royale. "This is nuts," Sikes grumbled to himself. He jogged across the parking lot anyway, though, figuring he could at least stay warm in the lobby until the next bus came along.

The interior was dark and badly decorated. Oddly colored sofas and coffee tables, looking like leftovers from the Bates Motel, were scattered unartfully across a carpet whose pattern had long ago been obscured by dirt and traffic. Overhead, dust webs clung to a huge chandelier that no one had bothered to reach for cleaning in decades, and a lumpy gray rock nearly as tall as Sikes stood under glass in one corner. Someone had sliced the rock open to display the purple crystals inside, but a thick accumulation of dust kept them from looking as impressive as Sikes suspected they really were.

The boy at the front desk sat with his back to Sikes, his attention firmly fixed on a palmtop television hanging from a ventilation grate by a twisted length of aluminum foil. Sikes tried to repress a sting of guilt when he saw the tiny Newcomer on the screen and remembered where he was supposed to be. He hoped Cathy wouldn't be speaking until at least some time this evening, when he might have a chance of getting back in time to hear her. She'd kill him if he didn't.

Pushing those worries from his mind, he briskly slapped the little bell on the desktop.

The boy didn't turn. "Yeah?"

Sikes rattled the crumpled paper in a bid for attention. "I'm looking for Chuck's," he began, and the kid jerked a thumb over his shoulder.

"The basement."

"What?"

"The basement," the kid said, with some irritation. "Go to the elevator and press B."

Didn't seem to matter what city you were in, a smart-ass was a smart-ass everywhere. "Gee, thanks," Sikes drawled. "I really appreciate all your incredible effort."

The kid leaned over to turn up the volume on his TV. "No problem."

It wasn't worth it.

The elevator groaned a little on its way down the single floor, then took forever to open its pitted doors onto the concrete and cinder-block basement. Directly across the hallway, a floor-to-ceiling wrought iron gate marked the entrance to a gym. A sign proclaiming Chuck's was crookedly hung above the doorway. A high-class place, indeed.

"Hello?" Sikes called, looking through the grillwork. "Anybody home?" He tugged experimentally on the gate. It rattled fiercely but didn't move.

"We're closed!" somebody yelled from out of sight down one of the hallways beyond the gym's front desk.

"It's two in the afternoon," Sikes countered.

"Tough shit, we're still closed." His voice drew clearer as his shadow appeared on the wall ahead of his arrival. "We close early Fridays, especially when—" Then he rounded the corner, arms loaded with sweat suits and towels, and slammed to a stop when he saw Sikes waiting for him.

Sikes grinned at him with malicious delight. "Well,

hello, Darren. What's a sleazeball like you doing in a nice place like this?"

Darren Pickett dropped everything he was carrying and ran.

Sikes grumbled. "Oh, man, I hate it when they get stupid." At least with Pickett this didn't come as any big surprise. "Now I'm gonna have to chase him and knock him down."

Planting one foot against the grillwork, Sikes caught the top of the gate and hauled himself up and over. The space near the ceiling was narrow enough that George would never have made it through. Sikes grinned to himself as he thumped to the ground on the other side; at least there were some advantages left in being a scrawny human amidst all that Tenctonese brawn.

Sikes caught the door frame on his way into the hall, using it to swing around the corner after Pickett without slowing. He expected the hallway to end in a fire door, probably left ajar from Pickett's hasty departure. Instead, he had to nearly plant both hands on the floor to keep from sliding headlong into Pickett. Good thing he was bent over, too, otherwise Pickett's first swing with the unloaded weight bar would have taken his head clean off.

Sikes scrabbled backward and bounced to his feet again. He felt a secret surge of relief when Pickett chose to stand his ground instead of following. "What are you doin', Darren?"

Pickett uneasily shifted his grip on the bar, aneorexic frame trembling with either excitement or terror. Sikes hoped it was the latter. "Leave me alone,

Sikes," Pickett insisted frantically. "Jesus! Don't you have anything better to do than follow me all the way from L.A.?"

"You kidding? I live my life for you, Darren." He tried to take a step forward but stopped when Pickett's whole body jerked with tension. "You swing that at me again, and I'll break your arm."

"I'll sue! You're a cop!"

Sikes grinned at him. "Not here, I'm not. I'm just a concerned citizen, protecting myself from a crazed out-of-state bigot."

That at least enticed Pickett to hesitate and lower the bar by a small degree. Sikes thought about trying to close the distance between them again, then saw how rapidly Pickett was breathing and decided maybe he'd wait. "What are you doing in Pittsburgh?" he asked instead.

Pickett squinted his dark eyes down to suspicious slits. "None of your business."

Sikes made a guttural buzzing noise. "Wrong answer! Try again."

"Dammit, Sikes!" the Purist exploded. He shook the empty bar as though not really aware he still held it in his hands. "Why do you have to rag on me like this? What did I ever do to you?"

"You mean besides the occasional riot charge, gay bashing, and illegal firearms?"

Pickett released the bar long enough to swipe one hand across his greasy, pulled-back hair. The bar's unsupported end clanked heavily on the floor. "This is America. I can think anything I want about other, inferior people."

"We're not talking about racism," Sikes said with a scowl. "We're talking about crimes." He lunged forward before Pickett could recover, clamping both hands around the bar and muscling the Purist straight back against the wall with the bar crammed into Pickett's chest. Sikes was a good six inches taller than the Purist, so had the advantage of better leverage as well as surprise. "Let's talk about felonies."

"I can't breathe!" Pickett wheezed.

Sikes ignored him. "Kidnapping—that's a felony. So's murder. And how about breaking and entering? Or do you want to negotiate on that one?"

Pickett squirmed beneath the bar, his face squeezed up into an ugly knot of pain. "I didn't do any of those things," he protested in a tight, breathless voice.

"But I'll bet you know who did."

"No!" He heaved once against Sikes's greater weight and strength, then collapsed back against the wall with a groan. "I don't do that kind of stuff, Sikes, you *know* that!"

Sikes wasn't sure Pickett would like hearing all the things Sikes knew about him. "It just seems like an awfully big coincidence, is all—you showing up here in Pittsburgh right about the same time the Newcomers do."

Pickett shook his head. "I'm here 'cause I got paid!"

"Paid?"

"Paid!" He glared up at Sikes in almost humorous defiance. "Some local dude who cares about this country's future got hold of me through the UPP. He knew the slags were coming for their propaganda parade, and he wanted somebody with experience to organize protests. That's all I've been doing—protests and tracts."

Sikes studied Pickett's ratty little face for almost a full minute. He didn't like the glow of honesty he saw there. "What's his name? What's he look like?"

Pickett spat on the front of Sikes's jacket, and Sikes thumped him once against the wall in return. "Even if I knew, I wouldn't tell you!" Pickett insisted, eyes clenched shut. "It's my duty to the human race not to give in to bleeding heart liberals like you, who would sacrifice our sacred place on this earth just to—"

"Oh, shut up." Sikes took a step back, jerking the weight bar out of Pickett's hands as he did so. The skinny Purist seemed intent on pressing himself even flatter to the wall, as if afraid of whatever Sikes would do next. "Are you telling me you came all the way across the country to work for some guy you've never even seen?"

Pickett shrugged awkwardly, looking as though the stupidity of that was only just occurring to him. "I knew he was a slag-hating fascist," he said in a significantly calmer voice. "That's usually enough."

Sikes planted one end of the bar on the floor and leaned the length of it up alongside his cheek. "You think you could identify this guy's voice in a phone call?"

"You just don't get it, do you?" Apparently reassured by Sikes's relaxed posture, Pickett eased away from the wall and struck a haughty pose. "I'm not gonna help you snag this guy."

"There's a good chance he's an accomplice to murder!"

"It's not murder unless it's a human."

Sikes hissed a curse he'd learned from George and resisted whacking Pickett with the full length of the weight bar. "That may be your opinion, but it sure as hell isn't the law's. You could get hauled in just for withholding this kind of information."

Pickett sneered. "Not by you," he said smugly. "You're not a cop in this state, remember? And if you try to take me in, I'll have them arrest you for kidnapping."

The reality of that threat made Sikes's stomach roil. "I can still make a citizen's arrest."

"I'm not committing any crime," Pickett countered. He seemed to be enjoying himself immensely. "I've got a paper that says I work here. I'm not on probation anywhere. In fact, you're the one who broke in here after I specifically told you we were closed, and then you threatened me with that stick." He made a move toward the house phone on the front desk down the hall. "Maybe I should call security and have them haul your ass downtown, hmmm?"

Sikes's first instinct was to roundhouse the shit and stuff him in a locker. He managed to quell that, though, and instead tossed the bar a little farther down the hall so that Pickett didn't have to go past it on their way to the entrance. "Fine. You let me out and I'm gone. I'm getting to where I can't stand the smell in here anyway." Besides, he had more than he came in with, and he could always send Protzberg's people out here later to lean on Pickett on their own time.

The Purist's grin was crooked and toothy as he

unlocked the gate for Sikes. "I think I could get to like Pittsburgh," he commented. "This is the most fun I've ever had with you, Sikes."

Sikes yanked the gate closed behind him, taking evil pleasure in how close he came to catching Pickett's fingers in the hinge. "Don't get too used to it," he advised, "'cause if I have my way, Darren, you're not going to be in Pittsburgh very long."

CHAPTER 12

IF ONE MORE person complained to him about what the FBI had done, George thought bleakly, he was going to hurl himself through the hotel's wall of windows and straight into the nearest river. Emma Bovary was the eleventh one since lunch, and the fourth since this coffee break had started five minutes ago. It didn't help that she was also the least logical.

"—it's not that I don't appreciate the protection." The model gave an exaggerated and distinctly human-looking shiver. The younger Tenctonese and human males who swarmed around her as mindlessly as midges made appreciative noises, although George wasn't sure if they were responding to the emotion or to what it did for her low-cut dress. He wondered how Bovary could stand to expose that much of her back in the cold hotel air. "After all, with people getting ripped to shreds every night around here, a girl needs as many strong men around as she can get."

George suppressed a snort, remembering how Ann Arbor had thrown around the FBI agents assigned to protect her. Even Emma Bovary, for all her painted china delicacy, could probably have broken any bone she wanted to in the men she was gazing at with such helpless appeal. With an effort, George refrained from pointing that out. He sipped his tea in grim silence, barely tasting the refreshing bite of soy sauce.

"But really, some things are just more important than personal safety," Bovary continued bravely. She took a deep, determined breath. "The clothes in my room are literally priceless, Mr. Francisco! They're unique originals, donated by professional designers for my exclusive use. I just can't take the chance that one of them will disappear if the FBI decides to move us again."

George sighed into his tea. "The FBI isn't going to move us to a different floor each night, Ms. Bovary," he said for the third time. With each repetition, he found himself using simpler words. "They just want to keep us safe from Purists breaking in our windows. And I don't think they want to steal your dresses."

"Oh, I'm not accusing *them!*" Emma Bovary cast an apologetic glance at the gray-suited young man at her right, and he reddened. For a minute, George wondered how she had picked the agent out so unerringly, then realized it must have been his clothes. "But with so many things disappearing in this hotel—I mean, the souvenir hunters are just having a field day! First it was the Frees' manuscript, then one of Leo da Vinci's chess pieces, and now poor Ann Arbor's medals—"

George frowned. "Other people had things stolen before Ann Arbor?" he demanded. "Did they report that to the police?"

"I don't think so," Emma Bovary said in surprise. "I mean, why should they? It wasn't anything really valuable, at least not before Ann Arbor lost her medals. Leo told me he has to replace his chess set almost every month." She shrugged and another appreciative murmur went up. "You get used to fans wanting little souvenirs when you're a celebrity." Bovary's beautiful violet eyes darkened with determination. "But I won't let them take any of my clothes! If you could just explain to the FBI how important that is—"

His patience exhausted at last, George opened his mouth to tell her exactly how important he thought her clothes were. Before he could speak, however, a hand tugged urgently at his elbow and he looked down to see Cathy's anxious face.

"George, Susan sent me to get you. She needs to talk to you right away."

George felt both his hearts miss a beat. Susan had gone up to their room at the beginning of the coffee break to call Albert and find out how Vessna was doing. Had there been bad news? "Excuse me," he said, cutting Emma Bovary off in mid-word, then turned and followed Cathy across the balcony.

"Bless you, *neemu*." Susan stepped out from the alcove that sheltered the ladies' room, and smiled at him. "You brought your tea."

George handed it to her, sighing. One glance at the color of his wife's blue eyes told him there was nothing

133

wrong at home. "So what did you need to talk to me about?"

"Getting you rescued from that Hollywood harpy," Susan said with a mischievous smile. She warmed her hands around the paper cup, shivering a little in the chilly air. "Aren't you grateful to me?"

"Yes," George admitted ruefully. He held an arm out, offering his warmth to her. Susan slid into his clasp at once, her silk-clad shoulders cold under his hand. "Couldn't you find anything warmer to wear than this dress?"

Susan chuckled. "I thought about wearing my Pillagers sweater, but I didn't think it would look right over fuchsia and teal silk."

"Cathy wore hers," George pointed out. The stylized penguin skating across the heavy black-and-gold sweater somehow managed to look casually elegant on the other *linnaum,* combined as it was with a metallic gold scarf and a short black leather skirt.

"Cathy is younger than I am, George," Susan reminded him tartly, "and a lot more trendy."

The biochemist shook her head. "No, I was going to wear a silk dress, too. But then I decided comfort was more important than fashion."

Susan chuckled. "No wonder you and Matt get along so well."

"Speaking of Matt—" Cathy turned her head to scan the balcony with a frown. The crowd was thinning out as people drifted back into the ballroom for the second session of talks. "I thought for sure he'd show up in time for the coffee break. Where did he go this morning?"

"To the downtown police station to help Captain

Protzberg interrogate some Purists." George glanced out at the midafternoon sun and frowned. "It must have taken longer than usual."

"Or something else came up that he had to deal with." Cathy sighed. "As it usually does."

Susan reached out and patted her hand. "Don't worry, dear. I'm sure he'll show up in time for your talk today."

"I know he will," George said firmly. He took Cathy's elbow and steered her back across the balcony with Susan still tucked under his arm. "Even Matthew wouldn't forget something as important as that."

"He wasn't here, was he?"

George met Cathy's gaze in the darkened ballroom, seeing resignation as well as disappointment in her eyes. She dropped into the empty seat next to him, crumpling her note cards in tense hands while the last echoes of applause for her talk faded to an appreciative murmur.

"No," he admitted, "but your talk was superb, whether Matthew heard it or not." Around them the audience stirred and settled, waiting for the next speaker to be fitted with his microphone while the cable news network took a commercial break. In the interim, static hissed and burst across the ceiling speakers, an electronic counterpoint to the crowd noise below.

Susan leaned across George, covering Cathy's clenched hand with her own. "I'm sure Matt wanted to be here. Police work just doesn't stop for other people's schedules."

"I've noticed that." Cathy managed a small smile.

"I didn't think it would happen while we were on vacation, though."

George thought about the last time he'd considered this trip a vacation and decided it had been somewhere over St. Louis. He sighed. "Cathy, for Matthew and me, this has turned into a busboy's holiday."

"Busman's holiday, George." Susan gave him an affectionate swat on the arm. "And I think you'd find some police thing to worry about no matter where we went for vacation."

"Humph." He sat back, trying to find a comfortable spot on the slick metal chair. The afternoon talks were winding to a close, and it was obvious that most of the audience were ready to break for supper. It made their enthusiasm for Cathy's discussion of female Tenctonese scientists even more impressive. When the next speaker launched into a discussion of Tenctonese contributions to the television industry, George drifted into contemplating how receptive the audience was likely to be for his own talk. Given all the interspecies police cooperation this symposium had already generated, he thought ironically, he might even rate a sound bite on the evening news.

"George!" Susan joggled his elbow in the darkness, her voice an urgent whisper. "George, my purse is gone!"

Used to these sporadic alarms, George didn't even open his eyes. "Did you look under your chair?"

"Of course I did. It's not there."

"Then how about under my chair? Or Cathy's?" Up on stage, the speaker was explaining how interspecies situation comedies could provide role models for other families. It sounded more like a sales pitch than a lecture, and George wondered if the Newcomer was an agent.

Susan's breath feathered his hand as she leaned over to see beneath him. "It's not there, either. And anyway, I distinctly remember putting it under the chair in front of me."

"Let me look." George ducked his head down between the closely spaced seats and deliberately widened his eyes, forcing his pupils to dilate to their maximum extent. He saw the backs of several trousered legs, a few kicked-off women's pumps, and a small army of discarded coffee cups, but no trace of Susan's handbag. Surprise jerked him upright, blinking against the brighter light until his eyes adjusted. "I can't believe it. Someone *did* steal your purse, Susan."

"I told you so."

"Maybe someone took it by mistake, thinking it was theirs." Cathy leaned over to add her whisper to theirs as the speaker began promoting the use of Tenctonese actors in commercials. "I've done that with briefcases sometimes in dark conference rooms like this."

"That's possible." George could see empty seats in the row before theirs, seats he knew had been occupied earlier in the afternoon. "Did anyone just leave from the row in front of us?"

Susan shook her head, looking annoyed with herself. "I was so busy watching Cathy's talk that I didn't pay attention," she admitted. "At least there isn't much money in my wallet. I just wish I hadn't put all my pictures of Vessna and Emily in there!"

"Thieves usually take the money and throw the rest away," George reassured her. He got up, careful not to intrude his head into the projected beam of light from the speaker's slides. "I'll see if anyone has turned it in at the hotel desk."

"Thank you, *neemu.*" Susan caught his hand and squeezed it gratefully as he slid out of the row. "You see, Cathy, there are advantages to having a policeman in your life."

Cathy made a sound that might have been the ghost of a chuckle. "You mean besides a refrigerator full of doughnuts?"

That young *linnaum* had been spending entirely too much time with his partner, George reflected. He hurried out of the room, barely avoiding the bearded cable news reporter who had jumped up to challenge the speaker about Hollywood cliches of Tenctonese life. A spontaneous burst of applause followed his question.

The balcony outside the ballroom had lost its sheen of sunlight, the shadow of Pittsburgh's sheltering hills already fallen over it. Mixed groups of Tenctonese and humans drank tea and chatted as they waited for the symposium day to end, while a soft twilight mist gathered over the melting snow outside. George scanned the crowd, hoping to find a plainclothes FBI agent who could take him downstairs to the main lobby. Instead, his gaze snagged on an elegantly gaunt *linnaum* who stood alone near the balustrade, looking into an open leather purse. A second purse hung unobtrusively from her elbow.

George frowned and shouldered through the crowd, police instincts keeping him silent until he was close enough to catch her if she ran. "Mrs. Vegas, may I talk to you?"

"Oh!" Photos spilled from between unsteady hands

as Lydia Vegas jerked around to meet him. George recognized the sweetly smiling face of his baby daughter and felt his frown deepen. The Overseer's wife didn't seem to notice, heaving what sounded like a genuine sigh of relief before she bent to pick up the pictures. "Oh, Mr. Francisco, you're exactly the person I needed to see!"

George dropped to one knee beside her, gathering up a picture of Emily dressed as Pocahontas for a school play. He held it for a minute, smiling despite himself at the sight of his ultramodern teenager in the archaic Earth costume of fringed buckskin and long skirts. Then he stood and helped the older *linnaum* to her feet.

"How can I help you, Mrs. Vegas?" he asked, handing the photos back to her and keeping his voice carefully neutral.

"It's this purse." She tucked the photos inside the leather bag and held it out to him, solemn as a ritual offering. "I found it in the trash can of the ladies' room just a few minutes ago. Could you return it to its owner for me?"

George studied her in speculative silence. "You could do that yourself, if you wanted to," he said at last. "All you'd have to do is look in the wallet and find out whose it is."

Lydia Vegas met his gaze, her gray eyes turned almost black by embarrassment. "I don't feel—I can't do that. The person it belongs to might think I'd stolen it."

Not the usual attitude of people who found lost property, George thought, but that didn't necessarily mean Lydia Vegas was a thief. The same lack of self-esteem that led her to marry a *kleezantsun'* might just as easily convince her she'd be blamed for someone else's crime. He sighed and took the purse from her outstretched hand, feeling her thin fingers quiver as he did.

"I'll make sure this goes back to the proper owner," he told her. "But I'd like you to report finding it to the police and the hotel management. They've had a rash of thefts recently, and the information might help them track down the culprit."

Lydia Vegas nodded, her eyes fading back to a more normal pale blue-gray. "Then I'll certainly make a report." She surprised him by reaching out to touch Susan's photos again, carefully tucking them into the open purse. "I wouldn't want anyone else to lose something so—precious."

George watched her walk away, baffled into stillness. After four years on the police force, he could usually tell when people were lying, but the combination of sincerity and insecurity in the Overseer's wife threw his intuition all awry. Something wasn't right about her explanation of finding Susan's purse, but George would be willing to swear in court that Lydia Vegas hadn't wanted to steal anything from it. Except, perhaps, the pictures of Vessna, he thought suddenly. With her own child lost to miscarriage late in life, she might have been tempted—

"Hey, George!" A familiar shout from below yanked George out of his whirl of speculation. He leaned over the balustrade to see Sikes standing in the main hotel lobby, his jacket still damp from the outside fog. Two hotel guards flanked him, inspecting a soggy piece of cardboard that might once have been a name badge. They didn't look impressed. "Tell these guys I'm with the symposium, will you?"

"I can vouch for him," George told the guards, and they reluctantly allowed Sikes onto the marble staircase. He took the steps two at a time, vaulting over the red velvet rope at the top before the guard there could unhook it. His tennis shoes left dark grimy spots on the carpet behind him as he crossed the balcony, and he smelled powerfully of diesel smoke.

"Nice fashion statement, George," Sikes said, tapping at the purse. "Doesn't match your belt, though." He turned to peer into the darkened ballroom behind them. "Cathy didn't give her talk yet, did she?"

"About fifteen minutes ago." Lips tightening with embarrassment, George tucked the purse into the crook of his arm to conceal it. "She was disappointed that you weren't there."

"Damn!" Sikes turned and slammed a fist down on the marble railing, then cursed again at the pain. "I can't believe I came all the way out from L.A. for this and missed her talk!"

"I can," George said frankly. "You do things like that to her all the time."

"I know, but this time she really wanted me to be there." Sikes groaned and buried all his fingers in his tousled hair. "Oh, George, I'm a dead man."

CHAPTER 13

Sikes sat with his stockinged feet propped up on the heater, a tepid cup of coffee trapped under his hands while he watched the darkness gather outside their hotel room window. He would rather have been inside the saunalike bathroom, talking to Cathy while she finished her before-bed shower, but a guy could stand only so much silence from the other side of a shower curtain.

He heard the water turn off and took his feet down from the heater to scoot his chair around. "I said I was sorry." He spoke in a normal tone, knowing his voice would carry just fine for Tenctonese ears.

Likewise, Cathy had learned long ago that she had to shout from a bathroom if he was to hear her. "I know."

Sikes dropped his head and counted to three. "I

really am sorry," he sighed. "I've been looking forward to your talk ever since we got here."

"Matt, you think the impact of women in the professional sciences is the most boring subject on the planet."

The accuracy of her comment stung. "Okay, so maybe the talk itself didn't have me dancing with anticipation. But I really did want to see you up there, looking so smart and beautiful, being proud of you . . ."

The bathroom door whispered open with a breath of steam, and Sikes thought she'd at least keep the discussion going long enough for him to convince her of his sincerity and thus win some forgiveness. Instead, she simply went about the business of folding away her clothes from today, neatly hanging up her Penguins sweater, laying out her clothes for tomorrow. Her face had taken on the completely unreadable, emotionless expression Sikes knew she must have learned for protection during her days as a slave. He hated it when he made her look like that.

"Cathy . . ."

She pushed a drawer closed without turning to look at him. "I'm not sure we should talk about this right now."

"God*dammm*it!" He thumped the Styrofoam coffee cup to the dresser top, earning a startled look from Cathy when sticky liquid splashed all over his sleeve and hand. "It was just a stupid talk," he argued, leaping to his feet to shake the coffee off his hand. "I tried to get back for it, okay? I spent six bucks on bus fares just trying to get someplace I recognized! I'm sorry I missed it, and I'm sorry you're mad, but I don't know what the hell you want me to do!"

She watched him curse and wipe his hand dry on the leg of his jeans but didn't move to help him or even offer him a towel. "I don't want you to do anything," she said calmly. "In fact, I . . ." As though suddenly thinking better of whatever she'd started to say, she turned abruptly back to the dresser and pulled out a drawer to inspect the contents. "It's not fair for me to want you to be . . ." She cocked her head, still looking at her underwear as she searched for words. ". . . different," she finally decided, "just because we share sexual relations. It's not like you've ever cared about what I do—"

"Oh, come on!"

"No, Matt, it's true." The firmness of her voice startled him and hurt in a way he hadn't expected it could. She faced him with her hands tucked under her elbows. He couldn't remember the last time she had looked so beautiful. "Tell me—do you have any idea what the project is I'm working on right now?"

He didn't answer, didn't even shake his head. She already knew he hadn't the faintest, or she wouldn't have bothered asking.

"Do you even know the name of the biochemist I'm working with?"

This time he looked away from her to the window again. He didn't even know why, just that he couldn't always stand to look at her when she told him the truth like this.

Behind him, Cathy sighed softly. "All you care about, all you've ever cared about, is catching the next bad guy." He wished she'd at least sound angry and not so goddammed reasonable and calm. "And that's okay—really. I knew the way you worked and thought before I even decided to get involved with you. But I'm not perfect." The heat of her body coming up close to his back inexplicably made him shiver. "It's just that, sometimes, I think it would be nice to know I matter to you at least as much as all this crook-chasing does."

He turned in surprise, nearly bumping into her, and took her face between his hands. "Oh, Cathy," he whispered, "you matter! You matter more to me than anything." He pulled her close, as tight as he dared, and squeezed his eyes shut against the horrible image of her disemboweled like Sandi Free. "That's why I was out there today, because the thought of anything happening to you scares me a whole lot more than anything you could do to me if I missed your lecture." He felt her smile against the side of his neck, and he smiled a little, as well. "We've got to catch these guys. *I've* got to catch these guys. I can't let them do this to anybody else, and if they try to hurt you—"

Her arms gripped him painfully. "Don't."

"It'd kill me, Cathy," he finished hoarsely. "I swear, just kill me."

"Matt, don't!" She pushed away from his embrace but didn't let go of his arms. "There's nothing going to hurt me. Not with you here." Her eyes, as strong and cool as milky jade, forced him to look at her and believe everything she said. He opened his mouth to protest, but she silenced him with a frown. "Not with you to protect me," she insisted, slipping her hands across his hips and into the back pockets of his jeans. "My big, strong policeman."

He snorted but answered her smile by resting his forehead against hers. "Good try, pumpkin head. But you and I both know you could whip my ass with one hand tied behind your back."

Cathy acknowledged that with a little shrug. "Very true." Then she ducked abruptly to cut his legs out from under him and sweep him up into her arms. Sikes yelped with surprise and clutched around her neck for fear of falling. But her hold was strong and steady. "I guess that means you can't resist me if I decide to use force to take advantage of you," Cathy commented with a sigh.

Sikes smiled, liking the way her mind worked. "Yeah, I guess not. Oh, well."

Sikes jolted awake in the darkness, overhot, muscle sore, and exhausted. He thought he jerked when he came out of his dream—something about hiding in Cathy's apartment while a dog from the K-9 corps tore at the outside door—but Cathy still sighed peacefully asleep beside him.

He clenched both hands in the bedclothes and listened. Nothing specific, nothing real. Just a feeling that itched along every inch of his skin, warning him that something was going on in the darkness that he didn't like. It was the same feeling that warned him where a shooter crouched in a warehouse, or hinted about just which cars he shouldn't approach without a gun in his hand. He wanted to shake Cathy awake, whispering like a nervous housewife, *"Honey, I think I hear somebody in the room!"* But that was asinine—anything he could hear, Cathy could hear better, and she was sleeping like a baby while he pissed in his shorts over nothing but a bad dream. He rolled over, burying his face in the pillow.

And Cathy bolted upright with a horrible gasp.

Just then, in the room adjoining their own, a woman's bellowed profanity followed an explosion of shattering glass.

"What is it?" Cathy gasped, wrapping herself in the bedclothes. "Matt, where are you going?"

He was out of bed without even realizing it, yanking at the door separating their rooms as if he really expected it to be unlocked. "Open up!" He pounded the door so hard he knew his fist would bruise. "Open up!" he shouted again in his deepest, gruffest voice. "This is the police, *dammit!*"

Cathy pushed between him and his first attempt at throwing his weight against the lock. "Let me—"

"Call George," he tried to say, but she glared at him and shouted, "Let me! I can break it!"

No sense dating a woman with twice your own strength if you didn't make use of it every now and again. He danced to one side, fidgeting unhappily as he darted his eyes around the room in search of some kind of weapon. Cathy wrapped both hands around the smooth metal doorknob, wrenching back with a grunt just as Sikes caught sight of the Bible he'd flung from the bedstand to the bureau the night of their arrival. He scooped it up, feeling a little stupid, and the door gave with a shriek and a crack as the doorjamb tore loose, lock and all.

There was a second door beyond the first, this one knobless and smooth. Cathy broke it in with a single slam from her shoulder, then jumped away when Sikes grabbed her arm and hissed, "Call George!" Relief throbbed through him at her brisk nod. Then she was out of sight behind him, and he had only a cheap Bible between himself and the blackened adjoining room.

He slipped into the room as quickly and carefully as possible, Bible high over one shoulder. Thumps and gasps pounded from behind a rumpled bed, and winter wind, as sharp as the broken glass beneath the window, tattered past the curtains to swirl painfully around the lightless room. Sikes tried to step past the glittering debris, and instead slammed his foot into some cold, heavy chunk of metal that sent him sprawling with a shouted curse.

Cathy's voice arrowed in from the other room, sharp with concern. "Matt?"

He struggled to all fours, suddenly terrified of who might have heard her, and shot a frantic look toward the violent sounds in the corner. A dark, big-headed silhouette already stretched above the humped out-line of the bed. Sikes felt his heart crowd up into his throat as it planted both hands on the bedspread and launched itself across the room.

He reared up on his knees to hit it, but it cleared the distance with inhuman speed and crashed into him before he could do more than draw back for the blow. The stench of Newcomer blood swarmed around him, spicy-sweet, and he coughed against the strength of the smell as the floor slammed him and knocked his breath away. A broad, sloping Newcomer head low-ered close to his, and Sikes swung at it. He struck a corded shoulder instead, and the Newcomer on top of him wrenched the Bible out of his hand and threw it aside without turning away from him. The book smacked the far wall with a sound like a gunshot. "Get off me, damn you!" Sikes whispered fiercely.

As if in reply, it twisted its head aside, drowning its deep eye sockets in shadow. Sikes had only the barest glimpse of its elongated jawline before it was thrown into the air with a mindless, guttural cry.

Sikes felt a dash of stinging heat across his cheek. *Blood,* he realized, *Newcomer blood,* just as his attacker ripped through carpet and curtains and glass to flee out the broken window. A drizzle of bloody spittle trailed behind it.

Sikes tried to sit up but couldn't. His chest still felt hot and tight from the Newcomer's blow, and he could feel the tingly beginnings of shock nibbling away at his fingers. Someone mumbled above him—

"Na tog toe sacka wrap'da . . . Na tog ma syka tam eckwa . . ."

—but it was sibilant Tenctonese, and the words meant nothing to him. Straining to see upward through the dimness, he could just make out thickly muscled legs and a powerful fist gripping a blood-stained iron dumbbell, then Ann Arbor swayed with a thick gurgle and collapsed atop him.

CHAPTER 14

A DISTANT CRASH shattered the midnight stillness as George burst out of his hotel room, still struggling to fasten the pants he'd grabbed when he heard the phone. He ran down the dimly lit hall, fear hammering in his blood. From the concierge's desk behind him, he could hear one of the FBI agents yelling questions, but he ignored her. The thick smell of Newcomer blood swirled out to meet him two strides before he skidded into the alcove that sheltered Ann Arbor's room. George felt both his hearts lurch in dismay. Was he too late again?

He pounded on the door of Room 1612 and heard the muffled sound of gasping through it. "Matthew! Cathy!" He battered on the door again, then lost patience and ripped it entirely off its hinges. It tore away with a shriek of stressed metal and splintered wood. Frigid air blasted through the opening he'd made, nearly choking him with the reek of spilled blood.

George stiffened, seeing the tangle of heaving bodies on the floor beside the shattered window. Two shining spots lifted from that huddle and focused on him—Cathy's eyes, pupils widened by the darkness. As George's own vision adjusted to the unlit room, he could see the biochemist kneeling beside Ann Arbor, blood-drenched hands pressed to the bigger *linnaum's* chest. A ragged slash ripped through the athlete's white T-shirt, exposing ropes of dark coral muscle and the ivory gleam of bone beneath the skin. Her left arm twisted at an impossible angle to her shoulder, the muscles around the joint already swollen to a hardened lump.

Blood spurted between Cathy's fingers as the athlete heaved beneath her. The pink liquid came out so frothy and bright that George knew it had to be flowing straight from one of the huge veins that fed oxygen to both hearts. His own chest wall clenched in horror.

"George, don't just stand there—pull Matt out!" Fear and frustration gave Cathy's voice the fragile sharp edge of glass. George realized that the heaving motion came from his partner, trapped under Arbor's considerable weight. He groaned at his own stupidity and lunged forward to lift the athlete's unconscious body with one hand while he hauled Sikes out with the other. The frantic sound of gasping eased at last.

"Is he all right?" Cathy's gaze was locked on Ann Arbor, but her anxious voice told George who she was really worried about. "He couldn't answer me before."

George steadied his partner against the icy night air, scanning him for injuries. Despite the dark red bruise on his chest and the blood trickling across his chin, Sikes did not seem seriously hurt. "I think he's just winded."

The human nodded forcefully, still too breathless to speak. A glare of light washed the room with sudden bright colors and made George's eyes sting. He swung around in time to see David Jordan burst through the open door, clad only in trousers and a scowl. The FBI agent cursed when he saw Arbor's blood-stained body, then handed his gun to one of the agents who had piled up like grim logs behind him.

"Is she alive?" Jordan strode over to examine the athlete, ignoring the blood-splattered carpet under his bare feet. One of his agents followed him while the others waited more warily in the hall. "How fast do we need an ambulance?"

"As fast as you can get one here." Cathy didn't look away from the bloody flesh beneath her hands, but the quiver in her voice betrayed her strain. Sikes scowled at her, then jerked free of George's support and went back through the splintered connecting doorway into his own room. "One of her pulmonary veins is cut."

"Kosak." Jordan glanced over his shoulder at the young man who'd trailed him in. George recognized him as the same man Ann Arbor had knocked out the day before. "Get the life-flight helicopter from Allegheny General. Tell them they can land on the hotel roof."

"Yes, sir." The male agent spun and launched himself down the hall at a run. His colleagues stepped aside to let him through, then took up their posts in the doorway again. George realized they were keeping a curious crowd of Tenctonese symposium guests from flooding into the room.

"Who did that?" Jordan demanded, jerking a thumb at the battered doorway. "You or the perps?"

"I opened the hall door." It occurred to George that the cold night wind was probably draining Ann Arbor of much needed heat. He yanked the coverings off the unmade bed, then carried them over to her. The unconscious athlete didn't stir as he tucked the blanket around her hips and legs, then began ripping the sheet to make a pressure pad. "I assume Cathy broke the other one. The attackers came through the window."

"The hell they did." Jordan's voice shivered with disbelief. "We moved to the sixteenth floor, and they *still* came in the window?"

"Yeah, some protection that turned out to be." Sikes emerged from his room fully dressed, with a heavy peacoat slung over his arm. He ignored Jordan's glare, crossing the room to drape his coat over Cathy's bare shoulders. "What are you going to do next, move us to the roof?"

"The roof!" Jordan started to cross toward the open window, then yelped and leaped back as glass crunched under his bare feet. "That's how the Purists must have gotten in—they rappelled down from the roof. Go see if there's a rope hanging out there, Francisco."

George bound the last of his pressure bandage down and began to rise, but a human hand fell on his

153

shoulder and stopped him. "Broken glass can cut Newcomers just like it can cut you," Sikes told the FBI agent caustically. "Get someone with shoes on to do it."

Jordan grunted. "You have shoes on."

George could see his partner's mouth tighten in response. Unusually for him, however, Sikes said nothing. He circled Ann Arbor without looking at her blood-stained chest, then put a hand on either side of the shattered window and leaned so far out into the darkness that Cathy gasped. "I don't see any rope."

"The Purists probably took it with them when they climbed back onto the roof." Jordan didn't seem to notice Sikes's uncharacteristic silence, but George did. He gave his partner a sharp look. "I'll get dressed, then see if I can spot any sign of forced entry on the roof. Starling, you and Wampler go up and make sure the copter doesn't blow away all our evidence." "Yessir." The two agents ducked through the crowd of curious onlookers and disappeared into the fire stairs. With characteristic good sense, the Tenctonese stayed out of the room even after the agents were gone.

Jordan glanced at the spreading pink stain across Ann Arbor's bandaged chest. "That life-flight crew should be here any minute," he said. "Can you guys hold the fort until then?"

"I think so," said George, when neither of his companions spoke. Cathy was intent on her bloody, urgent work, and Sikes still stared out at the night, an odd expression twisting his wide mouth.

Jordan nodded and turned away, then stopped abruptly in the doorway. He swung back to scowl at Sikes. "That *red* blood on your lip," he said, as if he'd just realized what that meant. "You caught part of that fight with the Purists?"

Sikes shrugged without turning away from the broken window. "Just the end of it."

"You get a good look at any of them?"

"Nope."

Jordan nodded again, accepting that flat statement, but George knew better. He turned to eye his partner with sudden suspicion. Cathy spared a quick glance up from her bloody hands, as if she had sensed the lie, too.

"Too bad," was all the FBI agent said. "We could've used an immediate witness. Now we'll have to wait and talk to Ann Arbor in the hospital." He glanced at the still form on the floor and frowned again. "If she lives."

Jordan disappeared into the hall, leaving uneasy silence behind him. The wind clawed through the jagged glass, snuffling at them like an invisible animal. Then George said, "Matthew" just as Cathy said, "Matt" in identical chiding tones.

Sikes turned away from the window and glared at them both. "What?"

"You saw something," Cathy told him.

"Something you didn't tell the FBI," George added. He meant to be admonishing, but it came out with exasperation. "Why not? What did you see?"

Sikes gestured at the window without answering. "George, come here—no, dammit, you don't have shoes on. Go into my bedroom and look down at the outside wall for me."

Fiercer exasperation tugged at George, but he flattened his lips to a thin line and ignored it. Leaving

Cathy to her vital task, he strode into the connecting door, threading his way through the carelessly flung clothes on the floor until he got to the curtained window. "All right," he said, raising his voice so Sikes could hear. "I'm looking out."

There was a pause. "George, could you climb that wall?"

"From the ground?" George frowned at the smooth metal ribs that separated the windows, seeing no breaks or crenellations that might have provided handholds. "No, Matthew. I don't think any Tenctonese could." He retraced his steps through the room and stood staring at his partner from the connecting door. "You saw a Tenctonese in here tonight," he said, not making it a question.

"Yes." Sikes spoke through clenched teeth, as if the answer had been shaken out of him by force. "I mean, no. Oh, hell, I don't know." He swung around from the shattered window, scowling. "I saw someone who *moved* something like a Tenctonese. That doesn't mean I saw a Tenctonese. Or that I have to blab it to some fed when I'm not sure."

"You don't want them to think that a Newcomer is behind all these murders, do you?" Cathy didn't look up as she spoke, but her tense voice melted into affectionate warmth. George saw his partner's face darken with a mulish look of embarrassment.

"I just don't want anyone jumping to conclusions, that's all," Sikes growled. "It'll make catching the bastard that much harder."

"The FBI—" George began.

"The FBI couldn't find a plastic bag in a garbage dump, much less figure out who's really behind these murders!" Sikes gave him a grim look. "We're going to have to do this ourselves, partner, and you know it."

George frowned, self-doubt clawing at him. It was one thing to track a killer with the full authority and resources of the Los Angeles Police Department behind him. It was quite another to do it unofficially and against legal prohibitions, with only one belligerent human to help him. Especially when the lives of his wife and his partner's lover depended on their success. "I don't think—" he began, but the sound of Susan's voice out in the hall stopped him.

"They should be in here." His wife glanced in from the hall, her strained look fading as soon as she saw George. She stepped back to allow the white-jacketed medical team to swing their wheeled stretcher into the room. Emergency medical technicians and nurses converged on Ann Arbor, taking only a few minutes to clamp the pulmonary vein and release Cathy from her long vigil. The biochemist stood up, swaying with cold, and was promptly dragged into Sikes's arms, blood and all. He carried her back to their room, looking defiantly careless of who saw them.

George lingered in Ann Arbor's room, Susan standing silent and concerned at his side as the emergency team worked over the injured athlete. They exchanged information in the efficiently abbreviated language of medical personnel everywhere, but George sensed an underlying uncertainty beneath their professional calm. It occurred to him that this was probably the first time they'd seen a Newcomer, much less tended one.

He stepped forward, clearing his throat with a click. "If I can be of any assistance—"

"Blood," said the nearest crew member succinctly. George looked down at the short black-skinned female in surprise, not having guessed that she was the one in charge.

"What can I tell you about it?" he asked.

"How to get it." The woman frowned at his uncomprehending look. "We're going to have to replace what's all over this floor, and we don't exactly have a lot of this pink stuff in stock." She tilted her head. "I assume you guys have blood banks in L.A.?"

One of the taller men looked up from an instrument before George could answer. "We're not going to have time to get blood flown out from L.A. Her blood pressure's dropping too fast."

George looked over his shoulder at Susan, asking a question with his eyes and reading the answer in hers. He turned back to the black woman. "I don't believe that'll be a problem," he told her quietly. "Tenctonese were bred to reduce the rejection factors in their blood. There are thirty-five potential donors in this hotel, and you have two of them right here."

"What the hell do you mean, we can't talk to her?"

It was interesting, George thought, how humans reacted differently to stress. Of the two law enforcement officers assigned to this case, he would have thought David Jordan, the federal employee whose political future rode on his success, would be the one shouting at the doctor. Instead, Jordan leaned quietly against a tiled hospital wall while Jen Protzberg confronted the head of Ann Arbor's surgical team. Despite the fact that she no longer had any official responsibility for the safety of the symposium guests, real frustration snapped in the Pittsburgh detective's voice.

"Anyone feel like explaining why the hell we *can't* talk to her?" This time it was Sikes whose shout rattled the metal gurneys parked outside the operating room. The irritation in his partner's voice came as no surprise to George. After waiting through the predawn darkness for the operation to be over, Sikes had reached the point of sleep deprivation where irritation replaces fatigue. Of course, with Sikes that never took very long.

It didn't help that they had left Susan and Cathy back at the hotel, exhausted from donating blood. Even through the numb tiredness of his own blood loss, George could feel an echo of Sike's anxiety. In his case, it made him wish everyone would just stop shouting and let him go back to the hotel.

The older woman who headed the surgical team glared back at Sikes, not intimidated by his bellow. "This isn't something we decided on, dammit! Your precious witness is in a coma."

"Coma?" George frowned up at her, forcing his eyes to focus against the glare of hospital lights. "You mean *riasu?*"

The surgeon grunted, scrubbing one hand across her lined face. "That's what the Tenctonese doctors we teleconferenced with during the surgery called it. They said it was some kind of healing trance. According to them, it was a good sign that she slipped into it, although it scared the hell out of our anesthesiologist."

George nodded. "Attaining *riasu* means she has enough strength to begin healing her injuries. Given how badly she was hurt, she could remain in trance for several days."

"Damn." Sikes slapped a hand on the nearest gurney, hard enough to send it crashing into the wall. The surgeon gave him a disgusted look and spun back into her operating room. *"Now* what are we going to do?"

"First," said George, "we're going back to our hotel."

Jordan sighed and detached himself from the wall while Protzberg fished the keys to her car out of her rumpled jacket. "And then we're going to cancel the symposium," Jordan added grimly.

"Finally!" Sikes slammed the wall with his fist again, this time in fierce satisfaction. He grabbed George and hauled him through the trauma center with long, eager strides, heading out to the Doctors Only space where Protzberg had parked. "It's about time someone around here woke up and started thinking."

Bracingly cold air washed away George's lethargy as they left the hospital, emerging into a fog-wrapped dawn. He took a deep breath of the river-damp, coal-smoke smell of Pittsburgh. "Yes," he said clearly. "It's time someone started doing that."

"George." Sikes threw him a warning look as they slid into the backseat of Protzberg's car. "George, don't start getting any brilliant ideas about this case. It's too late."

"It's not too late, Matthew, it's exactly the right

time." George leaned forward intently while Protzberg edged her car into the morning flow of traffic. "Mr. Jordan, would you be willing to order a news blackout for the attack on Ann Arbor?"

"Why?" The FBI agent sounded dubious.

"Because then whoever attacked her will come back to attack her again."

Sikes snorted. "George, you don't know that! These murders have been random! Even if they didn't manage to kill Ann Arbor, they'll just find someone else to attack."

"No, they won't." George swung around to face his scowling partner, energized by the certainty now buzzing past his fatigue. "I think there's some connection between the murders and the thefts that we've been having. Ann Arbor reported her medals stolen, remember, and Emma Bovary said the Frees lost a manuscript."

"Oh, there's a reliable source." Sikes sprawled back against the torn seat of the police sedan, looking disgusted. "Why the hell would Purists want to collect souvenirs of the people they're killing?"

"Why do serial killers do any of the things they do?" George asked slowly. He held his partner's eyes, reminding him wordlessly of what he'd seen the night before. Sikes glowered. "Maybe I'm wrong and there's no connection, but maybe I'm right. If we don't release the news about Ann Arbor, the killer might come back to finish the job he started. If we stake out her room and wait, we'll catch him, or them."

Silence fell in the car. George glanced toward the front seat as they swung into the hotel driveway, catching Protzberg's eyes in the mirror. She looked thoughtful, and the little he could see of Jordan's face at least wasn't frowning. "Well, is it worth a try?"

"It's worth a try," the FBI agent said slowly. "I'll put the news blackout in effect if Protzberg will staff the stakeout." The Pittsburgh detective nodded at once. "But I'm warning you, Francisco. One more murder, and this symposium is history."

CHAPTER 15

"MATT, IS MY Puffins sweater in there?"

Sikes, still groggy from being up since sometime last night, smiled slightly from beneath the shower's hot spray. "Penguins," he called back. "And if it is, it's awfully wet."

The shower curtain billowed inward with a rush of chill air, and he realized Cathy had come into the bathroom when an alien-smooth hand darted into the stall to swat his bare bottom. "Ten thousand comedians, all out of work."

He blinked his eyes open and twisted to grab her wrist but caught only a jet of water when she jumped away with a squeal. Her movement jerked the plastic curtain outside the tub, spilling water all over the tile. Cathy laughed as she tried to maneuver out of his reach and away from the puddle at the same time. "Matt, don't! You'll get me wet!"

Sikes grinned but desisted. It was enough just to hear her sounding happy. With everything that had been going on lately, the sparkle of alien laughter was something he hadn't heard in what seemed like forever.

He flipped the curtain back inside the tub. "Find your sweater?" he asked, reaching for the soap.

She gave a little sigh of frustration. "No. I must have left it in Lydia's room last night. Damn."

The unaccustomed curse surprised Sikes almost as much as the information. "Lydia's room?" He poked his head around the curtain, stopping her just before she closed the bathroom door on her way out. "I thought we told you and Susan to stay here."

Cathy frowned as she swept at the water spots on the breast of her blue-green dress. "Yes, well," she said easily. "We're not *sardonakked*, we don't have to do everything you tell us." She glanced up with limpid green eyes before he could shout at her. "What's the difference between staying here and staying in any other room? Whoever's killing us will come wherever they want. Maybe there's safety in numbers." She shrugged, not looking like she believed herself. "Besides, Lydia was upset by everything, and we didn't want to leave her alone."

He could have yelled at her for caring about anybody else's emotional state when it put her at physical risk, but he knew it was pointless. Retreating back behind the shower curtain, he turned up the hot water to try and hide his irritation. "I'll check with Lydia on my way down," he said gruffly. "Now you get going before you're late for the first talk." He was running late and would no doubt be getting later still.

"You'll be down in time for coffee break?"

"You bet." He closed his eyes and stepped fully under the spray again. "Just promise to find some food I can eat, okay?"

"You bet." Her very voice smiled, and he couldn't help but smile with her. Sometimes it was really good to have a significant other.

Other times it was just good to have a shower. He didn't hear her leave through the outside door, so he didn't have that as a signal of closure to turn off his attention; he worried for a moment that she hadn't arranged to meet George and Susan before going down, that no one would know when she left or when to expect her. He drove that away by scrubbing his hands over his face and groaning. She was smarter than that, she wouldn't take the danger lightly. Leaning his shoulder against the cool tile, he closed his eyes and let the water pound all thought out of his head.

That lasted for maybe twenty minutes before he caught himself falling asleep and decided it might be safer not to pass out on the porcelain. Cranking the water off, he tried to pretend he felt awake and invigorated as he fumbled for a towel. Just enough coolness had already crept under the door that a chill prickled up his legs and back as he hurried to dry himself and retain some warmth. He wondered if Cathy would hate him if he just went back to bed instead of joining her downstairs.

The deep rumble of a bureau drawer opening sounded from the sleeping area.

Sikes paused in his drying and frowned. "Cathy?"

She didn't answer, but the drawer scraped again, then crashed to the floor as though pulled out beyond the limits of its runners. Sikes turned the knob with one hand and pushed the door open with his shoulder. "Cathy? Are you—"

Wind streamed in from the wrenched open window, and a naked Newcomer crouched on all fours amid Cathy's scattered clothing, its face pressed almost flat to the ground in her underwear and stockings. Sikes felt a throb of panic knock his breath away as some subconscious instinct connected the misproportioned body type to the reek of Newcomer blood. He jerked back into the bathroom and slammed the door behind him.

". . . Oh, shit . . . oh, shit . . ." He collapsed against the sink cabinet, hands in his hair. It was the thing from Ann Arbor's room, of that much he was sure. Boy, did that make him glad he hadn't mentioned the Newcomer resemblance where somebody like Jordan could hear. This thing might be of Tenctonese stock, but it wasn't any Newcomer as Sikes understood the race. Built more like a dog than a *gannaum,* with no ear canals and no genitalia, *binnaum* or *gannaum.* He was gonna have to ask George about this one.

Assuming he ever got the chance to talk to George again.

Overwhelmed by a need to do something besides be cornered naked in the bathroom, he stooped to dig through the pile of dirty clothing he'd worn since the night before. The wool sweater he jerked on straightaway, then had to fight with his blue jeans to extricate his Jockey shorts and socks. The socks smelled like hell, but—

He froze, one foot suspended half in a sock, half out. The smell. It was out there sucking down Cathy's smell. It was going to wallow in the very essence of her until it could find her anywhere in this city of two million people, then hunt her down and kill her just as it had the Frees, just as it had tried to kill Ann Arbor. Sikes suffered a stab of fear so intense it brought tears to his eyes. He finished yanking on his socks and jeans while cursing hoarsely under his breath.

You're stupid, Sikes, he told himself as his fingers fumbled through tying on his tennis shoes. *This thing eats Newcomers for lunch—there ain't nothing you can do to hurt it.* Not without a gun, at least, or maybe a good, fast car. But he also couldn't hide in here and let that thing have its way with Cathy. Even if he couldn't save her, he could at least die buying her time.

It was on the bed when he eased open the door a second time. Cream-pink blood smeared the sheets and pillowcases, and the creature itself was burrowed as far under the covers on Cathy's side as it could go. Sikes nearly cried out, thinking insanely that the blood must be Cathy's. Then he remembered the gory dumbbell in Ann Arbor's hand and realized she must have hurt the thing last night when she hit it. Grim satisfaction supplanted a little of his terror. It could be hurt—this was good. He was able to feel at least somewhat more steady as he edged across the foyer to pull the heavy peacoat he'd given to Cathy off its hanger.

The creature started at the sudden jangle. Its outline shuddered beneath the covers, then the blanket tore free from the end of the bed and its head burst forth to point toward Sikes. It was blind, completely eyeless, with its teeth askew from the broken bone protruding beneath its lower jaw. Sikes clutched the peacoat against his chest, clawing at the doorknob behind him, trying to get it open while still giving this horror a chance to catch Cathy's scent on the coat. *Follow me, you bastard, follow me, follow me . . . !*

It exploded from the bedclothes just as Sikes turned the latch. Adrenaline sang like fire through his nerves, and he scraped out the door while it was only a fraction open, trying to haul it shut behind him on its stiff, sighing hydraulics. The beast helped him by slamming into the door from inside. It closed with a thunderous *bang,* and a crack as wide as his thumb shot from door frame to floor.

"Jordan! Golitko!" He caught the pillar by the concierge's desk and spun himself into the sixteenth-floor reception area, hoping for at least one zoot suit with a gun. The place was empty. Sikes shouted a profanity and kicked one of the chairs across the lobby. Of course—they were downstairs with the Newcomers, protecting them against marauding humans, not protecting humans against marauding Tenctonese monsters. For one wild instant he thought about trying to get down there and explain in time to have Jordan or someone ready to blow the thing away. Then he thought about how fast it had come at him, and how strong it must be to tear a Newcomer's arms from their sockets, and he knew that if it managed to reach Cathy before he made the FBI understand, no amount of shooting would save her. He had to get the monster out of the hotel.

He looked down the hallway at the fire door, and started to run.

Sikes burst outside to frozen rain and a blinding fog.

At first, he felt a sense of dizzying relief. The fog seemed to even the odds somehow, with both of them stumbling around unsure of what the other was doing. Then he remembered that the thing behind him was blind and tracking him with otherworldly senses he could only begin to guess at. He suddenly wished he'd paid more attention when the department gave those stupid lectures about how to work with bloodhounds while they followed a trail.

He struggled into the peacoat while he ran, not paying any attention to his direction since he didn't know the city well enough to orient himself anyway. Somewhere distractingly nearby, he heard a chorus of dogs explode into howls so high and panicked his tongue went numb. He tried not to think about what had excited them or how distorted the fog must make the noise. He just kept his eyes on his feet, fighting to sort out the ground a few steps ahead of where he ran as he passed from concrete to asphalt to concrete again. He heard something crash into the bushes lining the sides of the hotel, then the slap-patter of bare feet on concrete and a wet, insistent snuffling. His feet hit snowy grass just then, and he put down his head and ran.

A waist-high obstacle crashed into his knees with a metallic rattle, and he was airborne only long enough to flip headfirst over himself into the snow. Clawing chain-link fingers caught at his coat hem and the cuffs of his pants as he twisted and struggled to regain his feet. His hands clenched uselessly on clots of icy snow, granting him no true leverage. Then, while something's low growling rended the hedges to his left, Sikes jeans leg tore loose with a soft purring, dropping him free. He lunged down the snowdrift that had built up to hide the fence, rolled, and came up again running.

Traffic sounds grumbled dangerously close on all sides. What could only be a truck roared up and over him, riding some invisible overpass as Sikes pelted across a low footbridge over a decorative pond too filled with ice and dry leaves to be a drowning danger. He thought he must have hit some kind of public park, and hope twinged weakly inside him. God only knew if he could outrun this thing, but he at least had a chance as long as the way stayed flat and open. Hearing his pursuer scramble through the pond full of leaves a handful of yards behind him, Sikes allowed himself to think just briefly about reaching some kind of safety. Then he hit the end of the pier.

Arms pinwheeling, he tried to grip the edge of the dock with his toes. He didn't even know how he'd come up on it—it was just grass, a brief expanse of smooth cobbles, and now the cold iron hitchings above the equally gray and cold roil of filthy river. Did the whole damn city end in rivers? Turning, he ran along the dock in search of a boat, or a policeman, or something he could use to put distance between himself and the monster. But the place was abandoned, just as he should have expected on a weekend with such foul weather. He couldn't see a damned thing, and all he could hear were the cars somewhere above him and his own ragged panting. When the stone dock abruptly gave way to a concrete bridge piling, Sikes jumped for the lowest iron fitting without pause. If he could get to the traffic, he could at least hijack a car and try to run the damned thing over.

It caught up to him when he was less than thirty feet up. He didn't hear it or see it, just felt an incredible weight on his shoulders as it leaped for the tail of the peacoat. He clutched the bridge hard with his right hand and tried to hang on while extending his left arm so the thing could drag away the coat. It pulled the sleeve free with little effort, but Sikes's grip wasn't strong enough to hold them both. He knew he was a dead man the minute his fingers lost their grip on the icy metal.

He hit the ground on top of the monster, but still felt the impact like a gunshot to the chest. Coughing with pain, he tried to scramble away on all fours; the thing beneath him twisted with lightning speed and was on him. Huge hands scissored closed on either arm, and a handlike foot ground into each thigh, pinning him. Gagging, Sikes turned his face away when it bent forward to snuffle him from eyes to crotch.

It smelled disgustingly like Cathy, like all Newcomers, with their musky carnivore breath and their sweatless, bone-dry bodies. It was their color, too— pink and hairless, with a delicate line of spots down its spine suggesting the tail it had never developed. But it smelled too strongly of the blood it had spilled so recently, and the nostrils that caressed Sikes's face were so different from Newcomer anatomy that it was hard to reconcile them with the people he knew. They were flat and flexible, as big as its entire face. The sticky membranes felt like flies' legs against his skin. Sikes bit his tongue to keep from crying out, but the smell of human blood just seemed to intrigue it all the more. It lingered at his mouth for a very long time before butting its head into the front of the peacoat like a dog in search of a treat.

The thumping of his heart nearly deafened him. Sikes thought about trying to hit it, then the horrid mess made of Ann Arbor's shoulder flashed in front of his eyes, and he knew it was hopeless. The best he could hope for was that it would rip his head off first and render him insensate.

Instead, it jumped away from him to clench both hands in the heavy coat. It tumbled him out of the fabric with a savage rip, and Sikes rolled nearly into the water before he could catch himself. Shivering, he raised up into a crouch at the foot of the piling and thought invisible thoughts while the monster methodically shredded the peacoat to strips small enough to hide in one of his hands.

Oh, Cathy . . . ! he thought desperately, achingly. *It thinks the coat is her—it thinks it's killing her!* He didn't know if this would save her, but the thing's apparent stupidity let him believe that saving the rest of the Newcomers wasn't completely hopeless. He wondered where it would go—where it always went— after it finished its mission.

Its only answer was to gradually slow its movement until it was standing still and silent over the remnants of the rain-soaked coat. Then it cocked its head as if listening, huge nostrils stroking the breeze that poured from the river over Sikes's left shoulder. The intensity with which it turned toward him was even more palpable than what he'd felt in the room. It had caught his smell, he realized with a silent shriek of terror. It knew who he was now, and it wasn't finished in its work.

Sikes didn't even pause to look down at the ice-clotted water. He just dashed to the edge of the river and jumped.

CHAPTER 16

"GEORGE." SUSAN SWIRLED a cup of lemon-pepper tea under his nose, pulling his attention away from the rain-streaked wall of windows across from the balcony. The subdued chatter of morning coffee break couldn't hide the note of anxiety in her voice. "George, you *do* remember that you're giving your talk later this morning, don't you?"

"Mmm-hmm." He straightened from the balustrade and took the paper cup from her, curling his fingers around its welcome warmth. As usual, the symposium ballroom had been much too cold during the morning session.

"Are you sure?" Susan eyed him over the top of her own cup. "You haven't said one thing about it since you woke up."

"I've been thinking." George's gaze swung back to the window and its view of Pittsburgh. Fog clung to the gray winter hills, slowly shredding and reforming as rain pelted through in visible waves. "There's something bothering me about the connection between the thefts and the murders, Susan. I just can't put my thumb on what it is . . ."

"Finger, George," said his patient wife. "You can't put your finger on it."

"That's what I said." George shook his head, annoyed with the vague sense of urgency overwhelming him. "It feels like I've forgotten something important, something I shouldn't have."

Susan frowned at him. "Well, if you ask me, I think what you've forgotten is your talk."

"Has anyone seen Matt?" Cathy paused beside them, looking chilly but elegant in teal silk. Her tea steamed forgotten in her hand while she scanned the crowd. "He said he would come down for the coffee break, but I haven't seen him yet."

"Neither have I." The nagging feeling in George's head intensified as he turned from the balustrade to face her. "I assumed he was sleeping in. We were up all night at the hospital."

Cathy shook her head. "No, I called up to the room and no one answered." A rueful smile glimmered on her face. "Matt always answers the phone, even if all he does is snarl and hang up."

"True." George frowned, considering where his wayward human partner could have gone. "He might have stopped to talk to David Jordan on his way down here or dropped in to see how well the Pittsburgh police have staked out Ann Arbor's room."

"Or gone out to get a doughnut," added Susan brightly.

Cathy laughed, some of the color returning to her eyes. "Yes, why didn't I think of that?" She sipped at her tea, looking grateful for the warmth. "Is it colder in here today, or is it just me?"

George opened his mouth to reply, but before he could say anything, shouts of alarm exploded from the hotel's main lobby below. Warned by some internal instinct, he swung around to look over the balustrade. Hot tea splattered the carpet as Cathy's cup went flying, but it took George a moment longer to see the tall swaying figure trapped inside the revolving doors. Caught between front and back openings, Sikes leaned his forehead against the glass as if he didn't have the strength to push further. As George watched, he slowly folded into a wet and awkward heap.

"Andarko!" George vaulted over the balustrade to the marble stairs below, reaching the main lobby just a few steps behind Cathy. As he got closer, he could see rivulets of water running down the glass door in spasmodic surges, pressed out of Sikes's sodden clothes by the weight of his shaking body. Shoving past stunned bellboys, George grabbed at the brass handle and forced the revolving doors into motion despite Cathy's cry of protest. The back panel caught Sikes and swept him forward until he toppled through the opening wedge toward them. He smelled like dead, wet weeds and blood.

"Matt!" Cathy dropped to her knees beside him, frantically tugging at his water-logged wool sweater to see where he was hurt. Fighting the instinctive panic that the smell of blood created, George forced himself to glance away from Sikes's body to the water puddling on the marble floor around him. No trace of

iron-dark red stained it anywhere. George grunted in relief and leaned over to pull Cathy's hands away.

"He's not bleeding," he told her when she fought against him. "That's Tenctonese blood you smell, not human."

Cathy subsided in his grip, looking scared but much less frantic. "But he's unconscious!"

"That's hypothermia, from being so cold and wet. He must have fallen into the river." George pushed her aside and swept Sikes's shaking body into his arms. Icy wetness soaked through his sleeves, and he shuddered, guessing how it would feel to be soaked in water of that temperature. Even for a human, it must be achingly painful.

Dripping water patterned the carpet as he carried Sikes across the lobby. When he would have turned into the first-floor elevator alcove, Cathy caught his elbow and dragged him to a stop. "George, where are you going? We need an ambulance!"

"We'll call one after we get him up to your room." George freed himself and swung around the corner. "If human hypothermia is anything like ours, we need to get him dry and warm as soon as possible." He scanned the row of elevators and sighed with relief when he saw Susan standing between the doors of the nearest one.

"I told the FBI to make our elevator come down here." She held the door open as George ducked in. He turned sideways to fit Sikes's long legs into one corner, leaving just enough room for Cathy to squeeze in beside him. She crowded close to Sikes, making a small, helpless sound as she felt the shudders that racked his unconscious body.

"Oh, Celine, he's so cold!" She took his hands, tucking them beneath her arms to warm them as the elevator rose. Her teal silk dress dampened down the sides as water soaked out of his sweater sleeves, but Cathy didn't seem to notice. Tears stroked mascara shadows down her cheeks. "If he were Tenctonese, he'd be dead by now."

"Then be glad he's human." Susan leaned across George and pressed two fingers against Sikes's neck, shivering as water ran down her wrist from his sodden hair. "His heartbeat is slow, but very strong. I don't think he's going to die."

The elevator doors slid open onto an empty security desk and the sound of distant, worried voices. George swung Sikes out of the elevator, then started down the hall with both females close behind him. Halfway to the far end, he paused and frowned. "Cathy, isn't that your room those policemen are coming out of?"

He could hear the startled breath she took behind him. "Yes. It looks like someone broke the door."

"And the window," George said grimly. Wet as he was, he could feel the cold skeletal fingers of wind combing the hall, even from this far away. "We'd better go back to our room before the police see us." He caught the surprised glance Cathy threw him and smiled, just a little. "I know it seems illegal, but we can always answer their questions later. We have to take care of Matthew now."

Susan rummaged in her purse for her key while they retraced their steps, then hurried ahead of them to unlock the door. Cathy stayed beside George, her green eyes pale with shock. "Our room," she said numbly. "Purists broke into *our* room. And then they took Matt and threw him in the river. Why would they do something like that?"

"Maybe because he was human. Maybe because they weren't Purists." George angled his partner's long body through the hotel door and set him gently on the carpet. Susan had already turned up the thermostat and gone to gather towels from the bathroom. George matter-of-factly began stripping off Sikes's water-logged clothes. "The only way we're going to learn the answer is to thaw out Matthew and ask him."

It wasn't easy. The icy river water clung stubbornly to Sikes, even after they'd wrestled his clothes off and rubbed at his clammy skin, using George's T-shirts and Susan's flannel nightgowns when all the towels were wet. They gave up at last and stuffed him in bed under extra blankets, with Cathy on one side and George on the other for maximum body heat. It took a long time for his shivers to subside and for a tinge of pink to creep back into his pale skin. A police siren wailed in the distance while they waited and reminded George of the one thing they hadn't done.

"Ambulance! We forgot to call an ambulance." He sat up in bed, then saw Cathy and remembered how little he had on beneath the sheets. He slid down beside Sikes again, embarrassment tightening the skin around his eyes. "Umm—Susan, can you reach the phone?"

"Not from the end of the bed." His wife looked up from where she sat rubbing Sikes's feet through the blankets. "Can't you get it?"

"Not without—" George broke off uncomfortably.

Cathy laughed, reaching across to give George's shoulder a friendly squeeze. "You really don't need to be shy, George. After all, Susan's seen most of Matt by now. But if you want, I'll close my eyes while you call the ambulance."

"No ambulance . . ." The hoarse mutter came from the bundled lump in the blankets between them. George rolled onto one elbow to frown down at his partner. Sikes's eyelashes fluttered, then fell closed again as if the effort were too great. "No . . . ambulance," he repeated stubbornly.

"Matt, you need to see a doctor." Cathy touched a hand to his stubbled and still-pale cheek. "Didn't they hurt you when they threw you in the river?"

"Didn't get thrown," Sikes muttered without opening his eyes. "I jumped."

"You *jumped?*" George sat up in surprise, heedless of his bare back this time. He thumped a hand on Sikes's rib cage through the blankets when the human didn't reply. His partner groaned. "Why did you jump into a river in the middle of winter?"

"It seemed like a good idea at the time." Sikes opened his eyes at last and scowled up at him. "George, what the hell are you doing in my bed?"

"Getting you warm, along with Cathy and Susan. And for your information, Matthew, *you're* in *my* bed."

"Oh." Sikes looked blank for a moment, then shivered and clenched his eyes as if returning memory had called up an emotion he didn't want them to see. "Oh, shit, that's right. That thing tore up our room."

"What thing?" demanded George.

The human shivered again, more convulsively this

time. Cathy wrapped her arm across his chest to warm him, but George guessed this wasn't a physical chill.

"It *wasn't* a Newcomer." Sikes's voice was low but certain. "It looked like one, but it wasn't. Same naked head, same skin, same god-awful strength. But it acted like an animal . . . like a dog. A Newcomer dog."

Sudden, sick fear curled through George's stomach along with incredulous recognition. He shot a glance at Susan and Cathy but saw only puzzled looks on their faces.

"Newcomers don't have dogs," Susan reminded Sikes from the end of the bed. "There were no animals with us on the ship at all."

It took George a minute to find his voice again. "There was one." This time, Susan and Cathy turned their puzzled looks on him. He ignored them, focusing down at Sikes. "Matthew, did this thing—this dog— have eyes?"

"No." Sikes shivered again. "No ears either, I don't think. All it had was a big sloppy nose like a bloodhound." Intent on facing the memory, Sikes missed Susan's almost soundless gasp. George heard it, though, and saw comprehension bleach his wife's blue eyes to gray. "That's how it hunts, I think, by tracking smells like a bloodhound. It was after Cathy when it came into our room, but I took her coat and fooled it into chasing me."

George closed his eyes, memories of wild flights on distant planets flooding through him. "And did this thing smell like blood? Like Tenctonese blood?"

"Yeah." Sikes glanced sharply at Cathy, as if he'd felt the intake of breath so quiet George barely heard it. Shock had turned Cathy's eyes even more colorless than Susan's, to a green so pale it was almost silver. "You guys know what this thing is, don't you?"

"I'm afraid so." George groaned as the pieces fell into place: the thefts, the impossible break-ins, the violent attacks. Even the overwhelming smell of blood that had accompanied each murder. "I can't believe I didn't recognize it, but it shouldn't exist on this planet! We destroyed the last of them on the ship during the Days of Descent."

"The *kleezantsun'* could have made others." Despite the pulsing heat of the room, Susan had wrapped her arms tightly around herself. "After the ship landed."

After a moment, Cathy nodded. "The technology exists on Earth," she said, an odd breaking quiver in her voice. "All they needed to save was an embryo."

"An embryo of *what?*" Sikes sat up, scowling at them. "What the hell was that thing chasing me this morning?"

"A thing genetically designed to chase," George told him bleakly. "An animal the Overseers engineered to track down escaped slaves on colony worlds. A *levpa.*"

"*Levpa.*" Sikes grimaced, as if the alien word left a bad taste in his mouth. He huddled back into his blankets, eying George suspiciously. "You've seen this thing, haven't you? You knew what it looked like and how it smelled."

George didn't answer. Noticing that Cathy had closed her eyes for the moment, he slid out of the bed and reached for his pants.

"George used to run away whenever he got sold to one of the planets we visited," Susan told Sikes. An echo of long-ago dread swept through her voice, like a ripple from a distant storm. George heard it and yanked a dresser drawer open harder than he had to, searching in vain for a dry undershirt. "That way, the colony would send him back to the ship as a trouble-maker before he got left behind. The *kleezantsun'* always sent their *levpa* after him."

Sikes cursed. "Then why the hell didn't you recognize it, George? Why didn't you know what had to be murdering the Newcomers here?"

"Because it never ripped slaves apart when it caught them!" George swung away from the dresser and glared at him, guilt and anger roiling together inside his chest. "Would I be here now if it did?"

"Oh." Sikes shoved lank, damp hair out of his eyes, fury fading into a thoughtful frown. "So normally, this *levpa* thing just caught you and kept you until the Overseers arrived? Sort of like a bloodhound from hell?"

"That's right." George took a deep breath, trying to evict from his mind the memory of a sinewy body locked against his, pinning him to an alien forest floor while wide, wet nostrils snuffled blindly across his face. "The *kleezantsun'* always told us that they could have ordered it to kill us if they'd wanted to. But we were too valuable. I never saw them do it."

"Until now," Sikes said flatly.

George nodded, closing his eyes against the torrent of painful memories. "Yes," he said softly. "Until now."

CHAPTER 17

BACKED UP AGAINST the bed's flimsy headboard, his knees pulled to his chest and the blanket crumpled in his lap, Sikes scrubbed both hands over his face as if that would help erase the smell and feel that still clung to his skin like spider silk. His fingertips were cold. He told himself it was the chill that had him shivering despite the Newcomer heat smothering the room, but he knew that was a lie when he opened his eyes to Cathy's hollow expression and George's stiff back. The sight of their subtly alien features made him shudder with revulsion.

He disguised his reaction by gathering several folds of the blanket closer around him. "Okay," he sighed gustily. They were people, just like him. He was ashamed of himself for thinking otherwise. "So somebody's got this *levpa* thing, and they're sending it to tear up Newcomers. Whoever it is has to know all

184

about you guys, which means they're probably from L.A. How the hell did they get a *levpa* out here? Getting it past airport security must have been a bitch."

"It followed us," George said tonelessly. "It followed us on foot."

Sikes couldn't help barking a disbelieving laugh. "From *California?*"

George's shoulders jerked with tension, and Sikes immediately regretted his outburst. "If it was given a scent and told to follow it," the *gannaum* stated with grim certainty, "it would follow until it died." He turned a bleak look over his shoulder at Sikes. "And if you don't think it could track us while we were in an airplane, or that it couldn't cross the continent that quickly, then you've never tried to outrun one before."

And, besides, Sikes told himself, *it could just as easily have been brought by car, or sicced on somebody who* wasn't *on the airplane who would have been easier to follow.* Either way, the question of how it got to Pittsburgh wasn't nearly as pressing as the question Why?

When no one said anything, Sikes elaborated, "Why go to all this effort anyway? Putting together a *levpa,* shipping it clear across country—just to kill a couple random Newcomers? Why?"

Susan just continued to stare fearfully at the fog outside the window, and George went to sort a clean shirt out of those hanging in the alcove by the bathroom. Sikes could hear Cathy's soft, rapid breathing, but nothing else from that side of the bed.

"Maybe they want to kill all of us," Susan said at

last. She turned pleading silver eyes to Sikes, and he felt his heart turn over with despair for lack of having anything soothing to tell her. "If the *levpa* can find just a few of us in this whole city, what could it do to the thousands and thousands of us left in L.A.?"

Sikes shook his head, fighting for confidence despite the enormity of her suggestion. "It would be easier just to car bomb every auto in Slagtown." He waved a hand at George when his partner came back into view, a heavy sweater balled up in his hands. "Hey, George, you got some pants I could borrow?"

George nodded absently, then tugged the sweater over his head while answering Susan. "Matthew's right. The *levpa* can only track what it's already smelled. That means its owner would have to steal some personal item from every Newcomer in Los Angeles. That would take centuries." He opened a drawer at random and pulled out a pair of trousers. "This thing has to have some more specific purpose."

"All we have to do," Sikes said, leaning forward to take the pants from George, "is figure out what that purpose is." He hesitated, pants in one hand, the other poised to push back the covers so he could crawl out. Susan looked surprised when he raised expectant eyebrows at her, then her eyes darkened with embarrassment, and she scooted around on the bed to face her husband, granting Sikes a sort of privacy. He glanced at Cathy, still huddled beneath the blankets with her arms hugged across her stomach, and thought better of disturbing whatever troubled her thoughts just now. It must be hard for her to realize that she'd come so very close to dying just like Sandi Free. He hated the thought himself. Swinging his legs over the other side of the bed, Sikes hurried to pull on George's pants with hands still weak from cold.

"I don't know enough about this *levpa* to tell you how to guess at its thinking," Sikes said, pushing to his feet. "But I do know that if we want to figure out why it's doing anything, we have to start by figuring out who—" A tingle of gray numbness caught him mid-thought, and he had to brace himself against the wall to keep from stumbling. It only half worked—his elbow thumped loudly against the plaster, and he caught his head awkwardly in one hand.

"No." George's hands clenched hard and warm on his bare shoulders. "We start by getting you to a doctor." He pushed Sikes back onto the bed, and it was all the human could do to keep George from laying him flat atop the covers.

"I'm fine," Sikes grumbled, shoving aside George's hands. They both glanced up when a knock sounded at the door, but Susan rose immediately to answer it, so Sikes turned his attention back to fighting with his partner. "I don't need a doctor. I just need to sit for a minute and let my head clear." Voices mingled tensely out of sight in the hotel hallway, and Sikes guessed what was about to come even before Susan led the others into the room. "Coffee would help, too."

"Sikes? You in here?"

Sikes elbowed George away in earnest, and the alien took the silent edict, stepping back to stand beside the headboard so that Jordan wouldn't see him ministering to his partner. "I'm in here," Sikes called, even as Jordan and Golitko stepped into view, all gray-suited and serious.

Jordan glanced over the combination of half-clad

human and half-clad aliens, then fixed his gaze on Sikes as though the others didn't matter to him. Golitko merely looked embarrassed.

"Are we interrupting something?" Jordan asked with politic neutrality.

Susan frowned with confusion, and Sikes suppressed a smile. "Just make it quick."

Jordan nodded and dug his hands into his pockets. "Those Purists," he said, "the ones we've been hunting. You know they broke into your hotel room?"

Sikes raised an eyebrow in feigned surprise. "Did they?"

"They did." But Jordan's eyes narrowed as though he wasn't buying the sham. "Tore out your window and busted the hell out of your door. Don't you know anything about it?"

Sikes shook his head and pulled his feet up to tuck them under his knees. "I was gone this morning," he said contritely. "Got a little wet by the riverside, then came up here. I've been here ever since."

Jordan hunched his shoulders with displeasure, staring at Sikes in the cold, gray manner every FBI agent used to prove he wasn't fooled by lousy liars. Ironically enough, Sikes had found that lying well didn't much change their expressions, so putting forth the effort hardly seemed worth it now. He followed Jordan's gaze when the agent flicked a nod toward the other side of the bed. "What about her?"

Pain caught Sikes by surprise when he turned to look over his shoulder and saw Cathy with her face hidden behind both her hands. The pillowcase beneath her face was dark with subtle wetness, and the rapid rise and fall of her prominent rib cage kept time with sobs, not breathing. Sikes clenched one hand in the sheets beside him, afraid to reach for her while Jordan could see. "She's fine," he said thickly. "She's been with me." He made himself tear away from her suffering to scowl across the room at Jordan. "Anything else?"

Jordan shook his head but didn't take his eyes off Sikes and Cathy as he nudged Golitko back toward the door. Before turning to go, he asked coolly, "You'd tell me if you knew anything, wouldn't you, Sergeant?"

Calling on his rank was a low blow, and Sikes didn't like it. "Hey, Jordan, whose side do you think I'm on?"

It was supposed to be an easy question, but Jordan considered it without speaking just long enough to make Sikes's heart labor. "We'll be down the way," the agent said at last, not answering Sikes's question. "You and your girlfriend might want to think about staying here for the night. If that's okay with Mr. Francisco."

George nodded, his face unreadable. "Thank you, Agent Jordan. We'll be careful."

"Yeah." Jordan brushed another disapproving glance across Cathy. "You do that." Then he followed Golitko to the hallway, pulling the door shut behind them sharply enough to swirl the air in the wake of its slam.

Sikes rolled away from their retreat without even waiting for the sound to die. On hands and knees, he scrabbled over the rumpled covers to the trembling form on the other side. "Cathy? Honey?"

Her crying was more audible now, but when he crouched above her to stroke the back of her head, she gasped and jerked away from him with a cry. "Don't touch me!"

Sikes froze, wrestling his fear for her under control before reaching for her again. "Hey . . ." George caught his arm, but Sikes shook him off with a growl. He brought his face down close to Cathy's, letting her feel his warmth this time, smell his worry. "Hey, it's me . . . Cathy? . . ." They touched, temple to temple, and she rolled over into his arms.

He gathered her up as close to him as he could—not in a lover's embrace, but the way he would a little child, with her head against his chest and his arms all the way around her so that nothing in the world could reach her without going first through him. She pressed tight against him, oblivious to her nakedness even though she shivered like a frightened puppy. Sikes was glad when Susan silently drew the blankets up over Cathy's exposed shoulders, but didn't break his attention even long enough to thank her for her care.

"Cathy, baby, what's the matter?"

She drew in two short, hiccupping breaths and balled her hands into fists so tight they trembled. "I know where it came from," she whispered against his chest. "The *levpa*—I know how they bred it!"

Sikes felt George's solid presence move up close behind his shoulder. "Who, Cathy?" he asked, very gently. *"En?"*

She shook her head, crying, and Sikes pressed a hand against the side of her face to nestle her under his chin. "Cathy, what do you know about this thing?" When even that garnered no answer, he said softly, "You've got to help me. I'm scared it's going to kill you."

She reached up to twine her shaking fingers with his, but didn't open her eyes. "The *kleezantsun'* . . ." Her body rocked in painful rhythm with memories only she could see. "On the ship, they were so . . . *proud* of their *levpa*. Sometimes, they would barter *levpa* into slave sales to the colonies because they could get a higher price if there were *levpa* to ensure that no one could run away." She looked up at him then, and her eyes were nearly colorless with horror, with soul-deep remembrances of things Sikes could barely imagine, much less believe. His own stomach twisted in sick sympathy for what she must keep hidden from human sight every minute of every day.

"We couldn't carry excess cargo on the ship." Her voice was calmer now, almost without emotion. She'd retreated behind that wall Sikes hated so much, the wall that separated her present from her past. "Our food was always in premeasured nutrient packs, and fluids were strictly controlled so that the *kleezantsun'* could alter our rations for punishment or reward. Even excess *sansol* weren't allowed. They kept the *binnaum* hidden and only bred us when they needed to meet a quota. Even then, they monitored the pod's sex and genetics and used outstanding purchase orders to decide which ones would be allowed to grow to term."

Still silent, Susan slipped onto the bed beside Cathy and threaded her arms around her to clasp hands with George, who knelt behind Sikes. It frightened him sometimes to think of the things they'd shared before knowing him—things he could never be a part of, no matter how much he loved them or how long they stayed. He wasn't comfortable wondering how many children with Cathy's beautiful eyes or Susan's wonderful smile had never been able to join their parents in Earthly freedom. He hated knowing that only an Overseer's unfathomable whim had even let Cathy be born in the first place.

"When they needed to order a *levpa* . . ." She shifted a little, huddling more tightly. "It wasn't like a Tenctonese pod—the *kleezantsun'* could keep the *levpa* embryos in cryogenic storage almost forever. They had to implant them into preprepared wombs, though, ones that had already been serviced by a *binnaum,* but where the original pod had been . . . evacuated." Oddly, she turned to look at Susan. "We carried them just like a normal child, only instead of passing them on to our mates, they were given to a *kleezantsun'* from some other ship to incubate. It bonded the *levpa* to the *kleezantsun',* they told us. Even though it grew inside our bodies like our very own child, the *levpa* would grow to love only the *kleezantsun'* who birthed it, and it would hunt us down and kill us if we ever tried to see it again. . . ."

She fell silent, so still against him that Sikes feared for her. "And you think somebody saved some of these during the crash somehow?"

"Oh, Matt, don't you see?" She disentangled herself somewhat, and twisted to look up at him with pale desperation. "It *has* to be attached to a *kleezantsun'*— it has to have a master somewhere."

"But, Cathy," George said softly from behind Sikes, "the only *kleezantsun'* anywhere near Pittsburgh was Ross Vegas."

She nodded, eyes glistening with horrified tears. "And it's *his,* George, it has to be! I don't know where he got the embryo, but he had everything he needed to grow it—This is Ross and Lydia's unborn child!"

They finally called an ambulance, but it didn't come for Sikes. He stood crammed into a glassed-in alcove near the revolving lobby doors, watching a mini crowd gather beyond the waiting vehicle and hating them all for their morbid fascination.

He'd left Cathy upstairs with George and Susan. Jordan had let him into his ruined hotel room long enough to gather an armful of clothes. He'd found a pair of once-worn blue jeans, the underwear discarded from last night's lovemaking, and the LAPD sweatshirt he'd been letting Cathy wear to bed ever since they got to Pittsburgh. He had to make do with his own soggy tennis shoes and a pair of Cathy's socks. With as much of her scent on him as he could contrive, he'd come down here to be alone while George and Susan did everything they could to purge Cathy of her own smell until the ambulance came.

They knew not to let anyone touch her and not to let Cathy touch anything while they transported her from place to place. Then came a shower in Emma Bovary's room, with the water running right up to the moment the medics with the isolation suit arrived. She touched nothing in the model's room, and the water would wash all scent of her down the drain so that any odor she left behind would be little more than the perfume of passing by. It would have been better to bathe her in her own room, or the Frees', or even Ann Arbor's. But all those were locked off by the FBI, and they were the last people Sikes wanted to know about what was going on.

So, even now as Sikes waited, somewhere above him medics were transferring Cathy, wet and naked, into a hermetically sealed environment, ending her scent trail in a hotel room that she would never see again, leaving the *levpa* only one strong remnant of her trail to follow when it returned to the hotel in search of her.

Sikes. With Cathy's socks, and Cathy's sweatshirt, and the bitter smell of Cathy's musk still fresh upon his skin. He was warmer now, if still chilled deep inside, and a trip to the hospital would just lead the *levpa* into a crowd of people who wouldn't know how to protect themselves from an alien monster. It wasn't the first time he'd been half frozen—he'd be fine if he just kept moving, and he'd *have* to keep moving if he wanted to survive the night.

Still, he wished with burning desperation for a gun.

The elevators across the lobby chimed, and a flurry of nervous FBI agents flocked out ahead of the medics. Cathy followed between them, her steps slow and clumsy in the over-large protective suit, her arms raised just a little to either side as if searching somewhere out there for balance. They'd told the convention organizers that she'd developed some sort of infection. They didn't know what, and it seemed best to keep her in isolation until it could be verified that it wasn't something the humans could contract. She'd be kept in an airtight room away from strangers, protected from the *levpa*'s nose by every obstacle modern science could throw between them. Sikes hoped it was enough and had to beat down a rising swarm of guilt because he couldn't think of anything better.

She looked up at him just as the party reached the exit. Her eyes had darkened back to moonlight green, trusting him, believing him when he told her he'd do everything in God's power to keep this thing away from her. Sikes wanted to smile and reassure her, but he could only watch in helpless fear as George hurried ahead to lever open the handicapped access doors to help her to the outside.

I love you, she mouthed, reaching out to him as she went by.

Sikes blinked back tears and didn't move. To come close to her, to touch her, would contaminate her with his deadly scent. And that would kill her. "I love you, too," he whispered in reply. But he didn't think she heard him.

George spoke to her a moment as they helped her into the ambulance, then he shooed the gathered reporters away. Sikes stayed willfully separate inside the hotel, his hands pressed against the frost-patterned glass. His breath left no marks to be seen on the window, but his scent swelled all around him on the air, settling onto the plants that hung above him, soaking like blood into the carpeting below.

CHAPTER 18

"THERE YOU ARE!" Kathleen Westbeld pounced on George as soon as he turned away from the revolving glass door, before Cathy's ambulance had even disappeared from view. He took a step back, startled by the vengeful fury in the television producer's face. She held a clipboard across her chest, but the way her rigid hands clenched on it suggested she would prefer to use it as a weapon rather than a shield.

George blinked at her, feeling distinctly underdressed in his sweater and slacks next to her severely tailored wool suit. "Is there something I can do for you, Ms. Westbeld?"

"You *could* have done something for me forty-five minutes ago, Mr. Francisco," she snapped at him. "You *could* have shown up for your talk."

"My talk!" George felt the sickening jolt of adrenal hormone hit his blood as he realized he'd missed the most important engagement of his life. Oddly enough, the first thing he thought of wasn't the criticism of the Newcomer community or the affront to the human symposium organizers. It was the disappointment that Emily and Buck must have felt, waiting proudly at home to watch their father on television and never seeing him.

Sikes cleared his throat beside him. "Sorry, George," he said uncomfortably. "I guess that means you're not going to get elected Newcomer of the Month again."

"No, it means my children probably think I'm dead." George looked around the marble-encrusted hotel lobby for a phone in vain. Such prosaic necessities were probably hidden away in alcoves to keep from clashing with the decor. "I'd better go up to my room and call them right away."

Westbeld caught at his arm, not looking quite so angry anymore. "Hey, wait—we're not morons here, all right? The only thing we said on TV was that we'd rearranged the schedule to accommodate your work with the Pittsburgh police on the Free murder case."

"Thank you." George took a deep, relieved breath, feeling as if his reputation had just been handed back to him. "That was very magnanimous of you."

Westbeld shrugged. "Don't thank me. Nancy Thompson suggested it. She said she saw you handling some kind of emergency during the coffee break." The producer's level eyebrows pulled together into a frown. "It would have been nice if you'd called and told us you couldn't make it."

"Hey, he was so busy he didn't even remember to call an ambulance for me," Sikes informed her.

Westbeld gave him a baffled look, and he sighed. "Never mind. Come on, George. We have to go find Lydia Vegas."

"I've got you tentatively scheduled for tomorrow at three forty-five," Westbeld called after them as they moved toward the marble stairs. "I'm warning you now, Mr. Francisco, that's the last talk of the symposium. If you miss it, I won't be able to do anything for you."

George glanced back at her, remembering the rose pink smear of blood and flesh that had been Sandi Free. "If I miss it," he said soberly, "nobody will be able to do anything for me."

"And now, turning to the dialectic of kidney transplants and the ethical dilemma of cloning antirejection drugs from Tenctonese DNA—"

Under the whirring of the slide projectors, Sikes's whisper sounded horrified. "Jeez, George, have *all* the talks been like this?"

George paused in his scan of the crowded ballroom to frown at his partner. The dim light didn't hide the human's sincere disgust. "You should know the answer to that, Matthew. You *did* attend the first morning session of the symposium."

"Yeah, but I managed to sleep through all those talks." Sikes fiddled absently with the coffee cup he'd grabbed as they crossed the balcony lobby. Torn paper strips lay in a ragged semicircle around the corner in which they stood. "You see Lydia yet?"

"No." George went back to scanning the crowded ballroom, forcing his eyes to widen despite the bluish beam from the slide projector. Up on stage, the elderly

Tenctonese philosophy professor began another digression into the moral question of hair emplacement surgery for Newcomers. As far as George could tell, he hadn't advanced beyond his first slide.

Sikes grunted. "Maybe she's not down here."

"She didn't answer her room phone." Up on stage, George could see Kathleen Westbeld and Nancy Thompson conferring with bent heads over a copy of the program schedule. He wondered if they would turn off the slide projector to stop the professor or just cut to a commercial. People were already starting to trickle out for the afternoon coffee break. As they did, a faintly scarred cheek caught George's gaze on the far side of the room. He moved along the wall until parallax gave him a view of the rest of Lydia Vegas's profile. "There she is, sitting beside that pillar."

"Got her. I'll go left, you go right." Sikes strode across the front of the ballroom, his tall shadow darkening the screen momentarily as he cut through the projector beam. George circled more carefully around the back of the room, working his way through the stream of exiting guests. He reached Lydia Vegas two steps after Sikes, in time to see her flinch and gasp when the human touched her shoulder.

"What is it?" The Overseer's wife stared up at him like a startled child. Even in the darkness, George could see the flicker of fear that paled her eyes. "What do you want?"

"We'd like to talk to you, Mrs. Vegas," George said before Sikes could answer. "We'd rather not do it in public."

"Oh." Lydia rose obediently from her seat, a spike-thin shadow in the darkness. George spotted a side door that he knew didn't lead to the lobby and headed for it. It opened onto an empty maintenance hall, lined with spare tables and metal carts and stacks of extra chairs. Lydia Vegas followed them in, then paused uncertainly on the threshold.

"Here, have a seat." Sikes pulled a folding chair from the nearest stack and kicked it open for her. He threw another one at George, then leaned back against the wall in stony silence. Knowing which role his partner intended to play in this questioning, George arranged the chairs so one faced away from him, then sat in the other. "Well, are you coming?"

After a moment's hesitation, Lydia Vegas stepped forward, letting the ballroom door sweep shut behind her. The sound of amplified voices hushed to a background rumble. "What did you want to talk about?" she asked, huddling her sweater around her as she sat. It was even colder in here than it had been in the ballroom.

"About the thefts we've been having in the hotel." George tried to keep his voice unthreatening but firm. "Specifically, about your role in them."

"My role?" To her credit, Lydia Vegas managed to sound surprised, if somewhat breathless. If he hadn't known about her husband's activities, George might have attributed her fear simply to her own insecure personality. It occurred to him for the first time that a timid person had some advantages in lying to authority.

"Yes." He held her faltering gaze until she dropped it to her thin-boned hands. "I caught you with my wife's purse yesterday, Mrs. Vegas. And Cathy Frankel knows she left her sweater in your hotel room last night. You told her this morning that it wasn't there."

"But that doesn't mean—"

"It does to us," George said. "And then there are Ann Arbor's Olympic medals and the Frees' book manuscript. We don't have any evidence to link you to those thefts now, but I suspect that if we ask around—"

"Did you get them the same way?" Sikes interrupted, his voice harsh. "Just found them conveniently lying around?"

George thought she would continue to deny it, but her thin shoulders heaved in one great sigh. "Yes," Lydia admitted, in a voice that shook with pent-up tension. "I shouldn't have—but they were so easy to take. It was almost as if they were asking to be stolen." She lifted her radiation-scarred face to look pleadingly at George. "Please don't arrest me. It's a psychological problem from the years on the ship when we never had enough food or water. When I see something lying unattended, I can't stop myself from taking it. It's something I'm being treated for."

Sikes lifted an eyebrow behind her, wordlessly asking George if he believed that story. George shook his head and resumed the interrogation. "Mrs. Vegas, you say you steal things because you just can't help it. Can you prove that?"

Lydia blinked at him. "Without my psychiatric records, I don't see how—"

"People who steal compulsively also hoard the things they've stolen. If we examine your room, will we find all the stolen items there?"

Her gray eyes paled again. "I—I don't know. I don't always remember what I do with them."

Sikes leaned forward, planting both hands on the metal back of Lydia's chair. The Tenctonese female jumped as she felt the impact. "Do you remember giving any of them to your husband?"

"My husband—" A visible shudder ran through Lydia. She caught herself with an effort, folding her hands tightly in her lap. "My husband has been kidnapped. For all I know, Mr. Sikes, he could be dead by now."

"Dead, my ass!" Sikes slammed at the nearest metal cart and sent it crashing into the wall. "Don't give me that dogshit! The only dead Newcomers around here are the ones Ross Vegas has had killed!"

"That," said Lydia with dignity, "is ridiculous."

Silence fell in the dimly lit corridor while George and Sikes traded stymied glances over her leopard-spotted head. The human spread his hands, silently asking whether to continue the verbal badgering. George considered the tense figure of the Overseer's wife, then shook his head at his partner. It was time to try something different.

"Mrs. Vegas." George drew his chair so close that their knees touched, then lowered his voice until she was forced to lean forward to hear him. The intimate stance wove an illusion of trust between them. "You told us that you lost a child last year, that your husband miscarried it. Is that right?"

"Yes." A shadow of buried sorrow darkened Lydia's eyes. "Yes, we did. But I don't see what that has to do with this."

"It has everything to do with this," George said somberly. "Tell me, did you have problems with the pregnancy before you transferred the pod? An episode of premature labor, perhaps, early in the first few weeks?"

"How did you know about—" She bit her lip, stopping the flow of unguarded words, but George had heard enough to know he was on the right track.

"Your husband took you to the hospital when it happened," he continued. "Probably the hospital attached to his biotechnology company." Her soundless gasp told him he had guessed right again. "They had to put you to sleep to stop the labor, but when you woke up you were still pregnant. They told you everything was all right, but you never felt right after that, did you?" He reached out and caught her gaunt hands, feeling them knot convulsively inside his grip. *"Did you?"*

"No." The Overseer's wife took a long, almost-sobbing breath, then freed her hands with a jerk. "I don't have to listen to this," she said, suddenly frantic. "It has nothing to do with—"

"Oh, yes, it does." Sikes shoved her back into the chair when she started to rise. George trapped her chin with his hand, forcing her to look up at him. He could feel tears catching in the corrugations of her scarred skin.

"Lydia, your husband lied when he told you he miscarried. You lost your child a long time before that, when you were put to sleep at that hospital. Ross Vegas took it away and replaced it with something else." Her eyes were almost silver now, the pupils huge with shock. George tried to think of more compassionate words, but found none. "Lydia, he used you to make a *levpa.*"

A visible shudder ran through the Overseer's wife, and horror spasmed on her face as if a mask had cracked and fallen off. She doubled up with a gasp, then let out a thin, screeching cry that seemed to go on forever. Sikes scowled and turned away, looking uncomfortable. George merely waited. Lydia fell silent after a while, shuddering as she fought for breath and composure. She managed to straighten at last, staring at George through a ruined smear of makeup.

"That's what's been killing them, isn't it?" she asked. "The *levpa?* It's been tracking them down from the things I've stolen."

"Yes." George eyed her grimly. "You knew they were going to be murdered?"

"No. No, I didn't, not at first." Lydia took a deep, steadying breath. Now that she wasn't lying for her husband, her voice had actually gotten stronger. "Ross told me he'd found a group of Purists here who wanted to help him send all of us back to quarantine. He said they needed the personal belongings for their religion. I thought they were the ones breaking into people's rooms, getting crazy and killing them when they were only supposed to be scaring them away." Lydia shivered, looking even smaller and more fragile now than she had before. "Purists hate us so much . . . that's why we have to go back to the desert, you see. We'll never be safe, living among humans."

"And will we be safer living among *kleezantsun'?*" George snapped at her, his patience gone at last.

"I will be," Lydia said simply.

Sikes cursed behind her, his voice tight with rage. "And for that, you've murdered two innocent Newcomers."

"I haven't murdered anyone!"

"The hell you haven't." The human detective swung her metal chair around and glared at her, ignoring her startled click. "If it hadn't been for the things you stole from the hotel, your *levpa* kid couldn't have killed anyone. You're an accessory to murder, lady."

"But I told you, I didn't know they would be killed!"

"You might not have known when you took the Frees' manuscript," Sikes admitted grudgingly. "But the Frees were *both* dead by the time you stole Ann Arbor's medals. No jury in the world is going to believe that you didn't know she might be killed because of what you did." He gave her a relentless look. "In the eyes of the law, you're as guilty as your husband."

George leaned forward as Lydia choked down another, almost soundless sob. "You don't have to go to prison with him. If you cooperate, and tell us where he is—"

"Na nteeka wask!" The sudden break into Tenctonese seemed almost unconscious and convinced George she was telling the truth. "Ross never told me where he was going. He just gave me a phone number to call, to let him know when they canceled the symposium. He was going to come back then."

Sikes scowled at her. "But you must have had some other way to contact him, somewhere you could go to meet him."

"I didn't go anywhere," Lydia said. "How could I? We've been trapped inside this hotel the entire time we've been here."

"Then how did you give him the things you stole?"

Her smile tugged bitterly at her radiation-scarred cheek. "I send them out in the hotel's dry cleaning bags."

CHAPTER 19

SIKES JAMMED HIS hands into the pockets of his leather jacket and reminded himself for the fifth or sixth time that he couldn't pace while he was supposed to be hiding in the bushes. Instead, he fingered the plastic trigger of the water pistol in his pocket and jiggled one knee like a grade-schooler waiting for his turn at the bathroom. The pine needles under his feet felt slick and spongy from the accumulated evening fog.

"Matthew." George angled a look of pale annoyance at his partner through the twilight. "Hush."

Sikes scowled at him, feeling his cheeks sting with slight warmth. "What? I didn't say anything."

"You don't have to," George sighed, turning his attention to the hotel entrance across the street from them. His words rolled out on breathy clouds of steam above the collar of his camel hair coat. "Your frittering is loud enough to make up for it."

"Jittering, George."

The Newcomer twitched a nervous little shrug. "Whatever. If Ross Vegas comes with the dry cleaner to pick up the package from Lydia, he'll hear you for certain. Stand still."

Sikes grunted an unamused almost laugh but made an effort to quell his fidgeting. At least for the moment. "He ain't coming with them, George. The whole point of not telling Lydia where he's at is so nobody runs the risk of bumping into him." He shook his head and squinted down the street at an unmarked van three blocks away. Its white sides stood out brightly beneath the first blossoming streetlights. "No, he's got some yo-yo to pick up for him. You'll see."

George didn't answer right away. Sikes kept his own attention on the distant van, letting himself be distracted by George's insistent elbow only when the vehicle turned down a street headed away from them and disappeared over a rise. Turning, he followed a jerk of the Newcomer's chin to where a dark red step van paused with two wheels rolled up onto the hotel's sidewalk. The side proclaimed Chuck's Cleaners in tall yellow type. And beneath that, Chez Royale.

Sikes watched the driver clamber from behind the wheel and jog inside. "Son of a bitch . . ." He kicked a spray of pine needles toward the street. "Son of a bitch, I should have known."

George glanced at him, frowning. "Known what?"

"That's the place Darren Pickett's working," Sikes said, stabbing a finger toward the van. "Chez Royale. It's a hotel a little ways outside of town, and I thought he was working in the gym. Son of a bitch!"

George fell silent, his eyes darkening with the distraction of inner thought.

Sikes started to pace, just short little steps, two or three to a direction, more to vent his frustration than because he thought it would help to move around. "I knew Pickett had something to do with this—I just *knew* it! When Protzberg said they didn't find him at the gym, I figured he split town."

"Matthew?"

"It never occurred to me he was working at the goddammed cleaner's!"

"Matthew?"

Sikes slammed to a stop. "What?"

George didn't look at him, attention still focused on some unknown distance. "I smell blood."

"You smell . . . ?" Sikes's stomach clenched around a stab of primitive terror. "Your blood?" he asked hoarsely. "Or mine?"

"Newcomer blood."

Right. "Let's get out of here." He caught George by the elbow and started across toward the abandoned van at a run. He tried not to think about where the *levpa* might be waiting or how quickly it could take him down if it decided to come at him right now.

"Where are we going?" George asked when Sikes stopped him by the side of the van and caught the big door handle in both hands.

Half on the lookout for Pickett, Sikes heaved the door open and shoved George inside. "Pickett knows where Vegas is. We're gonna let him take us there."

He hopped in after George, then squatted to pull the door shut and snug it gently into its latch. The inside of the van was hung with blankets, suits, and overcoats, some of them sheened with the glossy clear of plastic bagging, others looking stiff and grimy as they started on their way to be cleaned. George ducked between a row of bridesmaid dresses and crouched on the wheel housing. Sikes sat with his back to the driver's seat and the water pistol resting beneath his hand on one knee.

The van shuddered when someone jerked wide the driver's door, letting in a chill rush of outside air. Sikes fought off a shiver, then held his breath until the door slammed, the van lurched into gear, and the wheels bumped gently off the curb. Even then, he waited for Pickett to switch on the radio and start to sing before he rose up to his knees and pressed the pistol against the back of Pickett's neck. "Hello, Darren."

Pickett screamed.

Sikes reached over Pickett's shoulder to knock the Purist's hands back onto the steering wheel. "You wreck this thing," he growled, "and I'm gonna shave your head and tattoo spots clear down to your ass."

Pickett clutched the steering wheel, but Sikes caught hold of his oily rattail to keep him from hunching away from the touch of the water gun. "You're gonna kill me, Sikes!" Pickett whined, struggling to steer the van back into line with the road. His cheeks were starting to flood with color after his fright. "One of these days, I swear, I'm just gonna pack up and die because you hassled me to death or gave me a heart attack or made me slit my own wrists or something!"

Sikes smiled. "Aw, Darren, I'll bet you say that to all the cops."

"Let go of my hair, man!"

"Uh uh." Sikes settled himself more comfortably behind Pickett's seat, ignoring the other man's whimpers of protest as he shifted his grip on Pickett's hair. "Why don't you just keep driving, and we'll talk for a while." It was surprisingly soothing to see the speedometer at a steady forty miles per hour while he thought about the *levpa* sniffing up his trail somewhere back at the hotel. "Where's he staying, Darren?"

Pickett slid his eyes as far as he could to peek nervously over one shoulder when the sound of George crawling out from under the bridesmaid gowns distracted him. Sikes gave his hair a warning tug, and he quickly flicked his eyes back to the road. "Man, this is kidnapping."

"Is not."

"Is so! You got a gun to my head, and you're making me go someplace I don't wanna."

Sikes held the gun away from Pickett's cheek, letting its bulging green-and-orange outline register in the Purist's peripheral vision. "This gun?" he asked. He squeezed the trigger and sprayed a rosette of water all over the dash. "What? You thought I'd blow your brains out with a squirt gun?"

"Oh, man, this bites . . ."

George frowned as he settled behind the empty passenger seat. "Matthew, what on earth is that for?"

Sikes tossed the gun like the cowboys always did in the movies. But the water weighted it differently than bullets, and he ended up catching the barrel instead of the grip, getting a handful of water for his efforts. "I bought it in the gift shop while you were taking care of

Cathy," he said, stuffing the pistol back into his jacket and wiping his hand dry on his blue jeans. "I filled it up with salt water, and I'm saving it to use on Vegas."

George's eyes dilated with shock. "Matthew!"

"Oh, don't 'Matthew' me," Sikes shot back at him. "He's got a two-hundred-pound Newcomer pitbull chasing me all over this city, and I don't even have a gun! What did you expect me to do?" He shifted uneasily, looking out the windshield over Pickett's bony shoulder. "Besides, I'm hoping it works on the *levpa,* too."

"Just be careful where you point it."

Sikes made a little sound of amusement. "Don't worry, George. I won't forget it's loaded."

"Uh, look . . ." Pickett half turned to look at Sikes, then winced when the movement pulled on his hair, and looked back at the road. "If you guys wanna talk about this, why don't you let me take you some-where—"

Sikes enjoyed the way a clap on the shoulder made Pickett squeak. "What a smart idea. We even know where we want you to take us."

The Purist started to nod, then seemed to remember Sikes's grip on his hair and thought better of it. "Name it."

"We want to meet the man who sent you to pick up this bag," George said. He reached around the passenger seat to heft the gray paper parcel Pickett had thrown there upon climbing in.

Pickett glanced sidelong at the package, then sighed. "You guys are makin' me nuts."

"You don't even want to know what you're making me," Sikes replied.

"I'm doing this for my job, and there's nothing illegal—" Pickett launched into his explanation in that strident, overloud voice that seemed to come part and parcel with most preprepared lies. It was all Sikes could do to not bounce the Purist's forehead off the steering column.

George ended up saving Pickett from both Sikes and himself by interrupting, calmly but firmly, "You were called to the hotel to pick up dry cleaning for the woman in Room 1603. This is the fourth time you've picked up goods from her since the symposium began —one on Wednesday, one on Thursday, one on Friday, one today. You never bring anything back to her, and she never pays you for the service. Instead, you're paid by someone anonymous several hours after you deliver each package."

Pickett sat very quietly, staring past the windshield at a stoplight. Sikes could see the reflection of it in the glass as it turned from emerald to amber to red. "Where are you dropping the stuff off?" Sikes asked.

"He told me it wasn't nothing illegal."

Sikes exchanged a glance with George and even took the Newcomer's hint when George held up a finger telling him to wait.

"I mean, the lady just gave me the stuff," Pickett went on. The light turned green, but he made no move to start forward. "It's not like I stole it or anything."

"Your employer has been using those items to locate Newcomers and murder them," George told him plainly.

"No." Pickett shook his head, his mouth pulled down into a frown. "I'm not messed up with anybody's murder—I don't do shit like that."

"You may not," Sikes said, "but the slag who hired you does." He was pleased at the shocked frown Pickett shot at him via the rearview mirror. "You've been getting used by an Overseer, Darren. He thinks you're just some dumb *tert,* and you've been proving him right at every turn by running back and forth with his packages like a carrier pigeon."

"I'm not working for a slag."

"Prove it," Sikes countered. "Take us to your drop-off point."

Pickett didn't answer right away but pressed down the gas and started the van moving even though the light was red again. "I'll take you there, but it ain't gonna tell you much." He swung onto a wide thoroughfare, pulling a narrow frown. "I mean, what the hell would a slag be doing at the zoo?"

"The zoo?"

Pickett nodded, and Sikes was too busy squinting across the darkness at the entrance to worry about yanking on his rattail. "I leave the packages right here by the gate, then drive off. I guess after that he comes to get them."

George seemed to be having a lot more luck scanning the gloom. "So you've never actually seen him?"

Pickett shook his head, and Sikes added, "We've been over all this before."

"So you don't know for certain that your employer *isn't* Tenctonese?"

"And you don't know for certain that he *is.*" Pickett tugged the package out of George's hands, prying open his door. "I'll drop it off—you'll see."

As he hopped out into the night, Sikes strained to

keep his eyes on Pickett's lanky figure. It wasn't easy, what with all the outbuildings, fences, and trees in the way. "This *is* a pretty weird place to be hiding," Sikes admitted to his partner. "Maybe we're wrong."

George shook his head, expression grim with concentration. "We're not wrong." He glanced away from Pickett only after the Purist tossed the package into the grass beside the driveway and started back for the van. "Vegas and the *levpa* need raw meat and warm housing. Where else could they find both without attracting attention? This is really a very clever location for him." George slipped his hand around the handle on the passenger side door.

Startled, Sikes lunged between the seats to catch at his coat sleeve. "What are you doing?"

"Getting out." George's eyes in the darkness seemed honestly confused. "Someone has to stay to see who comes to collect the package, and Pickett's already told us he's expected to drive away."

Sikes grumbled, jerking a thumb toward their returning driver. "And what am I supposed to do with the lipless wonder meanwhile?"

"Drive around the block with him." George opened his door even as Pickett climbed in the driver's side. Sikes didn't like the way the Purist glanced hopefully around the interior, as though expecting his passengers to both pile out and leave him. "When you get back, we'll compare notes and decide what to do from there."

Something about this division of labor made Sikes's stomach itch with unhappiness, but he couldn't think of anything to reasonably object to, so said nothing. He waited until George had crawled out into a copse

215

of low-hanging greenery, then forced himself to turn away and thump a fist on the back of Pickett's seat. "You heard him," he grumbled. "Start driving."

Pickett sniffed and put the car in gear. "You know, this is really beyond the call of duty in my role as a Purist—"

"Shut up."

The road circumnavigating the zoo didn't make a block like any Sikes had ever seen. It looped and banked, but never made an honest corner, and at least twice the stop signs they either ran or passed seemed uncertain which avenue they were supposed to service. There was little traffic, and even less light, with the thick, skeletal remains of trees hugging up close to the road on one side, the tall chain-link fence marking the boundary of the zoo on the other. Sikes found himself studying every wind-tossed tree limb, every flicker of shadow, wondering if he'd truly be able to recognize the *levpa*'s outline against the makeup of earthly nature. The thought alone set his heart to pounding, and he slipped the plastic pistol out of his pocket like a cheap talisman, its tear-flavored water his only hope.

When they finally circled back to the service entrance where they'd begun, Sikes didn't even realize it until Pickett slowed to a stop near the same NO PARKING sign with the same corner curled back by some careless driver long ago. Sikes squinted to try and see the package where Pickett had left it in the grass.

"Well, either way, I'm right." The Purist sounded ridiculously smug. "Either the guy paying me is your normal slag-hating Purist or he's a slag like you say, and I'm right that they all think and act just the same."

Sikes twisted away from the window, scowling through the darkness into Pickett's beady eyes. "What are you talking about?"

Yellowed teeth flashed palely as Pickett grinned and pointed toward the bushes by the side of the road. "Your annoying alien partner." Sikes tried to find George's pink face in the foliage, and it took him a moment to realize why he couldn't, and what it meant.

Someone had come to fetch the package for Ross Vegas. And now, just like the package, George was gone.

CHAPTER 20

Sikes was going to kill him.

Five minutes after Pickett's van had driven away, George watched the stocky figure of Ross Vegas emerge from the zoo and knew he had to follow him back inside. It wasn't instinctive anger that drove him, although he'd certainly been buffeted by it when he saw the *kleezantsun'*. It wasn't the knowledge that his partner, as infuriated as he might be, would almost certainly have done the same thing if he'd been here. It was the simple fact that if George didn't move soon, he'd freeze to death inside this cold and dripping screen of evergreens. As long as he had to move, he might as well track the Overseer at the same time.

Banishing the unpleasant thought of what Sikes would say when he caught up, George watched the *kleezantsun'* slide out through the scalloped darkness of the zoo's service entrance, skirting puddles of orange-white mercury light. Vegas paused when he reached the road, dropping into such a dense pocket of tree-cast shadow that no human eyes could have seen him. Even George could only guess from the occasional glint of his face that he was watching the serpentine road around the wooded park. When no traffic passed for several moments, Vegas took two long strides over to the chain-link fence and scooped up the crumpled paper dry cleaning bag. He tucked it carefully under his parka, then retreated back into the zoo.

After a cautious moment, George rose from his damp hiding place and followed. The careless ease with which the Overseer had come out to pick up his delivery had already told George that there were no intruder alarms at the entrance. George ducked through the unstaffed gate, careful to walk on the frost-hardened grass beside the asphalt so his footsteps wouldn't echo.

The fast cadence of Tenctonese footsteps led him down a driveway into the zoo, bypassing the shadowy, dung-scented buildings near the entrance. George had hoped the Overseer would head for one of those storage sheds, where it would be easy to keep him under observation until Sikes arrived. The meager warmth generated by tightly stored hay and straw would have been enough to keep a Tenctonese warm through the frigid Pittsburgh night. But maybe only slaves knew the tricks of hiding in the cold— troublemaking slaves who used to run away from their owners. A *kleezantsun'* like Vegas might have been forced to use a more obvious nighttime shelter, like one of the refreshment stands or zoo offices.

The driveway ended against a thinner path of asphalt, curving out of sight behind darkly clustered trees to left and right. George followed the sound of Vegas's footsteps onto the downhill, right-hand path. After a few meters, the fringe of grass became a more tangled edge of hemlocks and hedges. The natural, untended look, George realized wryly. He picked his way through, slowed by the undergrowth but unwilling to trust the hard surface of the path. He could still hear the Overseer's footsteps ahead of him, although they were getting more faint as the distance between them widened. Then, without warning, the sound stopped altogether.

George plowed to a halt beside another dung-scented building, guessing from the deep whuffles and stamps inside that this one was not a storage shed. He stilled his breathing, trying to block out the nearby animal sounds enough to hear where Vegas had gone. He expected the scrape of a window forced open, or the sullen crack of a jimmied door. Instead, what he heard was the faint skitter of feet on stone, then the thump of a body landing on grass-softened ground. The footsteps resumed again, muffled now by more than distance.

Vegas must have jumped into one of the enclosures, George realized. He glanced over at the placard outside the darkened building, trying to place the unfamiliar name he saw there. His mind conjured a picture of orange-spotted herbivores with towering necks and awkwardly sloping legs. Fairly sure he could outrun such beasts even if they came out of their shelter, George hurried down the path and vaulted the low stone fence.

The drop on the other side was longer than he'd expected, and ended in the shock of ice-cold water. Wet to his knees and fiercely angry at himself for not looking over the fence before he jumped it, George staggered across the protective moat to the trampled grass on the other side. It would have been an easy distance to jump, if—like Vegas—he'd known it was there. He only hoped the splash had not betrayed him.

He looked around to get his bearings before he moved. He could no longer hear Ross Vegas, just the nearby rustle of tall seed-tufted grass and the shrill singing of wire fence in the wind. The moated enclosure rose in a long grassy hill, broken by the occasional darkness of small buildings. From somewhere farther away, George heard a wolf answer the wind's howl with one of his own. The wailing cry broke into a flurry of yips, then fell to silence again.

Shaking the worst of the water off his feet, George cut across the enclosure in the general direction Vegas had taken. He'd have to assume that the Overseer had taken this route because it provided a shortcut to his hiding place, not as an evasive procedure. If that didn't work, he could always circle back to the entrance gate and look for Sikes. The human must have returned by now.

Trudging up the gentle slope of the enclosure, George tried to ignore the wet squishing of his shoes while he sorted out the myriad of smells blowing toward him. The ground around him steamed with digestively fermented hay, obviously the product of grazing herbivores, overlain with the pervasive reek of bird droppings. When he reached the crest of the hill, however, George caught a more familiar gamy scent. He paused and frowned, trying in vain to match it with his dim memory of Ross Vegas. It wasn't until he heard a deep snarling roar that he realized he was approaching the carnivore section. Somewhere below him Ross Vegas—and the *levpa*—must be hiding.

George quickened his pace, veering to skirt around one of the small buildings that had dotted his path. He had gone almost a meter past it when the building stirred and grumbled and reached out to poke at him with a long, rubbery nose.

"Andarko!" George swung around, startled by the immense size and bulk of the beast confronting him. Its smell told him it was a herbivore, but the massive swing of one tree-trunk leg and the dim gleam of its curving tusks suggested its evolutionary success had not depended on flight. He took a step back, calculating the distance to where he had entered the enclosure. Too far. The line of fence to his right was tall enough to match the beast's height and also looked unpleasantly electrified.

George swung around, trying to find a more promising line of escape. Beside him, the huge animal rumbled to itself in grunts and snorts too deep for human ears to hear. He hoped that didn't mean it was planning to attack. The closest stone wall he could see lay at the top of the hill, near the tiled roof of some large building. George started walking in that direction, careful not to come any closer to the huge mound of gray flesh now flapping its papery ears at him. It blinked little piggy eyes as he went past, then began to scrape one massive foot across the ground.

George made it halfway across the field before the vibrating ground beneath his feet told him that the beast had begun to follow. He glanced back over his shoulder, just in time to see it break from its ponderous walk into a frighteningly rapid gallop. Abandoning all dignity, George ran for his life.

CHAPTER 21

HE WAS GOING to kill George.

Sikes slammed Pickett against the driver's side door with his elbow, stretching past the seat to hook a finger through the keys and yank them from the ignition.

"Hey!"

"You're gonna wait here," Sikes barked, scrambling out the passenger door.

Pickett rolled down the window to shout at Sikes as he dashed for the zoo entrance across the street. "The hell I am! This is grand theft auto, Sikes!"

Why was it that petty felons always thought they knew the law better than cops did? Zipping the front of his jacket, Sikes slowed to a jog and angled toward the grass where Pickett had thrown the cleaning bag. A square as wide as both spread hands had broken frozen grass blades, but there was no sign of footprints in the frost nearby. That meant whoever had picked up the delivery had approached on concrete, reached the bag from concrete, and left by the same route. Sikes flicked a frowning glance at where the zoo driveway stretched past on his right and dove out of sight between the gates.

Clicking Pickett's keys together in his fist, he stood and drummed his foot while he considered. Was George really stupid enough to follow Vegas into the zoo alone? Was Sikes stupid enough to walk into wherever the *levpa* spent the night without George along to back him up? He still hadn't decided if he liked the answer to either question when the van behind him roared into sputtering life.

Sikes swung around in time to see Pickett's dry cleaning truck roll downhill a half meter, then catch its gears and grumble up the street and away. "Darren, you rat turd!" He drew his gun and aimed a half-hearted squirt after the van. "I hope they pull you over for speeding." One look at the hot-wired steering wheel, and any cop in the world would assume the van was stolen.

Sikes turned with a sigh and followed the driveway into the zoo. The place obviously hadn't been built to accommodate visitors at night—no streetlamps, no path lights, nothing to make picking his way through the dark any easier. Even the pathway was black, without so much as a white line down the edges to distinguish it from the bramble. Sikes alternated between walking with his hands crammed into his pockets and walking with them thrust a little out in front of him, not feeling safe in either position. He stepped off the path twice, recognizing the uneven turn of his ankle just in time to right his balance and keep from falling. The third time, he didn't make it and tumbled through the high grass into a stand of knotted wire fence.

A hissing string of curses spun out of him without his really meaning them to. Jerking to free his shoelaces from the wire, he caught his jacket cuff on a fence post and then his hair in the bushes. Only the heavy sound of animal breathing and sturdy footsteps just beyond the fence kept him from shouting out in frustration. He froze, blinking through the wire into the darkness and wondering if whatever the fence contained could actually reach him from here, and if he'd care.

He heard the jangle of keys for several seconds before consciously identifying the sound. Still, the sweep of light across his shoulders caught Sikes by surprise.

He ducked his head, trying to throw shadow across the whiteness of his face, and peered back toward the path through the fringes of his hair. He couldn't see the man, just the brilliant glare of his flashlight as it swept back and forth across the path. A security guard, he guessed, ambling from checkpoint to checkpoint with his flashlight, key ring, and clock keys. He rang like an overfull silverware drawer, and the noise he generated would have made it damn hard to sneak up on any trespassers. That was fine by Sikes. He quietly extricated his shoes and clothes from the wire, watching the guard with half an eye until the light finally passed on out of sight beyond the bend.

No sense following the watchman. Biting his lip against expected pain, Sikes crawled back onto the roadway without trying to untangle his hair. What pulled loose came with him; what didn't, he left behind. Boy, George had better appreciate this.

Sikes headed back the way he'd come, a little faster this time. Taking a cue from the security guard, he dug Pickett's keys from his pocket and bounced them against his leg as loudly as he dared. He might not have a flashlight, but he could at least win himself some measure of immunity by sounding like he belonged. Maybe he could mug a guard for a flashlight later.

The path wound raggedly uphill, past a low stretch of wooden decking and around the edges of a multi-tiered building with chains on its doors. Sikes didn't like the way the landscaping and overgrown weeds along the pathside hid everything not directly in front of him. He hated the broken canopy of skeletal trees, and the fat, long-tailed chicken type things that roosted there, fluttering with distrust and annoyance as he passed by. He hated the scratchy whispers of the grass against itself and hated most of all the way his heart pounded with fear every time his senses told him something whisked by just outside the reaches of his sight. If the *levpa* had managed to follow them here, would it stalk him like that? Or just attack him and rend him to shreds?

The underbrush ahead of him peeled back and gave the pathway room to expand. It flared out, opening into a concession area bordered by arches and winged lions, with other smaller paths radiating out to south and east. Sikes paused to think about Vegas and consider.

Above and behind him, an elephant bugled, and a burst of disturbed animal noises followed. Sikes spun, startled, and listened for the sound of approaching watchmen as a cue for whether or not he should try to hide. No flash of warning light, not even the urgent jangle of watchman's keys. Only the sound of footsteps pounding toward him from the other side of the plaza's wall warned him that someone was headed in his direction. And not a human someone—not with that power, and not at that speed.

His heart seized into a fist between his lungs. If it was the *levpa*, he couldn't outrun it. If it was Vegas, he could at least try to fight. He moved into the path of approach and took a deep breath. Setting his legs wide, he slipped the water pistol out of his pocket and clenched it firmly in both his hands. Then he sank down until his hips rested even with his knees, dropped his left foot back by thirteen inches, and waited.

Whoever would have guessed that a twenty-five-year-old lesson in guarding home plate could save you from an onrushing alien? Sikes saw the flash of a dark silhouette clear the wall, and the Newcomer barreled into him without even checking his stride. Sikes took the force of the hit on his shoulder, just as his coach had trained him to do, and heaved up with all his might in the direction the runner was already aimed. He felt a flutter of protest in the small of his back but couldn't help grinning with evil pride when the Newcomer went flying, up and over, to crash with a breathless grunt on the asphalt behind him.

Scrabbling around to plant one knee on the Newcomer's broad chest, Sikes tapped the pistol against his forehead in warning. "Don't move or I'll squirt!"

CHAPTER 22

GEORGE STARED UP, his gut registering the barrel of a gun for a sickening moment before his mind saw the gaudy orange-and-green plastic. He let out a whistling breath of relief, then remembered what Sikes had put into his water gun and slapped it away with a fervent curse.

"George?" Sikes must have recognized his voice. He let the gun swing aside and dangle from his right hand, even though he still gazed uncertainly down at George. The winter night that was merely dusky for George must have been almost pitch black for the human. "Where the fuck have you been?"

"I followed Ross Vegas into the zoo." George scrambled up and looked around, trying to orient himself after his oblivious sprint across the enclosure. They stood on the edge of a cobbled plaza full of tables and benches, obviously the seating area for the small roofed restaurant beside them. The asphalt path continued on the other side, heading uphill and away from the direction Ross Vegas had been taking. They must be close to the carnivore section—George could smell the musky, almost familiar spoor drifting toward them on the winter wind. One unseen predator whined and padded quietly in the enclosure behind the refreshment stand.

"Why would Vegas go into the elephant pen?" Sikes swung around to scowl at the high stone wall behind them. The huge gray beast still stood on guard there, rumbling distrustfully at George. "It couldn't be for food. Even a *levpa* would think twice about trying to rip an elephant apart."

"He was taking a shortcut to somewhere down below." George waved a hand down the hillside, where occasional bad-tempered roars still echoed through the night. He circled the plaza, leaving wet footprints on the cobblestones as he looked for an exit to the lower tier of enclosures. "I think he was trying to avoid the security guards."

"Not a bad idea." Sikes tucked his plastic gun into his waistband and followed him. "I almost got snagged by one on my way in."

George paused just outside the plaza, beside a wooden platform that hung invitingly over a section of the brushy slope. "Maybe we should cut through the grounds here."

"Great idea, George." Sikes jerked a thumb at the labeled placard beside the fence. "I'm sure the cheetah would be real happy to see us. And don't try to tell me you could outrun *him.*"

"Not carrying you." George sighed and retraced his steps into the plaza. "Let's see if we can find a map of the zoo somewhere in here. We know Vegas must be hiding somewhere near the big meat-eating animals." He found a colorfully outlined map near the gift shop door and studied it, aware of Sikes squinting over his shoulder. "Something big, like lions or tigers."

"Or bears. Oh, my." Sikes sounded disgusted. "Why the hell can't all you Newcomers be vegetarians like Cathy? Then the only thing we'd have to worry about would be stepping in moose shit or scaring a flamingo to death."

George memorized the route to the feline exhibits, then stepped back and eyed his fidgeting partner. "You can wait here, Matthew, if you'd prefer."

Sikes snorted. "And hope the *levpa* doesn't find me?"

"If it reports to Vegas every night, it won't," George said quietly. "We already know Vegas sends it after a new Tenctonese each time he gets a delivery from Lydia, whether or not the one before was killed. The *levpa* will have someone else to chase tonight."

He'd tried to keep his voice dispassionate, but Sikes surprised him with a suspicious look. "George, what have you done?" When only silence answered him, the human cursed and reached out to grab the folds of the camel hair jacket. "Dammit, George, you said you were going to put a couple of clean towels into that dry cleaning bag!"

"I decided that would make Vegas too suspicious," George said stiffly. "After all, Lydia would be much more likely to steal something small, like a tie. And if the *levpa* didn't get a new scent tonight, I knew he'd just come after you and Cathy again." He managed a half-amused smile. "Don't worry, Matthew. Running away from *levpa* is old cap for me."

Sikes groaned. "I don't care how old hat it is, George, it's still stupid! If the *levpa* came after me, you'd at least have some hope of stopping it. If it comes after you, what the hell am I supposed to do?"

"Squirt?"

The human opened his mouth, but a long and strident ring broke the hush of distant traffic before he could speak. Dismay clawed inside George's chest, nearly choking him until he recognized it as the sound of a phone, not a tripped alarm. Beside him, Sikes spun around and scowled into the dark plaza as the phone rang again. "Think that call's for Vegas?"

"If it is, and it's from Lydia—" George didn't wait to finish the sentence. He bolted back into the plaza, rounding the corner of the refreshment stand just as the wall-mounted phone started its third ring. Grabbing it off the hook, he plastered himself back into the shadows along the wall just in case Vegas showed up. He snagged Sikes as his partner ran into the plaza after him and hauled the human into the darkness, too, ignoring his startled curse.

A tiny, familiar voice near his chest said, "George?"

"Susan?" George lifted the phone to his ear. "Susan, how did you get this number?"

"From Lydia, of course." His wife sounded tense and just a little impatient. "She and I are here at the hotel with David Jordan. He wants to know—"

"Susan, wait." George realized he couldn't listen for Vegas and talk to his wife at the same time. He handed the receiver to Sikes, who wouldn't have heard the Overseer coming anyway. "Here, tell Jordan where we are."

Sikes grimaced and took the phone. "At the zoo," he growled into the mouthpiece, then hung up.

George started to give him an exasperated look, then realized Sikes couldn't see it and cuffed him on the shoulder instead. Sikes glared back at him but said nothing. They waited until the human's watch had counted off ten minutes before they relaxed enough to speak.

"I guess he's not coming." Sikes transferred his water gun to his left hand and flexed his stiff fingers. *"Damn."*

"He might wait for a few rings, to make sure no security guard answers it first." George stared at the phone, remembering how loudly it rang and doing rough calculations in his head. "But it doesn't matter. Now we know where he's got to be."

"We do?"

"Yes." George swung away from the phone to stare at the map across the path, drawing a circle on it in his mind. "If Lydia calls him at this phone, he must be somewhere within hearing range."

"Shit, that's right." Sikes glanced around with sudden caution. "In one of these buildings?"

George gave him an ironic look. *"Tenctonese"* hearing range, Matthew. Approximately half a kilometer is what I'd estimate. Less, if he's hiding in a well-insulated building."

"So where does that put us?" demanded Sikes.

George pointed at the map, then remembered his partner couldn't see it. "Somewhere in the African savanna."

CHAPTER 23

THE SIGN OUTSIDE the rhinoceros exhibit read: Closed for Renovation. Sikes leaned as far over the observation deck's railing as he dared, trying to decide if he actually saw something moving through the enclosure's deep shadows. All he could make out for sure was the outline of a huge maned lion, pacing its limited domain another enclosure away. "You really think the rhinos would let Vegas shack up here?" The squat shed attached to the exhibit didn't look big enough to actually hide from the animals once everyone was crammed inside.

George had already turned back for the main pathway, tugging on Sikes's arm. "The last white rhinoceros died in the San Diego Zoo last year. This exhibit must be empty."

Made sense. Sikes jumped down the steps, too strung out on nervous energy to take them one at a time, and trotted ahead of his partner toward the gate to the rhino shack. A tall stockade fence lined the path, broken in the middle by a double door with a padlock as big as Sikes's fist and another Closed for Renovation tag. Sikes yanked on the lock—just in case it was defective—and was disappointed when it held like it ought to.

"Damn." He glanced aside at George. "You wanna just go over?"

George twisted the lock in one hand and snapped it in half. "No."

Sikes jiggled the parts loose as quietly and quickly as possible, then slipped between the heavy slats without actually pushing the gate wide open. George took a moment longer, pausing to shut the latch behind him in case one of the wandering security guards happened by. Sikes expressed his approval with a silent nod. When they were side by side again, Sikes let the Newcomer lead the way into the square concrete rhino building, but kept his squirt gun ready, just in case.

The hinges squealed appallingly when George pressed the door inward with his palm. As dark as it was outside, the building's dank interior was worse. There weren't even windows to cut the gloom, just four glazed squares of glass in the ceiling that barely let in enough moonlight to find the floor. Sikes pressed up close behind George, threading a finger through one belt loop for security. *Don't get ahead of me,* he pleaded silently. *Don't leave me where I can't see.* He didn't even protest when George reached back to take his hand like a mother keeping track of her child at the circus.

"It's empty." George's voice echoed flatly off the walls. Things were so close and narrow, it sounded almost as if he had shouted, even though he hadn't. "I can see spoor in the corner of one of the cages, though."

"And I smell blood," Sikes told him. "Newcomer blood."

"Yes." The warmth of George's presence moved away from Sikes, and he shuffled hurriedly after before George could even tug on his hand. Sikes felt something cold and indistinct pass close beside him on the right, and some indefinable change in the quality of the light made him glance upward.

"Hey, George, look at this."

He realized George had stopped when he bumped into his back. By then, he could almost make out the Newcomer's profile as George tipped his head to follow Sikes's gaze. "A broken window."

"Yeah." Sikes worked his hand uneasily on the squirt gun. "You think that's how the *levpa* gets in and out?"

There was a pause in which George might have nodded. Then he said aloud, "But there's no food in here and no heat. If Vegas is staying at the zoo with the *levpa,* he isn't staying in here with it."

Sikes tried very hard not to dissolve into grumbles as George bumbled him in a circle, pinning him briefly against the upright bars of a cage, then pulling him forward toward the door again. "So where are we going?"

Outside seemed remarkably bright after the eldritch interior. Sikes could almost imagine he saw the path and trees. "If he isn't hiding here," George whispered, "he's staying with the cats." He motioned Sikes to follow him back to the main path, then pushed the gate quietly closed behind them. "I'll go check with the tigers," he said, nodding at the stockade fence across the way. "You see if you can find him with the lions."

Sikes suffered a ridiculous urge to laugh. "George, I hate cats."

He assumed when George turned to him, it was with an expression of eloquent annoyance. "You don't have to play with them, just look into their enclosure and see if there's any sign of Vegas."

Sikes snorted, even though he already heard George padding away across the shadowed path. "Hell, I can't even see *you,* you stupid spongehead." Rubbing his thumb along the side of the water gun, he picked his way down the high fence until it swept to the right and disappeared.

Losing the fence helped a lot. Out from under its shadow, Sikes could at least see the frost-burned layout of the artificial savanna, guessing where the boundaries must be by the placement of buildings and the alignment of trees. A huge, obviously constructed rock did a valiant job of pretending to be natural as it separated the lions from the now extinct rhinos, and Sikes tucked the pistol into the front of his pants so he could clamber up the concrete using both hands.

It made a good vantage point. The posts that sketched the fences were easier to see, and Sikes could actually identify what had to be zebras beyond the cheetah's pen, and the long, awkward necks of giraffes rising up side by side with the treeline. Inspired by how well the giraffes stood out against the cloudy sky, he dropped to hands and knees to try and minimize his outline.

"A worthwhile tactic," a deep voice commented from behind him. "But a little too late."

Sikes tried to roll, but Vegas was predictably faster. He snatched Sikes's wrist in an iron-hard grip, jerking the human almost upright as he pried the water pistol loose from fingers already numb for lack of blood. Sikes swung his leg at Vegas's unprotected armpit, but without one foot on the ground to brace himself, the move only twisted him painfully in the Newcomer's grip and gained him nothing.

Not the least bit concerned about his reputation among the Tenctonese, Sikes shouted, *"George!"* at the top of his lungs and hoped it carried at least a half kilometer.

Vegas glanced away from his inspection of the water pistol. "Oh, is he here, too? I should have guessed."

Smash the pistol, you bastard, smash it smash it smash—!

Instead, Vegas pitched it negligently over Sikes's head into the lion enclosure some twenty feet below. "I hope you won't be offended if I tell you he's the one I'm most concerned with."

Sikes growled, one hand and one foot planted futilely against the Overseer's chest. "Oh, that'll be a big mistake, Vegas."

"We'll see, Mr. Sikes." And Vegas stepped to the edge of the rock to hurl Sikes after the gun.

CHAPTER 24

SIKES'S SCREAM ECHOED off the corrugated iron of the tiger house, drawing snarls from its shadowy inhabitants. George spun and dove back through the gate in the wooden stockade, his hearts pounding with urgency. If Ross Vegas had attacked Sikes, there might still be enough time to rescue him. The human had arrested enough Newcomers to know how to defend himself against their superior strength, at least for a while. But if it had been the *levpa*—

George forced himself to forget how fast Scott Free had been ripped apart and concentrated on keeping his balance as he hurtled down the sloping path. He rounded the turn that hid the rock-edged rhinoceros enclosure and saw an image silhouetted above it, clear against the cloud-black sky. Without stopping to identify it, George flung himself over the protective

239

stone wall and vaulted the man-made ravine between them.

He landed where he'd planned, a little above and behind the dim figure, but the combination of frost-polished stone and his own soaked shoes betrayed him. Slammed facedown by unbraked momentum, George slid clawing over the edge of the rhino enclosure. A frustrated hiss of metal whipped the air over his head. Twisting up, he saw Ross Vegas pull back a long steel pole looped with wire, the kind animal controllers used to restrain dogs at a distance. The sight of the weapon reassured George immensely. If the *levpa* had been here, the Overseer wouldn't have bothered to arm himself.

"Cha'dikav." Vegas thrust the animal restraint at George again, this time aiming lower. Knowing what the thin wire noose could do to his unprotected neck, George tried to lunge aside and scramble up onto the rock at the same time. The noose missed his head but caught his scrabbling left hand instead. Cold metal bit deep into his wrist, and the stocky Overseer grunted in amusement. "Caught again, *sansol?*"

"I may be *sansol,* but I'm not an animal." Rolling to his feet, George slapped his free hand out to seize the pole and shake it hard. The wire noose loosened as it had been designed to do, opening just far enough to free his blood-slicked hand before Vegas could jerk it tight again. George turned and grabbed the restraint with both hands, then yanked the Overseer toward him before Vegas could think to let his end go.

They collided and fell together onto bitterly cold stone, the pole jangling as it tumbled off the rock edge to their right. The momentum knocked George onto his back and gave Vegas the double benefit of leverage and weight. The older *gannaum* used it viciously, jamming both fists into George's unprotected armpits. Pain seared phantom fires across his vision, but George forced himself to move despite it, freeing his legs from the untrained sprawl of Vegas's body. He hammered one hand into the sensitive base of the other Newcomer's spine, then took advantage of Vegas's reflexive gasp and shudder to heave him over sideways. Still struggling, they rolled almost to the brink of the ravine before George managed to pin his opponent with a solid, arm-locked grip.

They strained against each other's strength in fierce silence for a moment, Vegas trying and failing to break free. His age and sedentary body counted against him now. He gave the struggle up at last and glared at George. *"Monk-suit sansol!"*

"Kleezantsun' vuka," George snarled back. Somewhere high and distant, the wolf howled again and was answered by a resounding ursine roar. "What did you do to my partner?"

Vegas grunted, his barrel chest jerking with the sound. "What humans have always done with each other for sport. I threw him to the lions."

A shrieking howl froze George's blood. He lifted his head to scan the hill across the ravine but saw only an empty ledge of rock where memory told him a tawny black-maned form should have been. He felt Vegas's chest heave again beneath him, but he was so busy looking for Sikes that he didn't realize what the Overseer meant to do until the familiar deep-pitched bark rang through the night. Memories of planet dreams crashed over George. That was the sound that summoned the *levpa*.

"Shut up!" George jammed his forearm between the Overseer's teeth, pushing the fabric of his camel hair coat deep enough to gag him. Vegas choked, then recovered his breath to stare up at George, his eyes dark and hot with triumph. A cold wind blasted over them and brought the first blood smell with it.

Designed to be a perfect hunter, the *levpa* made no sound as it approached. George tracked it, as he had tracked it on three planets before this one, by the instinctive fear it sparked in the animals around it. An elephant bellowed to their right, then the yowling cry shivered down the slope again. This time George recognized that it came from the cheetah enclosure Sikes hadn't let him cross. After that, there was only breathless, waiting silence—until something dripped on his back.

Behind him, the tiger shelter exploded with roars. George quivered and jammed his arm more fiercely into the Overseer's face to keep him from making any noise. Nostrils sticky as wet paper snuffled up his coat, then paused to drink in the smell of his left hand. A broken edge of bone scraped across his exposed skin, and George shuddered again, feeling drowned by the smell of blood.

Damp nostrils hovered over his fingers, ignoring the bleeding slash around his wrist. It wasn't until the beast nosed at his knuckles, though, that George realized it was smelling the minute trace of Sikes's jacket, left when he'd thumped his fist on the human's shoulder. Confused by the predominant smell of

George, the *levpa* lifted its head at last with a disappointed whine, then waited in silence for the hunting order that should have followed its master's call.

Vegas heaved under him unexpectedly, dislodging George's arm with a violent jerk of his head. The *levpa* sprang back from the struggle with a startled patter of feet. Hoping to drive the air out of the Overseer's lungs and silence him, George braced his arms under him and slammed his full weight down on Vegas. The knowledge that one croaked word could bring the *levpa* into the fight made him more ruthless than usual with his strength. He heard a muffled crack, then felt the flutter of released tension along Vegas's long chest bone as the lowest ribs broke away.

The Overseer choked over the word he had been forming and began to fight for breath. George leaned on his shuddering rib cage and gave him only enough air to survive. "Call your *levpa* off," George growled, hearing urgent splashes from across the ravine. "The signal that means the chase is over—give it to him now." He tightened the pressure a little when Vegas merely glared at him. "Do it, *kleezantsun'*, or I will kill you."

The Overseer held out until his face darkened from lack of oxygen, then choked and nodded reluctantly. George eased his arm out of the quivering rib cage and let Vegas recover his breath, keeping just enough pressure on him to make sure the Overseer knew he could crush him breathless again in a moment. Beside them, the *levpa* stirred out of its waiting stillness and turned its head toward the next enclosure. A frenzy of growls from that direction had suddenly crested into a roar.

"Roos!" Vegas spat the word out before George could stop him, turning it into a bone-deep growl. *"Roos nema!"* The last words rode a gasp of pain as George shoved his arm down against disarticulated ribs, but the *levpa* must have heard. With a hushed padding of hairless feet against stone, the beast leaped down toward the sound of a human yell.

CHAPTER 25

SIKES TRIED LIKE hell to twist over in midair. He had a vague memory of deep concrete moats running the edges of these enclosures, and the fear of broken limbs commanded his actions more than any conscious thought. Still, something caught at his leg as he fell, wrenching it at a dangerous angle, and he registered that it was the ground slamming into him too hard and too early just as his knee gave way in a sickening wash of agony.

Only the force of him landing kept Sikes from crying out. He didn't even have the air to breathe, much less scream, and the uneven knobs of grass and rock beneath him dug into his rib cage like angry fists. Overhead, pushed into the distance by pain, he could still see Ross Vegas silhouetted against the sky, looking after him. The damned bastard had thrown him past the moat and into the enclosure proper. Sikes didn't know whether to be terrified or laugh.

A hoarse, angry roar from behind and above him quickly answered that dilemma. Heaving up to his elbows, Sikes dug one hand into the scrubby grass and flung the other across him in search of a handhold with which to turn himself over. The answering splash of pain from his knee nearly made him vomit. He ignored it, just like he'd ignored hurt from the first time his old man had beat him as a child, and lurched unsteadily upright. The lion stood on its flat, rocky perch, head low, tail lashing.

"Aw, hell . . ." Sikes staggered in an uneven circle, balancing on one leg and bracing the knee on the other with both hands. Of course there was no exit, just a wide expanse of moat and a tall stone wall. If the lion couldn't get out, neither could he.

"Zoos suck," Sikes muttered, stumbling toward an outbuilding a dozen yards away. "They should leave the animals out in the fucking wild where they belong." The animal keepers had to get into the enclosures somehow, if only for medical care and feeding. The metal and concrete shacks, like those they had inspected at the rhino exhibit, seemed the only possible entrance. Gasping meaningless curses, Sikes limped for the building without bothering to look back at the lion. Either it would kill him or ignore him, he didn't know enough about lions to determine which.

The big cat angled into his line of sight at a stiff trot, growling breathily. Sikes stumbled to a stop and swore. He'd never make it to the building ahead of the beast. "Go on!" he shouted. "Get outta here!"

It paused, inspecting him. Somewhere inside the concrete building, a volley of muffled roars and grumbles boiled forth, the sounds of other lions, confined inside. Sikes backed toward the shallow watering hole nestled against one wall of the enclosure. "Oh, great—I get stuck with the only lion they've got to lock all the others away from." If he had his water pistol, he'd just shoot himself now.

A skim of ice fractured under his feet as he retreated, stinging his legs with frigid water that lapped higher with each awkward step. Abruptly, the stone bottom swept away beneath him, and he sat down hard enough to clack his teeth together. The sudden movement seemed to summon the lion. It darted smoothly forward, ears pricked for Sikes's splashing as he crabbed backwards into deeper water. It slowed as it approached the edge and roared at him.

. . . I'm a dead man I'm a dead man . . . ! The water came only as high as his waist, but it made his skin twitch with a chill that crawled all the way up his spine into his skull. Only his knee felt better for the icing, stretched out straight in front of him, straining against the confines of his blue jeans and pounding like a second heart. His hands, braced against the rock behind him, had lost their feeling as well as their heat. The lion settled into a crouch, rumbling.

Sikes stared into its wide, luminescent eyes, counting the snaps of its tail to left and right as they regarded each other. "We can't sit here all night," he whispered at last. Well, *he* couldn't. Despite the weather and the ice water, he was sheened with chilly sweat, and he knew that meant he had another twenty minutes, max, before shock overcame him and took him down.

"Do something, dammit." He was pretty sure he meant the lion. But when its only response was to flick an ear and blow a cloud of steam, Sikes shoved both hands through the water to shower an icy curtain all over the lion's head. *"Do something!"*

It plunged in with a stuttering roar that turned his insides pure liquid. It seemed distasteful of the water, its eyes squeezed shut and head drawn back, so Sikes dove sideways beneath the cover of its spray and scrambled for the edge of the pool. He only made it far enough to clap both hands on solid ground before a weight like a falling body struck him between the shoulders and smashed him back into the water. He took in a mouthful but valiantly didn't swallow. Then the lion bellowed from somewhere much farther away to his right, and Sikes was suddenly struggling to free himself, choking on shock and panic.

On top of him, the *levpa* gave a barking chatter and planted a hand on the back of his head to drive him under again. Sikes jammed his arms against the pool bottom and shoved back as hard as he could. His face crested barely long enough to drag in a choking breath, then the water all around him seemed to explode into froth and spray. The *levpa* howled in frustrated rage, and a power like the thundering of a mountain pounded ruthlessly on top of him, sweeping the *levpa* along with it.

Then was gone.

Sikes broke the surface with a horrible gasp. Coughing, shivering almost too hard to support himself, he looked around frantically for some sign of his alien attacker. It tumbled in a wailing ball with the lion, slamming the door of the outbuilding and inciting fresh sounds of savagery from within. Sikes dragged himself out of the water to huddle against the edge of the enclosure. *Ten minutes,* he thought. *I'm now down to maybe ten minutes 'til I die.* Out in the enclosure, the *levpa* tore away from the lion, only to be chased to the highest point in the landscape and dragged down again. Sikes silently rooted for the Earth creature while staggering unsteadily upright.

The outbuilding seemed ridiculously close now that both the lion and the *levpa* were occupied. Sikes stumbled into the door and nearly fell there, but caught the handle in an effort to stay standing. It was cold and rock steady—locked from the inside.

"Karrto!" It was a curse George had taught him, and felt somehow appropriate just now. Turning to press his back flat to the door, he clenched his teeth to still their chattering and scanned the dark enclosure. Lion and *levpa* had separated again, this time eyeing each other with much yowls and snarling while the *levpa* circled and the lion stared it down. The big cat seemed unhurt, but also disinclined to attack the alien again. Sikes felt his guts twist into knots thinking about what would certainly follow as soon as the *levpa* realized it was free.

Then his eyes caught on a soft reflection where only grass should have thrown back the light. The squirt gun, downhill from the *levpa* and half an enclosure away. *Well,* Sikes told himself, *you can die backed up against a door like a baby, or you can die trying to outrun a monster for a gun. What'll it be?*

Taking a lungful of air almost as cold as his fear, Sikes pushed away from the outbuilding and started to run.

CHAPTER 26

THE SHRIEKS AND roars and frantic splashes inside the lion enclosure twisted into a maelstrom. George struggled to his feet and hauled Vegas after him, one arm locked around the Overseer's heaving chest. The only way he could think of to save Sikes now was to thrust the *kleezantsun'* between the *levpa* and its prey. George eyed the man-made ravine between the enclosures and knew he couldn't jump it with the heavy *gannaum* in his arms. He had just decided to throw the Overseer in first and hope Vegas landed hard enough to knock the wind out of him when a sweep of brilliant light dazzled in his face.

"Stop!" yelled an amplified female voice from the asphalt viewing area below. "This is the police!"

George squinted into the incandescent glare, trying to spot figures in its blurred edges. He thought he recognized Jordan and Golitko in dark raincoats, flanked by a scatter of uniformed Pittsburgh police. Protzberg seemed to be the one holding the spotlight, judging by its distance from the ground, but there were two other dimly familiar figures in street clothes beside her. With any luck, George thought, they were zookeepers.

"Don't worry about us! Help Sikes!" George waved at the blurred tangle of violence in the enclosure behind him. "He's in with the lion!"

The wave was a mistake. Restrained only by the grip on his cracked chest, Ross Vegas grunted and shoved George off balance, tearing free when he fell. The Overseer leaped across the ravine to the top of the lion's enclosure wall and disappeared inside it while George skidded across frost-slick stone and cursed his shoes.

"Don't shoot!" That female voice, anxious as a class mother on a field trip, certainly didn't belong to Protzberg. "That's my husband!"

George blinked into the darkness after he caught his balance, finally seeing the two Tenctonese *linnaums* behind their bulky parkas. "Susan, what are you doing here?" he demanded, scrambling to his feet in shock.

A gaunt face lifted inside a fur-trimmed hood. "She came with me," called Lydia Vegas. Susan had her arm around the older *linnaum,* who looked oddly determined despite fear-silvered eyes. "I wanted to see—"

George didn't listen to the rest of it. A quick scan of the group showed him no one else who looked like they worked for the zoo, and he cursed. He kicked his shoes off and started shouting orders down at Protzberg.

"Get a guard—someone who works for the zoo!" He saw Golitko set off down the path at a run. "Break into the lion's shelter while you're waiting and see if you can get Matthew out." George backed across the rock to get a running start, feeling the bitter cold strike up through his sodden socks. "I'll take care of Vegas."

Wet socks were only marginally better than wet shoes at holding traction on sprayed concrete, George discovered. He was off balance and flailing when he took off and even more off balance when he landed. Fortunately, the far side of the lion's wall wasn't nearly as steep or as high as the side facing the ravine. George let his feet slide out from under him and skidded down it. He landed face first in the dirt, hard enough to lose most of his breath. He struggled to his feet, bruised and wheezing, then cursed when he saw the disheveled figure headed toward him.

"Matthew!" George took in his partner's wet clothes and the way Sikes hunched over one stiff leg when he hobbled, then hurried to catch him. Sikes shook him off impatiently.

"Squirt gun, George." The human's voice was hoarse with pain and the beginnings of shock, but his lurching progress toward the edge of the enclosure never wavered. *"Levpa's* here. Gotta get it."

George looked around and spotted the anomalous gleam of green and orange under a winter-bare tree. He pulled Sikes's arm over his shoulder, taking the brunt of the human's weight, and hauled him toward the gun. Frost-sharp grass prickled and clung to his wet socks, its crunching broken only by the occasional stab of a rock. Sikes shivered convulsively beside him, and George glanced at him in concern. "Matthew, did that lion attack you?"

Sikes grunted, a sound that might have been a laugh if his teeth hadn't been clenched so tightly. "Nope—it attacked the *levpa*."

"It's not doing that now." The near silence in the enclosure had caught George's attention at last. He turned his head to track the smell of Tenctonese blood. On the upper part of the slope, a tawny shape had retreated, snarling, onto its rock ledge, while two spotted heads bent together on the grassy slope above it.

The *levpa* was striped with its own blood now, gashes raked across its side and belly. Ripped flesh exposed one entire side of its jaw, and its left arm dangled helplessly against its hairless chest. Unconscious of its own thin whimpers, the creature butted its head affectionately against Ross Vegas's arm, then buried its eyeless face in the scrap of blue silk the Overseer held. George recognized yesterday's tie and felt both his hearts begin to hammer.

"Protzberg!" He picked Sikes up by the arms and heaved him the rest of way to the water gun, dropping him there hard enough to wring a yelp from him. "Where the hell are you?"

"Inside the fence," came back the faint reply. Sikes had stooped to retrieve the water pistol and was shaking it now to see how full the reservoir was. "We're working on the shelter door."

The *levpa* lifted its head, nostrils fluttering in the wind as it tasted the air. It caught George's scent almost at once, and its blind face swung eagerly toward him despite the pain it must be in. Hindquarters quivering like a terrier's, it waited for the command to strike.

George sucked in a quick, cold breath, resisting the urge to vault back over the high rock wall. It wouldn't stop the *levpa* from coming after him, even wounded as it was, and it would leave Sikes to the mercy of Vegas in the meantime. George hoped like hell that his partner hadn't exhausted all his water shooting at the lion.

"Protzberg!" he roared again. "Break in that damned door!"

"We're trying!" The police officer sounded disgusted. "It was designed to keep lions in, for Chrissake!"

"Then let Susan do it!"

The *kleezantsun'* laughed, brief and bitter, from atop the hill. "Too late." He dropped a hand onto the *levpa's* bare-skinned skull. *"Roos sansol!"* Vegas ordered, voice dropping to a bone-deep growl. *"Roos cha'dikav!"*

And the *levpa* sprang.

CHAPTER 27

SIKES SHOULDERED IN front of George, water gun straight-armed, his hand clutched in the Newcomer's coat to keep from falling. The stench of Tenctonese blood swarmed them, and a flash of mottled pink tore across the enclosure at a fearfully silent speed.

"Matthew, *no!*"

He squeezed off shots as fast as his hand could pump. No muzzle flash, no report, no dust kick to tell him where his shots were landing or how far they could go. He had just released George's lapel to steady the gun in both hands when the Newcomer snagged an arm around his waist and yanked them both roughly to the ground.

Sikes fought to keep his eyes on the *levpa,* struggling to sit up in George's embrace despite the alien's volatile curses. It flanked them silently, and Sikes twisted to fire just ahead of its dim outline and catch it in the spray.

"Stop it!" George hissed, tightening his grip. "Lie still!"

The *levpa* jerked suddenly sideways, squawking, and Sikes felt a throb of relief at the bitter smell of searing flesh. It scrambled back, its head shaking, and Sikes basted it with a few more scattered shots to hold it at bay. Beneath him, George extricated himself and crawled to kneel at Sikes's side.

Struggling up to one knee and one elbow, Sikes kept the gun trained grimly on the monster. His whole body shook too badly to keep the aim true, but the *levpa* seemed to understand his intent—it paced unhappily just outside the squirt gun's range, whistling with distress.

"Told you it would work," Sikes panted, tossing a sidelong grin at his partner.

The look George gave him in return didn't include a smile. "That won't hold it back for long." His own eyes tracked the *levpa's* nervous movements, attentive silver coins beneath the slope of his bare brow.

Behind them, Vegas barked a string of fluid Tenctonese. *"Roos, karr vot! Roos sansol! Roos nema!"*

The *levpa* lifted its head as though begging for strokes of affection, and its abortive lunge made George jerk closer to Sikes in a defenseless way Sikes had never seen in the alien before. Sikes aimed a quick squirt into the *levpa's* face. The stream went wide over one shoulder, but the creature halted.

"It's bred to hunt, Matthew." George's voice sounded breathless, his expression numb. "It won't break off until it's caught us."

Sikes didn't like his partner's hopeless tone. "I guess that depends." He split his attention from the *levpa* long enough to shout up toward Jordan and Protzberg, "Will one of you please shoot this damn thing?"

"No! *Nos eeb!*" The *linnaum*'s voice rang off the surrounding stone in utter torment. *"Nos cate'un!* Don't hurt him!"

Half sliding, half leaping down the poured concrete boulder, Lydia jumped the moat and crashed to her knees in the lion's den, never taking her eyes off the wounded *levpa*. Even from halfway across the enclosure, Sikes could hear the pitiful hitching of her tearful cries. *"Nem zoo, nos odrey—toe'e therma!"*

Freezing at the sound of her voice, the *levpa* stroked the air with its nostrils, every line of its body quivering as though it felt the cold as keenly as the bone-wet Sikes. Lydia crept toward it like a child toward a butterfly. Her hands framed her face in gentle wonder, her eyes dilated so fully that Sikes could see the reflections of the lion's pool inside them. Murmuring senseless sounds of comfort, she stretched out one hand to stroke the monster's skewed lips. The *levpa* reared back and snapped at her fingers.

Sikes tried to leap up, but George grabbed him by the back of his jacket and climbed atop him. "Don't!" He pinned Sikes's hand so that the water pistol pointed at the ground. "Leave them," he insisted in the human's ear.

Sikes, head spinning in shock and pain, dragged himself forward half an inch on his hands. "It's gonna kill her!"

"It's not." Apparently sensing his friend's discomfort, George rolled to one side but didn't unlock his arms from around Sikes's shoulders. Revitalized by violent movement, the pain in his knee refused to abate. "It's her child," George said gently. "That might save us . . . Let her speak to it."

Speak to it, hell. "George, if you guys could do anything about these things attacking slaves, you would have done it years ago." He didn't like the way he was trembling or the fact that George's fierce hold didn't feel any warmer than the ground beneath him did.

"There's nothing slaves can do to save themselves," Vegas said in tones so deep and guttural, Sikes almost didn't recognize the words as English. The Overseer had come up close behind them, and Sikes expected him to add his strength to the attack started by his brutal construct. He saw that same belief in George's eyes when George rolled over to glare up at the standing *kleezantsun'*. Vegas seemed content to ignore them, though, swaying slightly with weakness as he stared at Lydia and her monstrous child.

"It hates you," Vegas slurred harshly.

Lydia flinched as if under a lash, her hand withdrawing to her side.

"It was designed to hate you and everything about you. You are *sansol,* Jery'zan. Inferior."

". . . He's my baby . . ." She whispered the words almost in rhythm with the *levpa's* sighs.

Vegas laughed cruelly. "He is not. Your baby is dead, taken and killed to make room for this one's birth." He stepped wide to Sikes's right, and Sikes made a grab for his ankle as he went by. George was suddenly on top of him again, pinning his arm with one knee.

"Would you be happier if I just let you get yourself killed?" George growled in vexation.

Sikes scowled at him, burning with annoyance. "Yes!"

"Then I ought to let you do it."

Vegas spun with a vicious snarl. "Shut up, both of you! A slave and the cur of a slave! Your love of sentimental weakness is what makes you less valuable than my *levpa.*" He stooped to rip the pistol out of Sikes's grasp, heedless of whatever moisture still clung to its surface. "With this thing you would destroy more generations of work and training than you can even imagine—work that now can never be replaced."

Sikes felt his partner's weight lift abruptly as George scuttled backwards, out of the pistol's range of fire. "Just as you destroyed generations of Newcomers?" Sikes challenged, pulling his good knee up under him and trying to rock back onto that foot for balance. "Just like you'd destroy anything you can't make or control?"

"Useless things," Vegas answered. Behind him, Lydia sank to the ground with the *levpa* cradled in her lap, singing a baby rhyme Sikes had once heard Buck sing to Vessna. "Cheap labor to begin with, they're now useless things that breed like *anir'na* and no longer do as they're told." Vegas fitted his finger across the trigger and raised the pistol shoulder high. "Without the ship, what good are they?"

Seeing the Overseer's hand contract, Sikes threw

himself at the outstretched arm. He didn't hope for much, really, just deflection enough to keep George from taking a faceful of saltwater, maybe even a chance to knock the gun into the moat. Instead, he slammed into Vegas as though he'd jumped against a parked car and gained a splash of salty spray and a hard cuff across his face as a result. Head ringing, the inside of his mouth tasting sickly of blood, Sikes locked hands on the fist twisted in the front of his jacket and tried to blink his eyes clear.

"You're as bad as them," Vegas sneered, voice thick with disgust. He threw Sikes to the ground at his feet and planted one foot atop his rib cage. *"Sansol* in your mind. And, worse yet, *cha'dikav."*

"Yes," a tiny voice said from somewhere out in the darkness, *"cha'dikav."* Sikes wanted to look up and locate Lydia's delicate tones, but couldn't lift his head to do it. "The only worthwhile thing you could ever let us be." She took a long, wailing breath, and the *levpa* echoed her with a sigh. *"Roos,* my baby," Lydia sang gently to her child. "For me . . . *roos kleezantsun'."*

Vegas turned his head, eyes flashing wide and white, as Sikes felt himself spiraling helplessly down into numbness. The last thing he remembered was the Overseer's hoarse, abortive roar, then the sudden lifting of the weight atop his chest, and the glistening cloud of shell pink blood that misted the air where Ross Vegas used to stand.

CHAPTER 28

GEORGE WASN'T SURE the lions would ever recover.

Three tawny cats snarled and paced uneasily in their cages, while the darker-maned male stood and roared at the crowd that had crammed inside the heated shelter with them. Humans and Tenctonese and one very quiet *levpa* filled the small building to capacity. It was a good thing a zookeeper had arrived to let the two shy leopards out into their fenced enclosure, clearing the space in their cage for Lydia and her child, or they would all be stuffed into the building's office.

As it was, the tiny room was still crowded. George and Susan sat huddled for warmth on the cat-musky couch, while David Jordan tipped back the chair at the battered keeper's desk. Sikes took up most of the floor between them, sitting against the wall with his leg outstretched, a heap of used, wet towels beside him, and a cocoon of woolen blankets swathing him from neck to toe. His knee bulged like a pumpkin under the heavy cloth, packed in plastic bags of frozen lion chow that Susan had found in the shelter's freezer. All the zoo's vet had been able to do was rip the human's pants leg open for comfort and order him not to move.

"Well, I think we have this covered." David Jordan hung up the phone after a long and mostly incomprehensible conversation with some higher-up in Washington. He swung around to face them. "We'll release the news about Ann Arbor's attack and Vegas's capture simultaneously, and keep our mouths shut for now about the exact role of the *levpa*."

George frowned, remembering another FBI agent who'd tried keeping secrets from Newcomers. "You're not going to tell anyone about it?"

"Oh, we'll mention it." Jordan jerked a thumb out toward the crowd of zookeepers and police watching the *levpa* through the open door of the leopard cage. "I couldn't keep those guys quiet about something this weird. If we don't explain it, the next thing you know there'll be a story about killer alien dogs in the *Midnight Star*. But we'll just emphasize its tracking ability and obedience to its master's orders. After all, Vegas was the real murderer."

"Then how are you going to explain Vegas's death?" Bruises mottled the pale skin under Sikes's closed eyes, but his voice was still sarcastic. "Say the *levpa* munched him when the food ran out?"

Jordan scrubbed a hand through his dark hair. "No.

We'll say it killed Vegas when he attacked its—uh—first owner from the ship. People know how loyal dogs can be. They'll believe that."

Susan made a dubious noise, her hand tightening around George's bandaged wrist. "But no Tenctonese will."

George answered before Jordan could. "We Tenctonese know what Lydia's role really was without needing to humiliate her in public. It's the humans we must keep from mindless panic."

"Speaking of mindless panic—" Sikes opened his eyes to glare across the room at George. "Did you have to throw me into this building so damn hard? It sure as hell didn't do my knee any good."

"The lion—"

"—was sitting across the enclosure, counting its toenails and waiting for the *levpa* to leave!"

George frowned at his partner. "Matthew, you were wet, cold, and nearly unconscious. You needed to get warm as soon as possible."

"Yeah, right." Sikes leaned his head back against the wall and closed his eyes again. "I just hope you remembered to call me an ambulance this time."

"It's on its way." Jen Protzberg came through the office door, blowing warmth onto her fingers. In the hallway behind her, a body bag rustled as it was loaded onto a gurney and wheeled away. George bit down on a smile. It was good to know that L.A. wasn't the only city where the coroner's people arrived before the paramedics.

Protzberg leaned a hip against the desk and regarded Jordan quizzically. "So, what's the official word on Lydia Vegas? Do we charge her for killing her husband?"

The FBI agent developed a sudden interest in his watchband. "This is your jurisdiction, Captain. I wouldn't presume to tell you how to run it."

"In other words, the feds don't want her." Protzberg drummed faintly pink-stained fingers on the desk, then speared a look across at George. "You and Sikes are our only witnesses. What are you willing to testify to?"

George's mouth tightened to a flat, uneasy line. The warm pressure of Susan's hand around his wrist told him what she thought he should do, but his oath as an officer of the law officially required something else. Before he could decide how to resolve the conflict, Sikes saved him the trouble.

"As far as I'm concerned," the human said flatly, "she sicced her kid on Vegas to save my life."

Protzberg snorted, and even Jordan looked a little dubious, but Susan smiled down at Sikes. "That's what I think, too."

"Matthew." George pinched unhappily at the bridge of his nose. "We both know Lydia wasn't thinking about you when she gave that order to the *levpa*. She was distraught and angry and worried about this creature she thinks of as her child."

Sikes shrugged, then clenched his teeth as if even that slight movement had been painful. "I don't care why she did it, George, she still saved my life. And yours, too, for that matter. That's all *I'm* going to tell a jury."

"But—" George paused, weighing Lydia's previous

thefts against her help in tracking Vegas, her outright murder of her husband against the years of suffering he'd caused her. At last he sighed. "Very well. Given her background as a mistreated spouse, no jury in the world would convict her, anyway."

Jen Protzberg nodded once, then slid off the desk as a siren wailed to a stop outside the shelter. From farther away, George heard the wolf pack howl back at it. "We'll file it as justifiable homicide, then, and close the book on the whole case. That'll make the city comptroller happy." She gave George a crooked smile. "And I won't have to put up with any of you guys coming back out here for a trial."

"You'll still have to get a judge to rule on custody for the *levpa*," George reminded her. "It's safe as long as it's with Lydia, but it's still potentially dangerous. Some other *kleezantsun'* might decide to kill her and use it the way Ross Vegas did."

Jordan cleared his throat. "The FBI will be filing some motions on that point. When my boss found out how well that thing can track—"

Paramedics interrupted him, swarming into the office armed with stretchers and leg braces and infrared lamps. George entertained a brief hope of getting his feet warm and dry at last, then lost it when he and Susan were evicted to make room for more medical equipment. They left Sikes cursing in Tenctonese behind them and joined the crowd of zookeepers outside the leopard cage.

Two vets worked inside, stitching up the gashes in the *levpa*'s bare pink skin. The beast ignored them stoically, resting its bandaged, eyeless face in Lydia Vegas's blood-stained lap. Spray-on dressings covered most of the raw sores where Sikes had shot it with the water gun.

George went to join the competent blond woman Golitko had found to organize the zoo's cleanup operation, leaving Susan to keep watch through the bars. "How badly is the *levpa* hurt?" he asked her.

"The vets think it'll survive, but it'll need some surgery on its face." She watched a zookeeper release the bad-tempered male lion back into the enclosure now that the police officers had cleared it. He was still roaring. "They want to wait a couple days before they operate, so it can rest and regenerate a little blood."

George considered the significance of that statement. "Does that mean you're willing to keep the *levpa* here?"

"Willing?" The blond woman glanced up at him in quiet amusement. "Mr. Francisco, you're looking at the first and only alien animal on Earth. Any zoo on the planet would trade its pandas for a chance to examine it." She waved a hand at the two intent vets in the cage. "I've already got those two planning more metabolic tests and kinesiology studies than I've got budget for. I just hope we can come up with the right diet to meet its nutritional requirements."

"Levpa aren't fussy," George assured her, his mouth twisting wryly. "They'll eat anything a Tenctonese would eat—raw lion chow, wood chips, a bucket of live crickets or earthworms for variety." He glanced in at the gaunt *linnaum* in the cage. "Lydia will be able to tell you. I assume she's staying here with it."

The zoo official nodded. "We're already setting up a cot in the rhino shelter for her. We'll transfer them both over there as soon as we get the heat turned back on." She glanced at her watch. "I'd better run out and prepare a press statement so we don't get deluged with reporters when the FBI releases the news. And the local TV stations will probably want film coverage—"

George left her to her planning, and went to stand behind Susan. She smiled up over her shoulder at him, her blue eyes a little misty. "Look, George. The *levpa* will do anything Lydia asks it to, no matter how badly it hurts."

"That must be why the *kleezantsun'* never kept them on the same ships as their birth mothers." George slid his arms around her, sighing as she tucked her own warmer hands into his. "I seem to remember hearing rumors of a slave revolt on Ylime, where the *sansol* turned the *levpa* against their masters. Now I know how they—"

"George!"

The fierce bellow from the hallway broke the soft chatter in the shelter. Even the *levpa* raised his head alertly. Lydia stroked it and whispered something, and it lay back down with a sigh. Then she looked up at George through the bars, and laid a shushing finger across her lips.

"I wish . . ." he grumbled, and strode out into the hall with Susan trailing behind him. Sikes had already been loaded onto a stretcher and now blocked the doorway where his paramedics had apparently left him for the moment.

"Matthew." George shouldered past a knot of police and knelt beside his partner. "What's the matter now?"

"Keys, George." Sikes had managed to twist an arm

through the stretcher restraints and was trying to dig something out of his pocket. "Dammit, I can't have dropped the keys!"

George frowned as Dave Jordan pushed through the crowd to join them. "What do you need keys for? You're going to the hospital, not back to the hotel."

"Not my keys." Sikes fished out a ring with three keys and a silver swastika dangling from it and held it out on the tip of one finger. "Darren Pickett's."

"Vegas's Purist accomplice?" The FBI agent frowned. "We've already got an APB out on him. Why do we need his keys?"

Sikes grunted. "Because he's evaded us about a hundred times before, and I'm really tired of running into him out in L.A."

Enlightened at last, George reached into his pocket for a handkerchief and wrapped the keys carefully inside it. He handed them to Jordan, who still looked baffled. "Don't touch them," George warned. "You want the strongest smell to be Pickett's."

"Smell—" Jordan glanced over his shoulder and down toward the leopard cage. "You mean—"

"That's right." Despite his blue-gray pallor, Sikes grinned maliciously up from his stretcher. "Forget your APB. Let Lydia's kid find him for you."

CHAPTER 29

THE HUGE HOTEL ballroom roared with the combined applause of Newcomers and humans. Television cameras panned up and down the proceedings, and halogens bright enough to sear the back of your brain spotlighted a pleased but startled George on the tall and distant podium at the front of the long room. Snorting with disgust, Sikes let the doors swing closed on all the shouting and crutched his way back to Cathy on the sunlit balcony.

"Christ! That's the fourth ovation." He flopped onto the backless bench next to her, stacking both crutches under his braced and bandaged leg to keep it slightly elevated. "They wouldn't be applauding like that if they'd heard the speech he had originally."

Cathy smiled and slipped an arm behind his head to brush his hair away from his temple. "Matt," she scolded gently.

"If you ask me, they're all just happy this damn symposium is finally over."

"Oh, hush. It was a wonderful speech." Cathy had sat through it for both of them when Sikes finally gave up on finding a comfortable chair and went out to the balcony for the duration. "You should be proud of George."

"Yeah, well . . ." He wasn't entirely sure how he felt about George blabbing the whole story to the world at large and tried to tell himself it wasn't his concern. But he couldn't help worrying how knowledge of Ross Vegas and the *levpa* could hurt Newcomer acceptance, and it rankled him to think how the people he cared about might still be put in danger because of everything he'd gone through this weekend. "Your speech was better," he finally grumbled, "and they didn't give *you* four standing ovations."

"You didn't even hear my speech," Cathy pointed out, stroking his cheek with a sigh.

He leaned into her touch and smiled slightly. "But it's the duty of Newcomers and humans alike to share their knowledge with the rest of the community."

She pulled back, her eyes narrowed in a suspicious frown, and the ballroom doors across the balcony swept open with a swell of lights and sudden sound.

A flurry of dancing photographers proceeded the wall of people that poured out of the auditorium, snapping pictures, then darting away like mosquitoes on a sultry day. George, his hand clasped with Susan's, looked shocked and embarrassed to be in the midst of it all, but Sikes knew his partner well enough to recognize the sheen of pleasure in the alien's dark spots. Maybe going public with this excursion into alien-human cooperation hadn't been such a bad idea after all.

Using his crutches as a lever, Sikes pulled himself upright without Cathy's help and hobbled over to meet the Franciscos. George looked a little surprised to see him, as though he'd forgotten all about his crippled partner waiting damn near all morning in a cold as hell lobby filled with know-nothing reporters and Newcomer groupies. Sikes hopped into position beside the Newcomer, crudely matching their speeds, and grumbled bluntly, "Let's go, George. We're gonna miss the plane."

"But, Matthew—"

"Detective Francisco!" A trim, bearded man with a microphone and a severe suit elbowed Sikes aside to push in front of the Newcomer. "Do you feel Lydia Vegas and her child should have the right to return to Los Angeles if they choose?"

"They don't want to go back," Sikes said, then swatted George with one crutch. "Come *on*, George!"

"What Mrs. Vegas chooses to do will depend on the court's final decision," George explained, ignoring his partner except to reach back and firmly snag the flailing crutch. "For now, she's expressed satisfaction with staying at the Pittsburgh Zoo with her child." Trying to wrench back control of his crutch, Sikes hopped awkwardly along behind George and cursed.

"Is it true the Pittsburgh Public Safety Department has already used Baby Vegas to track down a wanted criminal?" another voice from the morass called.

George nodded to someone on his left, Newcomer hearing letting him unerringly locate the voice in the crowd. "Darren Pickett is an accessory to some of Mr.

Vegas's activities, but we don't know yet what he might be charged with. Captain Protzberg has brought him in for questioning." He tipped a warning frown at Sikes over one shoulder. "Hit me with that thing again," he whispered, dropping his hold on the crutch, "and I'll break your other leg." Sikes caught his balance with a grunt, but didn't object to the threat.

"Detective Francisco, Emma Bovary tells me that you, Mrs. Francisco, Detective Sikes, and Dr. Frankel have been, well, sharing a hotel room since—"

"That's it!" Sikes nailed the short, mustachioed reporter who'd asked that with a searing glare and scythed a crutch back and forth through the crowd to clear them an exit. "We've got a plane to catch," he shouted to everyone, "and Detective Francisco doesn't want to be responsible for pissing off his partner any further by making us miss our flight, does he, Detective Francisco?"

George's face fell. "But—"

The bearded reporter in the well-cut suit tugged on Sikes's jacket sleeve. "You can use my limo to get to the airport," he suggested in a conspiratorial whisper.

Sikes scowled and jerked his arm away. "So you can ride with us and interview him the whole way? No thanks, pal."

"Let me take you in my limo," the reporter expounded, tapping his pencil against Sikes's hip-to-ankle brace, "and I'll get you a first-class seat to take care of that leg."

Sikes nodded and pushed the reporter practically into George's arms. "Start talking."

* * *

"Matt, fasten your seat belt."

An hour and a half delay at the gate and three airplane servings of bourbon had left Sikes feeling cottony, and pleasant, and not caring a rat's ass whether they got back to L.A. or not. He opened one eye to peek over at Cathy and noticed through her window that the plane had started moving. Funny— he hadn't even noticed the engine noise. "Wait'll we take off."

She reached across his lap without even asking again, digging underneath him for the buckle's second half so she could click it closed across his hips. "I'm glad Ann Arbor won't be coming home for a couple weeks," she sighed. "I don't know if I could put up with six hours of you two on the same flight."

Cathy had managed to spend most of last night on Sikes's floor at the hospital, but only because Ann Arbor came up from *riasu* shortly after they wheeled Sikes off into surgery. Between shot-putting elements of her room into the hallway and filling the ward with an impressive bouquet of Tenctonese curses, she'd kept both the orthopedic nurses and Cathy busy picking up after her and translating. Sikes was still sorry he'd missed it all.

Instead, he got to share his plane home with a bunch of tall, studly jock types who were busy shouting and laughing about wiping the ice with some Los Angeles sports team or other starting Monday night. Sikes wasn't sure he liked the way some of them were chatting up George and Susan behind him, and he *knew* he didn't like the way one of them kept smiling and waving at Cathy whenever she looked in his direction. Sikes made a silent suggestion to the fellow in the universal sign language of the streets. The athlete raised one eyebrow in amusement, said something in French apparently meant to be insulting, and turned back to his teammates.

"Stop that . . ." Cathy closed her hand over his, pulling it back down into his lap in an obvious effort to keep him from causing more trouble with it. She used her elbow to lift the armrest between them. "Come here, you."

Sikes let her pull him over close to her, shoulder to shoulder, arms intertwined. She smelled musky and fresh, better than the antiseptic hospital, better than the first-class cabin full of sweaty hockey players. He tipped his head against hers with a sigh.

"Does your leg hurt?" she asked him softly.

He nodded. "Yeah." He'd mostly gotten used to it, but its steady presence still made him awfully tired. Even the bourbon couldn't change that.

"Anything I can do to help?"

He snorted, a little embarrassed with himself. "Stop making eyes at the Pittsburgh Puffins."

She was quiet for a minute, then disengaged her hand to reach up and toy with the ends of his hair. "You know . . ." Her voice was pensive, the movements of her fingers in his hair relaxing and small. "You don't have to get worried every time a reporter wants to talk to me or a hockey player makes me smile. You ought to know by now that I'm not attracted to humans just because they're good-looking, rich, or well-mannered."

Sikes turned his head to frown at her with some concern. "Boy, I sure hope this is leading up to a compliment."

She smiled, and shifted so they could face each other in pseudo-privacy. "Matthew Sikes," she said prettily, "I like you because you're smart and loyal and honest even when you think you don't know how to be. I like you because you're just like all the best *sansol*—you're *cha'dikav.*" She leaned forward and kissed him unexpectedly. "And because you listened to my speech, you sneak." She poked him with a finger, failing abysmally in her bid to look stern. "Where did you get it? And how?"

He smiled, liking the warm blush her sentiments and touch brought into his cheeks. "I got Kathleen Westbeld to bring me a copy while I was in the hospital. I watched it with Ann Arbor before you came to get me out this morning." He touched the back of his hand to her temple. "It really was wonderful."

Her eyes darkened to a lustrous emerald. "Thank you." Then, taking his hands in hers once again. "I haven't really thanked you yet for everything you did for me this weekend, have I?"

Sikes shook his head and did his best to look martyred and neglected. Cathy rewarded him with an equally insincere attempt to look contrite. "Then I guess I'll just have to follow you home tonight and take hopeless advantage of you until you beg me for mercy."

Sikes liked the sound of that. "I'm a cripple," he reminded her.

"Don't worry." Cathy tugged on his tie with a wicked smile. "That will just make it easier."

Glossary of Tenctonese words used in *Extreme Prejudice*

Andarko—	Celine's religious male counterpart
anir'na—	a small, fur-bearing mammal from Peshtwa'e, known for its crop-destructive abilities and for its practice of bearing a litter of 8–12 young every thirteen days
cate'un—	child
cha'dikav—	a troublemaker; literally "too intractable to be trained"
eckwa—	dead
eeb—	baby
en—	who
karr—	damn
karrto—	damn it

kleezantsun'— Overseer

ma— they
monk-suit— colloquial profanity; literally "excrement consuming"

Na— I
Nem— I'm
neemu— term of endearment; e.g., honey, sweetheart
nema— human
nos— my

odrey— darling

roos— kill

sacka— was
sansol— slave
sardonak— a Tenctonese aphrodisiac, binding those who take it in eternal loyalty and monogamy; *sardonakked*—the act of having taken sardonak together
syka— were

tam— all
tert— racial slur applied to humans
therma— mother
toe— it
tog— thought

vot— you
vuka— butcher

wrap'da— finished

zoo— here

Phrases

"Na nteeka wask"— I don't know.

"Vots garsa ot aeb' blafta lon coke see 'ser la su rom heef"—a slave's phrase from the ship; literally "Your struggle to change things only brings the rest of us more pain."